A BRUTAL RETRIBUT

A Brutal Retribution

By Diana J Febry

COVER DESIGN - HTTPS://WWW.ELIZABETHMACKEYGRAPHICS.COM
PROOFREAD BY HTTPS://PROOFREADERSTEVE.WIXSITE.COM/SERVICES

CHAPTER ONE

Billy Jackson was sitting in the bedroom window when he saw Jen's car speed around the corner and come to a screeching halt outside his house. His was the smallest room in the house, with just enough room to cram in a single bed and a second-hand wardrobe missing one of its doors. He didn't mind having the box room as it looked out over the street, which people in the know used as a shortcut, so he had a bird's eye view of what was happening outside. Jas had the biggest bedroom, which overlooked the rear garden, and his mother had the other double bedroom at the front of the house.

Three loud blasts of the horn pierced the tranquillity of the early evening street. Billy pulled back from the window to avoid being seen when he saw one of his elderly neighbours straighten his back from gardening and scuttle inside. The neighbour had been young once. He could have been a right hellraiser in his day for all he knew. He shouldn't feel guilty about him feeling intimidated. But he did.

He glanced at his bedroom mirror, shot out of his room and thundered down the stairs. He darted under his mother's arm in the hallway as she tried to kiss him goodbye. His stomach butterflies were in full flight. Tonight was going to be the turning point in his life. Everything would be different tomorrow. "Come on, Jas. They're here. Let's not keep them waiting."

"You will look after him, won't you?"

"Yeah, of course I will, Mum." Billy moved from side to side to look past his mother, searching for his younger brother. He didn't like looking too closely at the lines creeping across her face. Signs of her ageing and vulnerability were a betrayal of his childhood beliefs. As a boy, he had thought her the most beautiful and talented woman in the world, oblivious to the fact so did most men. Even into his teens, he had been happy to walk along the street with her, sharing jokes and sometimes holding hands. It was only recently he had become self-conscious and realised how uncool it was to be seen anywhere out with your parents, let alone openly enjoying their company.

Jas swaggered from the living room in his battered leather jacket and stopped by the hallway mirror to check his hair.

Angie clapped her hands. "Oh, my two handsome boys. Let me look at you."

"Give it a rest, Mum," Billy said. He ducked to one side as she swooped in to steal a kiss.

"Jason will give me a kiss, won't you?"

"Of course, Ma," Jas said, draping an arm over her shoulder and giving her a peck on the cheek.

Billy felt his frustration rise. He could never be so casual and duplicitous. He opened the front door, turned and said, "Come on, Jas."

"Bye, have a lovely evening."

"We will, Ma," Jas said, following Billy out the door.

"Don't wait up for us," Billy called back from the garden path

"Of course I will. I won't be able to sleep until I know you two are safely tucked up in bed."

Billy was pleased that the pulsating drumbeat coming from the car drowned out his mother's words and the screech of the rusty garden gate. He forced a bored expression to hide the excitement he felt inside and opened the rear passenger door of Jen's Mini Metro. The smoke and rich scent of marijuana made his eyes smart. He didn't have to look back to know his mum would be standing outside the front door waving them goodbye. It was the pits, having a single mum who was always fussing about them, even if she used to be stunning and turned everyone's heads. Sometimes, that made it even worse. He cringed when he remembered how he used to be. No wonder he had never been one of the cool kids.

How often had people told him when he was growing up, 'Hey, my dad fancies your mum,' or 'Where were you when the family's good looks were being handed out?' He always laughed, but the comments demolished his faltering self-confidence every time. His classmates were bad enough, but when he overheard adults say it, it shattered any lingering remnants of his self-esteem. He was the pug ugly one of the family, and that was that.

He hated his big, fat, ugly face. Last year, he nearly starved himself to death. His body had become even weedier, making his round face look more ridiculous. That was when they started calling him Moon Face and the Moon Beam. Somebody had shortened it to Beamer, which had stuck. He consoled himself it was better than some of the other names he had been called.

He wasn't fooling himself. He was only out tonight because of his little brother. While he had always been tall, lanky and ugly with acne, Jason's features had rearranged themselves differently. Even the girls in his year fancied him. He wasn't jealous. Well, only a bit. He loved his little brother. Always had done from the day his mother had returned from the hospital with him wrapped in blankets. He hadn't minded being left to babysit night after night. It had made him feel responsible and needed.

Jen had made it crystal clear that he was invited out tonight on the condition that he brought Jas with him. Jen, the hottest girl in his class, fancied Jas something rotten. Jas had creased up with laughter when he had told him. Billy would love just one girl not to think he was a stupid oaf, while Jas couldn't care less. He had plenty of other girls lined up waiting for him.

Billy was squashed into the back seat between Jas and Andy. He fumbled with his seatbelt through his blurred vision from the smoke wafting around the enclosed space. Andy was going out with Rosie, Jen's best friend. Like always, he was the odd one out. But at least he was going out on a Saturday night rather than sitting in his bedroom staring at the walls. He might even get lucky in a new place where no one knew him. The evening could turn out to be his best night ever. Stranger things could happen. "Put your seat belt on, Jas."

Everyone burst out laughing, including Jas.

"Did you bring your slippers, Pops," Andy sniggered.

Billy blushed and looked at his feet. There was no point replying. Rosie had cranked up the stereo, and the bass pulsating through his body made him feel sick. He fell to his right as Jen accelerated away from the pavement and spun the car around the corner at speed.

Andy gave him a shove. "Move over, Beamer. How can someone as scrawny as you take up so much space? Jen, can we get rid of him and pick up someone smaller?"

"Be nice to Beamer," Jen shouted to be heard over the music and the complaining brakes as the car squealed around the next junction.

Billy's knuckles were white as he held onto the seat to keep himself upright. He forced a grin, pretending he liked the speed they were going. "Where are we heading?"

"Out to a little pub, I know," Jen shouted. "The Wheatsheaf Arms in Mickleburgh. Make a note of it. Tonight will be the best in your miserable little life so far."

"Yeah! We'll give you a night to remember," Andy said.

Billy's stomach lurched. That sounded more like a threat. A sudden chill ran down his spine. Had he weirdly voiced his earlier expectations without realising? No wonder people thought he was a freak.

"It's out in the sticks, but there's a great band playing tonight. Everyone is going to be there," Rosie said.

Andy pulled his jacket from under Billy's bottom and leaned forward between the seats. "You need to slow down here, or you'll miss the turning."

Billy sighed in relief. He wasn't the only one thinking that Jen was driving dangerously fast.

Jen laughed and accelerated. She slammed on the brakes and

turned the steering wheel. There was a sickening smell of burning rubber, and the car tipped to the side as two wheels briefly left the road and then landed back with a thud. Billy fell to the right onto Andy again. He couldn't help it as Jas was crushing him from the left.

Once everyone had rightened themselves, Andy said, "Yeah. You might want to slow down a bit. I'm being squashed to death by this great heffalump."

"Give over, you bunch of sissys. I passed my test the first time. I'm an excellent driver," Jen laughed, accelerating again. She took the next corner at speed, going wide to make the bend, forcing the car coming in the opposite direction to brake sharply and swerve to avoid them.

As the car horn faded, Billy felt sure he was going to be sick. He looked across at Jas, who was laughing and giving the finger to the other driver who had blasted his horn at them. He wanted to say something but didn't want to look a fool, so he stayed silent. Up in front, Jen angled the interior mirror to look at herself. He swallowed his pride and said, "You should keep your eyes on the road."

Jen laughed and looked over her shoulder at him. "Some of us have a pleasant surprise when we look in the mirror."

Another oncoming car blasted its horn at them as they had strayed onto the wrong side of the road again. Jen hit her horn in retaliation as she swerved back to the correct side of the road. "Keep your hair on Grandad."

Holding onto the dashboard, Rosie said, "Settle down, Jen. They might have a point. I fancy getting there alive."

"Oh, for God's sake! I thought we were going out for a good time. What's wrong with you all?" Jen glanced over her shoulder again. "You're having a good time, aren't you, Jas?"

Jas grinned back, gave Jen a thumbs up and shouted, "Turn the music up. Let's get this party started!"

Rosie tried to turn the dial, but the volume was already at maximum. Billy pinched his brother's leg and glared at him. The maniac behind the wheel didn't need any encouragement. He was seriously thinking of asking her to stop and let him out. But he couldn't do that and leave Jas behind. His mum would kill him.

Andy fought gravity to pull himself forward between the front seats again. "A duck pond and a hairpin bend are coming up in a few minutes. You do need to take that slow unless you want to end up swimming with the ducks. You don't want to turn up with panda eyes and duckpond weed in your hair."

"Oh, shut up with your nannying," Jen said, maintaining her speed. "Talking of weed …"

"Sorry. I think I'm going to be sick," Billy said.

Jen turned again, shouting, "You cannot be serious!"

Billy felt his insides rising. He bent forward, tucking his head between his knees, feeling dizzy and ready to vomit. He realised it wasn't only his stomach contents on the move. His entire body was rising and rolling over and over. Unseen things were flying about, pounding him. A screeching of rubber and metal. The stench of burning rubber. A high-pitched shriek blasted his eardrums, followed by a deep roar, an ear-splitting bang and a shattering of glass. And then silence.

Slowly and painfully, he raised his head. The sun was setting, casting an eerie orange glow. Andy was crumpled in the footwell to his right, his neck turned at an impossible angle, staring at him through glassy, unseeing eyes. He could see only Rosie's legs in front of him. The rest of her body was lying across the shattered glass on the car bonnet. Jen's face was turned towards Rosie as if she was about to speak to her. The top of her head was a mangled mess of blood and bone where it had gone through the windscreen. Whatever she was about to say would never be heard.

Billy swallowed hard and turned to his left. Jas was slumped in his seat, looking forward. His face looked calm and untouched by the horror around him. How typical of him to walk away from the wreckage without a scratch. The world had thrown a protective ring around him as someone special who needed preserving for all the wonderful things he would achieve in his life.

Ignoring the searing pain from his legs trapped somewhere under the front seats, Billy twisted forward to see his brother properly so he could speak to him. The left side of his face had smashed through the side window and dragged along the road. His good looks were gone forever.

Billy turned away and looked into Jen's wide-open eyes. "Look at what you've done. Look. Look. Look at what you've done!" he screamed, over and over again until his voice grew hoarse and weak. When he couldn't scream anymore, he sobbed. "I'm so sorry, Mum. This is on me. Somehow, I'll make it up to you. I don't know how, but I promise I will."

CHAPTER TWO

Isabella Stainton slammed the door of her Fiat ICON Convertible. Stupid lecturer, who did he think he was, giving her a dressing down for late assignments in front of the whole class? He was only picking on her because he was jealous of her. Underneath his lefty, up-the-working-class drivel was plain, green-eyed envy like most of his ilk. It was all hot air and fake righteous indignation. He didn't care more than she did about anyone else. It was all just empty bluster to make him feel better about himself. At least she had the guts to be honest with herself. She was what she was, and she was fine with that. She didn't need to be pretentious and false.

She juggled her laptop and shopping bag to unlock the house door. In the narrow hallway, she caught the strap of her Mulberry Bayswater handbag on the rusty bicycle abandoned against the wall. Her shoulder was yanked backwards, and she nearly dropped her laptop. Daddy would be furious if she broke another screen so soon after the last one. She flared her nostrils and shouted, "Martin, get this pile of junk out of the hallway!"

Martin appeared in the kitchen doorway. "Okay Iz. Keep your hair on. I've just come in, and I'm moving it now."

Stepping over the workman, crouched down doing something with the radiator, Isabella said, "I've told you before about bringing it into the house. Get rid of it. And my name is Isabella!"

Martin shared a pained expression with the guy in overalls squatting on the floor and rolled his eyes. "Moving it now, my sweet. How was your day?"

"Dreadful, since you asked. Now, get that bike out of my sight."

Isabella pushed past Martin and plonked her bags on the kitchen table.

"Can I move my notes out of the way first?" Simon asked.

Isabella huffed and lifted her bags while Simon quickly gathered his sheets of paper together.

Suzie looked up from the counter where she was chopping carrots. "Did you leave anything in Busby for anyone else to buy?"

"It's just a few bits and bobs for Jule's party this weekend," Isabella said, fluffing up her hair.

"I would love to be able to afford something from there," Tilly said, peering into one of the bags. "I couldn't even afford their socks."

Isabella slapped at Tilly's hands. "Get your filthy mitts off my shopping! I don't want it ruined."

Tilly moved away from the table, looking upset, but didn't say anything.

Suzie gave Tilly a sympathetic look. "With your figure, you can look good in anything."

"I love the way you dress," Harry said.

"Oh, please. Pass me the sick bucket," Isabella said, crossing to the bread bin. "Grow a backbone and ask her out."

Harry blushed and mumbled, "I've studying to do. I'll see you all later."

"Not so fast!" Isabella spun on her heels with a look of fury. "Which of you heathens has taken my sourdough?"

"I've got a loaf of bread. Help yourself," Suzie said.

Isabella grabbed the sliced loaf from the bread bin and threw it on the floor. "You expect me to poison myself with that cheap, mass-produced junk?"

"Chill," Martin said, appearing at the doorway. "It's only bread," he added, scooping up the loaf of bread and putting it on the counter.

"That's it!" Isabella shrieked. "When Daddy bought this house for me, he said it would be fun to have some housemates. Well, it's not fun. You're all smelly, dirty, thieving and boring. I want you all out by the end of the week!"

"Come on, Isabella," Simon said. "Be serious."

"We all have exams coming up," Tilly said. "I'll go and buy you some more sourdough."

"You couldn't afford it," Isabella sneered. "I mean it. I want you out. Daddy didn't buy this house for you to abuse it and make me unhappy."

"Wow! I've never been accused of abusing a house before," Martin said, folding his arms and leaning against the doorway.

"And you're the worst," Isabella said. "If you're not gone by next weekend, I'll have you evicted for squatting. I want the house to myself."

"Calm down and think about it. Who would you have to take your bad moods out on?" Martin asked. "You would soon be bored and lonely. That, or you would go stir-crazy with no one to shout at."

"No, I wouldn't," Isabella said. "And if I do decide to share my space again, I'll vet people to ensure they are suitable. I'll put something in writing this evening. I've had enough of being surrounded by idiots. Get out of my kitchen and start looking for somewhere else to live. All of you!"

"That's not fair, Isabella. Tilly's right," Harry said. "We all have exams coming up next month, and then it'll be the end of the year anyway. You can't chuck us out without reasonable warning."

"Don't you dare try to tell me what I can and can't do! This is my house, and I couldn't care less about your stupid exams. It's not like any of you are going to make something of yourself. You haven't got the contacts or the class to start with. I want you gone by the weekend."

"Come on, guys," Simon said, tucking his notes under his arm. "I've had enough of living here. I saw an ad for a house share on the noticeboard in the Union bar. Let's go and see if it's still available."

"I'm in," Martin and Harry said.

Suzie and Tilly looked at each other before saying, "Us too."

As the other four filed out, Martin said, "Okay, we're leaving, but we've paid you rent until the end of the month, so we're staying until then."

"You can have your filthy money back. I don't need it. Go!"

"We'll leave once we have sorted some accommodation," Martin said, unfolding his arms. "Until we do, we have the right to stay here."

"Until the weekend, and that's final," Isabella said.

The workman appeared at the kitchen door. "Everything is sorted, Miss Stainton. The problem was with …"

"Oh, don't bother me with your tedious, little achievements. Am I supposed to be impressed by you doing what you're being paid to do? Send the bill to Daddy and shut the door on your way out."

CHAPTER THREE

DI Fiona Williams arrived home from a week at Stefan's with her mind in a blur. She dropped her overnight bag in the hallway and headed straight to the kitchen to switch on the coffee machine. She wanted a long hot bath and a glass of wine, but in half an hour, she was on call. She looked down at the diamond on her left hand and wasn't sure how she felt about it. When Stefan had given it to her, she had felt her heart might explode with happiness. Now, her feelings were more mixed. When she was with Stefan, all their problems were surmountable, but doubts emerged and grew as she moved away from him.

Waiting for the coffee machine, she ran upstairs to the spare bedroom in search of the antique jewellery box she had inherited from her grandmother. She had been so overwhelmed when Stefan proposed that she could hardly breathe, let alone speak. She'd never thought it possible to be so deliriously happy, and she wanted to hold onto the feeling and protect it from the outside world for a short while. A magical secret shared only by them. Stefan hadn't fully understood her need for time, but he had accepted they would keep the engagement secret for a short while.

While not on her finger in the privacy of her home, her ring had to be somewhere beautiful. And hidden. The jewellery box was perfect as it held a special, if distant, place in her heart. In all honesty, she barely remembered her father's mother and knew her only through her father's stories. Stories that were more real to him now than the present. She carefully slid the ring from her finger and placed it reverently on the velvet bed. She kissed the box for good luck and carried it to her bedroom, hiding it in a drawer under her socks.

She returned to the kitchen, wondering what a therapist would make of her behaviour. Her finger felt naked and lost, but she reasoned that she couldn't risk discarding the ring in a hurry and losing it if she received an urgent call. She carried her coffee mug to the living room, hoping for a quiet night without interruption. She switched on the television to watch the story play out on the screen while her mind remained full of thoughts of Stefan and where she slotted into the life he had planned for them.

Curled up on the sofa, Fiona was nodding off when the phone rang. She read the screen and banished the romantic notions that had crept into her mind when her guard was down before accepting the call. "Hi, Humphries. It's great to hear you're back to full duties. What's up?"

"We've got a call. I'll pick you up in ten minutes," Humphries said. "It's a nasty one with multiple casualties. I'll fill you in properly in the car."

"Okay. I'll be waiting outside in ten." Fiona shoved her feet into a pair of trainers and grabbed a jacket from the stand in the hallway. It was unusual for Humphries to be so curt. Either he'd had a big argument with his new wife, Tina, or it really was a bad one.

CHAPTER FOUR

Waiting wasn't Fiona's forte, so after pacing backwards and forwards between her living room and kitchen a few times, she wandered outside to wait for Humphries. Although it had been a pleasantly warm day, there was a chill in the air, so she quickly returned inside to grab a warmer coat.

She wrapped her coat around her, sat on her front garden wall and glanced down at her empty ring finger. It felt weirdly wrong after wearing the ring while staying with Stefan all week. When she shuddered, she wasn't sure if it was the falling temperature or fear of getting too comfortable with the ring and whether that reflected how she felt about Stefan. She wished she knew whether she was being silly or whether she had reasonable grounds for her fears.

She jumped off the wall and waved to the approaching car. Although Humphries infuriated her at times, they had always worked well together despite their differences, and she was pleased to see him back on full duties. He was also astute, so if she didn't get a grip on her romantic fantasies, he would know something was up and wheedle the secret out of her. She smiled and climbed into the front seat. "Where are we heading?"

"A house in Mickleburgh," Humphries said, turning the car around. "I've been warned it's a pretty grim scene. It's a group of students in their late teens and early twenties."

Any lingering happy thoughts flew out the window when Fiona glanced across at Humphries gripping the steering wheel, looking tense. If he'd argued with Tina, he would have been complaining about women in general the second she opened the car door. For him not to be cracking jokes about her week away with Stefan was also unusual. It wasn't as if either of them was new to this game, and they had both seen things that kept them awake at night. The scene in Mickleburgh was going to be a bad one. "Okay. What happened?"

Looking straight ahead, Humphries said, "Details are vague, but the house belongs to Miss Isabella Stainton. She's a first-year student at Birstall University, and she shares her house with other students from the university. It appears a gunman broke into the house earlier this evening while they were watching television and eating takeaway pizzas."

"Oh God," Fiona said. Things like that didn't happen in the twee village of Mickleburgh. From memory, the last known criminal in the village was an amorous goose terrorising residents and their pets. "Were any of them killed?"

"All of them except Isabella."

"Oh." Fiona gave herself a moment to let the situation fully sink in and get her brain in gear. "Did Isabella come home from an evening out and find them?"

"This is where it becomes a little strange. She was in the living room with the others but was left unharmed. A neighbour returned home from an evening out with his wife to hear her screaming. He finally broke in and found her crying hysterically in the middle of the room, surrounded by her dead friends."

Fiona's hand went to her mouth. "The poor girl. Where is she now?"

"She's been taken to Birstall Hospital, and her parents are on their way from Surrey."

"Has she said anything?"

Humphries shook his head. "Since she stopped screaming, she has been in a catatonic state. We won't get anything useful from her this evening from the sound of things."

"Did she tell her neighbour what happened?"

"No. She hasn't spoken to anyone."

Fiona again glanced across at Humphries. He was frowning as

he concentrated his full attention on the road ahead, but she had to ask, "Then how do you know she was there when the others were shot?"

"She was wearing pyjamas."

Fiona was troubled by the incomplete answers Humphries was giving. He was king of gallows humour, and it was odd for him to be so quiet travelling to what would be a harrowing scene. His brush with death hadn't been so long ago. His return to full duties was possibly too soon, and she would have to keep a close eye on him. "Everything okay with you?"

"I'm fine. It's been a long day," Humphries said.

Fiona wasn't satisfied with the response, but accepted that Humphries didn't want to talk about whatever was bothering him and turned her full focus to work. "How many students were there?"

"Five or six, I think," Humphries said.

Fiona blew out her cheeks. Why would someone break in to shoot five people and leave a sixth behind? It didn't make any sense unless the witness managed to hide. Or she was the shooter. "The girl who survived may have come in from an evening out and gone straight upstairs to get ready for bed and come back downstairs to see what her housemates were doing. That would explain the pyjamas," Fiona said. "Was the T.V. on?"

"I'm not sure about the T.V., but there was blood splatter on her pyjamas."

"Oh. Okay. It's possible she hid behind a piece of furniture after the shooting started, but it seems strange that she wasn't shot with the others," Fiona said. "We will need to speak to her as soon as possible. When we arrive, ask the officer with her to keep it low-key, but we will consider her as a suspect until we have more details. All the normal physical and mental health history checks."

"Will do," Humphries said. "Her medical records have already been requested."

"Is the neighbour still available?"

"Yes. He's waiting in the house next door with an officer."

"How about the pizza delivery guy?"

"The company have been contacted and are locating him."

"After seeing the scene, we'll talk briefly with the neighbour. The delivery guy can wait until the morning. I'll ring Gareth from community care first thing tomorrow to see if anybody capable of something like this has been released recently, but my gut feeling is that this is something personal and probably connected to the university." When Humphries turned towards Mickleburgh village, Fiona asked, "Do we know why they chose to live all the way out here if they're students at Birstall?"

"It's unclear, but there is a half-hourly bus service into town, and Isabella stables her two horses nearby."

"Average student, then," Fiona said, making a face. Humphries's not commenting on privileged backgrounds unnerved her. Usually, he couldn't stop himself from criticising the class system and all the inequalities it upheld. Sometimes, she was amazed he didn't refer to her as comrade Williams. "Do you know which team is there?"

"Tracey Edwards."

Fiona would have preferred to chat for the rest of the journey, any subject would do, but Humphries seemed to have other things on his mind. She stared out the window, accepting that while it would rein in her imagination, she couldn't force a conversation. In the circumstances, Humphries' sombre mood was the correct one. How could any of them expect to have normal, surrounded by so much darkness?

The silence gave her too much time to dwell on the scene they were approaching, and the dread of what she would see grew as Humphries drove them closer. Although they were trained to conduct themselves at distressing scenes and developed personal systems for internal processing, they were still people with the same feelings as everyone else. Some images could never be erased, and she anticipated this one would force itself into the top ten of her nightmares.

Fiona carried the same internal scars as her colleagues, and she felt their shared history of horrors held them together as a team. Hers were nothing special and never considered badges of honour. They were hidden deep within, but they were there all the same, festering away, buried deep in who she was and who she was becoming.

Not happy with where her imagination was taking her, Fiona desperately played her trump card to restart a conversation as Humphries drove along the unlit country lane. "Are you looking forward to the new DCI's arrival?"

"She won't be around for long."

"What makes you say that?"

"Haven't you done your research?"

"I haven't had time."

"Dewhurst will love her. She's a career officer like him," Humphries said. "She hasn't held a post longer than two years during her upward progression."

"That could mean she's good."

"Or she's moved on before the disastrous repercussions of her decisions come to light."

"That's what I love about you," Fiona said. "Your unwavering optimism never ceases to amaze."

Humphries turned the corner, and the usually quiet, leafy lane was lit up by parked vehicles and flashing lights. He parked as close to the cordoned-off area as possible, and they walked silently to the house. A young constable met them at the front garden gate, took their details, and indicated where they could grab protective clothing. Once they had changed into their suits, a tired-looking officer let them into the house.

Inside the front door, a long entrance hall with several doors on either side stretched out in front of them. They stepped around a rusty bicycle propped up against the wall and headed to a room on their left, where the main activity was based.

Holding a clipboard, Tracey met them at the door. "Be careful where you tread. The bodies will be removed shortly. I'm stepping outside for a break."

Sophie Howard, Tracey's second in command, joined them outside the door. "Do you want me to walk you through the victims?"

Fiona nodded and tried to prepare herself for the scene but was distracted by watching the experienced SOCCO leader leave. Tracey was known for being calm and methodical, and in all the years Fiona had known her, this was the first time she had seen her let her emotions get the better of her. She recalled their last meeting when Tracey told her that her eldest daughter was going to university to study law. That partly explained why she was struggling with the scene. It was easy to forget colleagues had lives and families outside of work, especially for someone as efficient and businesslike as Tracey.

Fiona was reaching a point where she wanted to go after Tracey rather than enter the room, and it was almost a relief when Sophie opened the door, removing the option to run. The scene couldn't be as bad as her imagination's gruesome picture.

Fiona focussed her mind on the room's details. A large openplan living area made of two rooms knocked into one. Three large matching sofas were arranged around an oversized low table strewn with pizza boxes, half-eaten pizza slices and wine glasses. Attached to the wall was a wide-screen television. Beyond the seating area was a dining room table and ten hardback chairs. Behind that, a glass sliding door led outside. It would be a familiar everyday scene without the blood splatter and smears. Her chest tightened, and bile rose in her throat as she counted the covered bodies.

"Was the T.V. on when you arrived?" Fiona asked.

"No, but I believe someone switched it off before we arrived." Sophie tapped her clipboard and stopped at the first covered body lying on the floor closest to the door. "Martin Kelley. Second-year student at Birstall University, studying Anthropology. One shot to the front of the head. From his position by the door, we're assuming he was the first victim, and he possibly let the attacker in."

"Or he was the first to accost the intruder," Humphries said.

"Also possible. We haven't fully assessed the door lock yet," Sophie said, moving towards a covered body slumped over the arm of the nearest sofa. "Simon Marlow. A second-year student studying Civil Engineering. Also shot to the front of the head but from a further distance. Possibly in the process of standing. Next to him is Harry Benningfield, who was studying to become a vet. He was also shot to the front of his head."

Sophie checked her clipboard before stepping over to the third covered body lying across the adjacent sofa. "Tilly Feakes. First-year student studying Geology. One shot to the back of the head from a similar distance." Sophie walked behind the third sofa. "Suzie Blackford. First-year student studying History of Art. One shot to the front of the head at close range while cowering behind the sofa." Sophie hugged the clipboard to her chest. "It will take some time to process this fully, but you'll have our report as soon as possible."

"Thank you," Fiona said, squeezing Sophie's arm. "We won't take up much more of your time. Do you know where the neighbour found the sixth student who survived? I believe she's called Isabella?"

Sophie looked to the ceiling, blinked back a tear and took a deep breath before turning toward the dining room table. "The neighbour said between the table and the sofas." Indicating with her arm, she added, "About here."

"Thank you." Fiona looked around the surrounding devastation. Her mind raced, piecing together the last moments of the students' lives. Her instinct was to close down those thoughts to protect her well-being, but her responsibility was to the victims. She needed to commit every last detail to her memory if she was going to catch the killer. Remembering to breathe, she systematically looked around the room for anything that seemed out of place other than the obvious. Something to explain what had happened. But there was nothing. "We're going to go next door to speak to the neighbour. Call me later if you want to talk."

Tracey met them in the hallway. "Sorry about that. I needed five minutes."

"Understandable," Fiona said. "Have you looked through the

rest of the house?"

"We're still checking, but it looks like the living room was the only place disturbed," Tracey said. "Everything suggests someone walked in, shot the occupants, turned and walked out. The 'why' is over to you."

Fiona grimaced and continued along the corridor. She stopped outside the house and leaned on one of the parked police cars. "Sorry, was there anything else you wanted to see back there?"

Humphries said, "You'll hear no argument from me about us not hanging around inside. We would only have been in the way." He formed two fists. "What a bloody waste."

Fiona closed her eyes and took a few deep breaths. "We'll see what the neighbour can tell us. I can't imagine what it was like walking in there with the T.V. blaring and the girl screaming. Must have been one hell of a shock." Fiona pushed herself away from the car and stopped. "I forgot to ask which neighbour it was."

"You stay there. I'll go and ask one of the constables," Humphries said.

CHAPTER FIVE

Fiona and Humphries walked the short distance to Plum Tree cottage to speak to the neighbour, Dan Lown. A uniformed constable opened the door and led them over uneven floorboards into a small snug, where Dan sat with two cats on his lap. He started to stand to greet them, but Fiona indicated he could stay sitting.

The constable asked, "Can I get you a cup of tea or coffee?"

"Two coffees, please. Both milk if you have it, one with sugar, one without."

The constable took the empty mug offered by Dan and slipped out of the room.

Sitting, Fiona asked, "How are you feeling?"

Dan shrugged. "I think I'm running on coffee fumes. I'm exhausted, but I don't see how I could sleep after what I saw. I'm too afraid to risk closing my eyes for five minutes. I assume it will get better with time. You must see awful things like that all the time. Do you have a system for getting to sleep at night you could share with me?"

"It's often difficult," Fiona admitted. "Is your wife asleep upstairs?"

"Yes. Thank God she didn't come next door with me. To think we moved out here for a more peaceful way of life. In my wildest dreams, I never imagined seeing something as grotesque as I did tonight. Especially somewhere like this," Dan said. "I gave my wife only the briefest of details. She's had a long day at work and was tired after the show, so I persuaded her to go to bed before she could ask too many questions. She's suffered from anxiety in the past, and I want to keep as much as possible from her. I was thinking of telling her it was carbon monoxide poisoning."

"I understand you want to protect your wife, but you might find that difficult. We will withhold as much as possible, but the press is likely to be all over the story," Fiona said.

"We try to avoid the newspapers whenever we can. They're so depressing."

Fiona wondered how wealthy you had to be able to cocoon yourself in village life away from the harsh realities of modern-day life in Britain. She doubted they were wringing their hands at the thought of losing their winter heating allowance, but that didn't detract from the horror he had seen earlier. "You were out this evening, I understand."

"Yes, seeing a comedy, would you believe, to celebrate my birthday. *Jack Absolute Flies Again.* It was incredibly funny. And then... We came home to this."

The constable reappeared to hand out coffees, indicating which had sugar, before quietly sitting in a chair in the far corner of the room.

"Do you feel able to tell us everything that happened this evening when you arrived home?" Fiona asked. She hated asking the question, knowing that he would be spending months, if not the rest of his life, recalling the scene and realising the picturesque village wasn't the safe sanctuary from all evil he once thought. They needed his account, and it had to be as accurate as possible, so the best she could do was be as gentle as possible and not hate herself too much afterwards. "While they may be unpleasant, please don't hold any details back from us."

Dan sipped his coffee and took a deep breath. "Our youngest son was in the play, and we had a drink with the cast afterwards. We arrived home around midnight in high spirits. We heard someone screaming as we were walking to our front door. We waited outside the door for a short while, deciding what to do. We hoped it was nothing serious and would stop of its own accord. When it didn't, I told my wife to go inside, lock the door and call the police."

"Have you had a problem before?" When Dan shook his head, Fiona said, "I wondered why you immediately thought that you could be in danger."

"My priority was to ensure my wife felt safe. She can be very nervous." Dan stopped to take another sip of coffee.

"I appreciate that, but people generally only call the police if they feel they are at immediate risk," Fiona said.

"If everything was okay, I would probably have returned before the call ended." Dan put his coffee to one side and shrugged. "We could always call again to tell them it was a false alarm."

Fiona wasn't entirely convinced and made a mental note to check if there was a history of emergency calls. "What happened next?"

"I walked around to next door to see what was happening. I had no clear idea of what could be going on or what I could do. But the noise was rather distressing, and I had to do something to stop it. I pushed the front door, expecting it to be locked, but it opened. The screaming was ear-piercing inside the house, but I couldn't see anything to explain why she was making such a racket. There were no sounds of movement coming from the rest of the house, so I carefully walked to where the screaming was coming from, shouting out 'hello' or words to that effect. Receiving no reply, I thought they had gone to bed and left the television on at maximum volume." Dan fell silent, picking up his coffee and staring into it.

Fiona waited for Dan to continue. When he didn't, she asked, "When you drove into your street earlier, did you see anyone leaving the area? By car or on foot?"

Dan clenched and unclenched his jaw. "A couple of cars passed us on the main road, but nothing after we turned off for the village. We were relaxed and chatting so I might have missed something, but nothing stood out as unusual."

"Any lights on in the other houses?"

"No, this is a very quiet area, and everything was in darkness. Allison, who lives on the other side of the students, is in America visiting her daughter and son-in-law. The only other house down this end of the village is where May and Clive live with their live-in carer. It's well set back behind trees, and they're in their nineties. These old stone houses are very soundproof. If they were in bed, I doubt they would have heard anything. Knowing May, if your flashing lights woke her up, she would be around here now in her dressing gown, wanting to know what was going on. Thinking about it, I'm not sure we would have heard anything if we had been in for the night watching television."

"Okay, thank you," Fiona said, pleased to see some colour had returned to Dan's face. "I was wondering where the inquisitive neighbours were."

"If you're all still here in the morning, I'm sure you'll be bombarded with questions. Everything they say about nosey neighbours in small villages is true."

Fiona felt a fraud for smiling at Dan, knowing it was time to return him to the scene inside next door. She held eye contact with him, hoping she looked reassuring. "What happened when you reached the room?"

A muscle twitched when Dan re-clenched his jaw. "I looked in and saw the carnage. There was so much blood. It was hard to tell which was pizza, which was … I averted my eyes and stared directly at the girl as I closed the gap between us. I was in shock and on autopilot, as I'm sure you can imagine. I don't know why, as it's not the sort of thing I would normally do, but I hugged her. She tightly hung on to me and, after a while, stopped screaming. We were standing there together like that when the police arrived."

"Did Isabella say anything between screaming and falling silent?" Fiona asked.

Dan shook his head. "When I stepped back from her, it was as if somebody had flicked the off switch. Although she looked directly at me, my presence didn't appear to register. She was there but wasn't, if you know what I mean. I heard a young officer speaking to her, but she wasn't reacting in any way. I don't know how to describe how she was."

"Okay, thank you," Fiona said. "Do you remember if the T.V. was on?"

"It was. I didn't want to look at … I couldn't keep looking at the girl, so I stared at the screen. Don't ask me what was on. One of the officers switched it off while another led me out of the room. I don't think I was in a much better state than Isabella for a while. I still feel numbed by the experience. I don't think I'll try to sleep tonight."

Fiona glanced over to the officer and back to Dan. "It might be an idea to contact your doctor for something to help you to sleep."

"My wife has some sleeping tablets somewhere, but I don't like taking things unnecessarily," Dan said. He put his coffee mug to one side and gripped the arms of his chair. "What if they come back? Shouldn't I be ready and alert?"

"I understand your fears, but in the circumstances, sleeping tablets might help, and there will be trained officers working through the night next door," Fiona said. "Did you have much to do with the students before this evening?"

Dan started to look less tortured as Fiona led him away from the scene again. "Like most people in the village, I wasn't too happy about them moving in, but they haven't been too much trouble. The lads are quite pleasant. One of them came around and fixed my lawn mower. Simon, I think his name is. And the other one, Martin, would always wave from his bicycle. I didn't see too much of the girls or the third lad. I've seen them as a group in the village pub a couple of times. That's about it, really."

"They weren't welcomed by the village?"

"Oh, there was no nastiness. We would have preferred a couple of a similar age to us. That's all I meant. We did worry about noise and late-night parties, but there has never been anything like that. They were a pleasant group of young people, just not our age group." Dan sipped his coffee. "I wish now that we'd been more welcoming."

"Did they have many visitors?"

"Rarely," Dan said. "Not staying with them, anyway. Occasionally, cars would stop by to pick them up, but I can't say as we took any notice."

"Before you went out this evening, did you see any additional cars next door?"

Dan shook his head. "We were both late home from work. We shot in and changed, ready to go out again, but I don't remember there being any extra cars out the front."

"So, there might have been?"

Dan closed his eyes and thought back. Opening them, he said, "No. Only their two cars were in the driveway."

A shrill ringtone filled the silence, and Humphries apologetically pulled the phone from his pocket and looked at the screen. "I'll take this outside."

"What will happen now?" Dan asked.

"Our people will be next door for several days. I expect reporters will turn up tomorrow, and they may hang around for a few days. If they do, I suggest you don't speak to them."

Dan shuddered. "Blood-thirsty ghouls looking for a front-page story. They won't hear anything from me."

Humphries walked back into the room and addressed Fiona. "There was some misunderstanding, and the pizza delivery boy has been kept at the shop waiting to be interviewed. Should I tell them we're on our way, or should he go home?"

"We'll see him now." Fiona stood and turned to face Dan. "Thank you very much for your time. We will probably want to speak to you and your wife again soon. In the meantime, try to get some sleep. Don't get up. We can see ourselves out."

CHAPTER SIX

Driving to the pizza shop in Turville, Humphries said, "What do you think? He was brave to go next door, not knowing what he might find."

"I don't expect he properly thought it through. He mentioned his wife's anxiety, but I think the move to somewhere quieter was as much for his benefit. Chances are he was marching over there to have a word about them keeping the noise down," Fiona said.

"Fair," Humphries said.

"I wonder if he expected some trouble from them. Otherwise, why did he ask his wife to stay indoors with the doors locked and call the police? I'll check tomorrow to see if there have been any previous complaints."

"He described them as quiet and said there were no wild parties," Humphries reminded Fiona.

"No one likes to speak ill of the dead," Fiona said. "Plus, I almost had the impression they had the police number on speed dial. I let his comment about being more welcoming go because I wanted him to focus on this evening, but I think there was some friction there."

"Are you considering him as a suspect?"

Fiona shook her head. "While a reluctance to have students living next door might explain him marching around there about the noise, I don't think tonight resulted from a neighbourly dispute. I did wonder if repairing his mower was an olive branch from the students, possibly following a previous complaint."

"Did you see the photographs dotted about the house?" Humphries asked. "Unless they haven't been updated for a while, their children will be of a similar age."

"Maybe they felt a sense of responsibility, and he went around there out of concern, but that doesn't explain why he sent his wife indoors to call the police. He's not on my list of suspects, but we'll still complete preliminary checks on him and his wife," Fiona said. "Do we know what the pizza shop owner has been told?"

"Just that there had been an incident at a delivery address and that we wanted to contact the delivery driver," Humphries said as he pulled into the Turville Business Park. The area was in darkness, and no other vehicles were on the road. "These places are a warren. I hope the directions are correct." After a few quick turns, he pulled up outside a small unlit unit.

"It looks empty, but we'll go and see," Fiona said, removing her seatbelt as she looked up at the small pizza sign. She rang the buzzer beside the metal door, and they stood back to wait. The speaker crackled into life, and Humphries announced who they were.

A stocky, middle-aged man with tattooed muscles opened the door to them. "You took your time. We've been waiting hours for you."

"Sorry, there was a misunderstanding, and we didn't know you were waiting," Humphries said.

"But we're here now," Fiona said. "Is the delivery driver still here?"

"Jay, yes. He's through here. I run a tight ship, and I vet all the delivery lads. None of them have any convictions. I don't want any trouble."

A skinny boy who looked to be in his late teens or early twenties was sitting at a counter drinking coffee.

"Hi Jay, I'm DI Fiona Williams. Do you know why we've come to see you?"

"Not really, no. I know I haven't done anything wrong tonight,"

Jay said defensively. "Something about a delivery I made."

"That's right," Fiona said. The boy looked terrified as well as defensive. She suspected he was more scared of a reaction from his boss than anything else. His presence, leaning against the wall with his thick arms folded, was unnerving. "Do you remember delivering pizzas to Clearview House in Mickleburgh?"

"The posh house in that village? Yeah," Jay said, picking up an electronic receipt.

The owner asked, "What is Jay accused of doing?"

"Relax," Humphries said. "He's not being accused of anything. We just need to check a few details."

Fiona reached for the receipt. "May I?" Taking it, she asked, "Do you remember anything about the delivery?"

"Not much. They're lying if they say I damaged their property or something. Nothing happened. I rang the bell, the guy came out and I handed over the boxes."

"Is it a regular delivery?"

Jay shrugged. "I reckon I've delivered to them five, maybe six times in the last few months."

"It will be on our records. Do you want me to check?"

"That would be really helpful," Humphries said.

The owner disappeared through a side door while Fiona read through the items ordered. There were only four pizzas on the order, but judging from the size of the boxes, that would easily be enough for six people. "Was the order always the same?"

"No idea. I just deliver it," Jay said, stifling a yawn. "Sorry."

"Can you remember anything about the man who came to the door to collect the order?" Fiona asked.

"Not a lot. Tallish and in his twenties. He didn't keep me waiting and was polite like. He opened the door as soon as I rang the bell and thanked me."

"Was it always him who came to the door when you delivered there?"

"I don't take that much notice of who answers the door, but I think there was another guy at least once. Similar age," Jay said.

"Oh, and a girl one time."

The owner returned with a computer printout. "Can you tell me what happened? Has there been a complaint against Jay?"

"No, nothing like that," Fiona said.

"Then what are you doing here?" the owner said, flexing his fingers. "I run a legit business, and I have a right to know why you've kept us here half the night."

Fiona started to apologise before Humphries said, "An intruder entered the house and assaulted the occupants after the pizzas were delivered."

"So, nothing to do with us?"

"We don't think so at this stage," Humphries replied. "But it's early days in our investigation."

"The last few months they've ordered pizzas from us about three Fridays a month. We don't tend to beat up our regular customers. It wouldn't be a good business model." The owner handed Humphries the printout. "Sorry to hear about the assault. We'll give them a discount on their next order."

"Could you give me the names of all your employees who have delivered to that address?" Humphries asked.

"It was probably mostly Jay, but if you give me some time, I could go back through the records and probably work it out."

"When you delivered the pizzas, did you see anyone else in the area? On foot or in a vehicle?" Fiona asked Jay.

"No. The place was in darkness as usual. I don't really like going out there because it's so isolated. I'm always worried about what would happen if the bike broke down."

"You're absolutely sure that you didn't see anyone else?" Fiona asked. "Or sense there might have been someone watching the house?"

"Not any more than usual," Jay said. "Like I said, going out there always gives me the creeps. They don't even have streetlights. It's like the back of beyond. In the winter, if it's windy, the trees make weird sounds."

"How soon after Jay was there did this assault happen?" the owner asked.

"Hard to tell," Fiona said, thinking back over the scene and shuddering. "They were about halfway through eating the pizzas."

"So, someone could have been watching me when I delivered the pizza," Jay said, chewing a thumbnail.

"Possibly. Are you sure you didn't see anything?"

"No. It was dark. I shot in there and straight back out again as I had other deliveries to make. The delivery times are on there," Jay said, indicating the computer receipt. "If they saw me, do you think they'll come after me?"

"Why would they do that?" Humphries asked.

"Cos even though I didn't see them, they might think I did. Being a witness puts a target on my back."

"We'll let you know if we think you have any reason to worry," Humphries said.

Fiona stood to thank the owner and Jay. "Thank you very much for your time. We're sorry to have kept you up so late, but what you've said has been extremely helpful. Someone will drop by to collect that list of employees tomorrow."

"Can you pass on our good wishes and tell them that we wish them well as valued customers?"

Humphries nodded and followed Fiona outside.

"It's nearly four o'clock," Fiona said. "After dropping me off, go home and try to get a few hours' sleep. I'll give a team briefing at nine o'clock tomorrow morning."

CHAPTER SEVEN

Seconds after Fiona's alarm clock went off, her telephone rang. Still half asleep, she reached for her phone on her bedside cabinet to answer it, knocking it to the floor. Swearing, she leaned over the side of the bed to grab it, sending a rush of blood to her head. "Oh, morning, Stefan. Anything wrong?"

"Everything is good," Stefan said with far too much energy for that time of the morning. "Did you see my message last night?"

Fiona sat up, rubbing her tired eyes. "No, what does it say? I had a late call-out last night. Or more like this morning."

"Oh. Okay. Sorry. I hope I didn't wake you," Stefan said. "Have a look at it as soon as you get the chance and let me know what you think."

"Will do," Fiona said, swinging her legs out of bed, wondering what he was so excited about. He already knew his position heading up the cold case reviews was permanent, and he would be based in Cardiff for the foreseeable future.

"Speak later. Sorry to have woken you. Love you."

"Love you, too." Fiona dropped her head, trying to build sufficient motivation to move. She had crashed out the second her head hit the pillow, but three hours of sleep wasn't enough for anyone. Let alone someone who needed to be bright and alert at the start of a major murder enquiry. She counted to three and launched herself off the bed.

Her cold shower had jolted her into life, but she doubted it would sustain her through the day without assistance. Slumped at her kitchen table, she nursed her first coffee of the day and looked for Stefan's message.

The message contained a link to a cottage. A beautiful cottage on a country lane not far from the sea, at a ridiculously low price. She massaged her temples. There must be something seriously wrong with it at that price. Did they really want to take on a major renovation project when they both had stressful jobs with long, unpredictable hours?

The explanation for the price came as a kick to the stomach. It was a two-hour drive west of Birstall, in Wales. What was Stefan playing at? They had agreed on a midway point for their first home together so neither of them would have too long a commute. That meant somewhere between the eastern fringes of Birstall and Chepstow, and she had argued hard that as she was regularly on-call, it should be far closer to Birstall than Chepstow. And not in Carmarthenshire. Even if it was a fantastic four-bed by the sea. She put her phone away to deal with it later.

The murders quickly replaced thoughts about the cottage by the sea as she drove to work. As she anticipated, press vans lined the pavement outside the station car park. She hoped her hastily applied makeup covered the dark circles under her eyes as she shielded those sleep-deprived eyes and her pasty skin from the camera flashes and drove into the car park. She ignored the shouted questions, locked her car and hurried inside the station.

When she arrived in the incident room, she went straight to the coffee machine, standing behind DC Rachael Mann. "Morning. I take it everyone heard about the shootings last night?"

"It would be hard not to," Rachael said, taking her cup from the machine. "As you'd expect, it's all the local media are talking about, but the national press has also already picked up the story."

"Yes, I ran the gauntlet of their reporters when I drove in," Fiona said. "What time did they arrive?"

"Before me," Rachael said, taking her coffee from the machine. "Dewhurst popped in a while ago looking for you. I think he's setting up a press conference. What happened? What's the background?"

"I'll update you with the facts once everyone is in," Fiona said, stepping up to the coffee machine. "I haven't seen the press reports yet. What are they saying?"

"The usual wild speculation about the suspect, with undertones of racism and police incompetence. And the university has called asking if they should increase security. Not much of a welcome back for you," Rachael said.

"It wasn't a scene I ever want to see again, and the thought of the press and other racists milking it sickens me," Fiona said. "Humphries was badly shaken by it last night. How's he been this last week while I've been away? I thought he was keen to return to full duties, but he didn't seem his normal self last night."

Rachael rolled her eyes. "It seems the honeymoon is well and truly over. While you were away, he had a night on the town with Eddie and Andrew. Let's just say Tina wasn't too happy with the state he returned in, and he's spent a couple of nights in Eddie's spare room. I think last night was the first time he was allowed back home."

"Ah, that might explain it." Fiona took her coffee to her desk to read the overnight reports and prepare herself for the briefing. She had hoped they would make an exception and do the postmortems over the weekend, but they were booked in for Monday. Two pathologists were assigned, but it would still take up most of the day.

She glanced up when Humphries arrived with hair still wet from a shower. He looked tired, but that was hardly surprising. She probably did as well. She would ask him later how things were at home. He was a good officer and friend but didn't always have the best work ethic, especially when it came to balancing home and work. With the case ahead of them, she needed everyone to be at the top of their game.

She was drinking her fourth coffee when she pulled her team together. Although they had heard about the shooting, she ran through the brief details again while pinning photographs of the five students to the whiteboard. She stopped while pinning the picture of Isabella on the other side of the board. "For unknown reasons, Isabella Stainton was in the house with her friends but was left unharmed. She's in Birstall Hospital being treated for shock. I will be heading there this morning with Humphries to speak to her. Whether she's a victim or a suspect is yet to be seen, but she is currently the only witness to the slaughter of her friends."

"Could she be responsible?" Rachael asked.

"She has no history of mental health problems, but I want us all to keep an open mind at this stage," Fiona said. "She's obviously been in a highly stressed state since the shooting and heavily sedated. We don't know yet how or why she was spared."

"It seems odd no one saw the shooter leave the area," DS Abbie Ward said. "The gunshots must have been heard."

"Not necessarily, but we need to find out," Fiona said. "Mickleburgh is an affluent village, and many residents are retired. When we arrived last night, all the surrounding houses were in darkness, and nobody came out to see what was happening. But we can't assume nobody saw anything. Uniform is sending a team out there this morning to knock on doors. There are less than a hundred houses in the village, so it shouldn't take too long to check whether anyone noticed anything last night. I expect a fair few of the residents were already tucked up in bed, and most of the houses are shielded from the road by trees and long driveways. Can you and Rachael keep an overview of that? The village has a popular pub, the Wheatsheaf Arms. It's worth you taking a trip out there to ask the landlord if there have been any new faces recently and the names of any drinkers who left after closing time. You can follow up on any witnesses in the village at the same time, if there are any. And on your way, can you pick up a list of delivery drivers who delivered pizzas to the house? The owner will expect you. All the details are in our initial report."

"Do we know if the victims drank in the Wheatsheaf?" Abbie asked.

"According to the neighbour, occasionally, so ask who they came in with and whether they have been involved in any incidents. The neighbour said there was some ill-feeling about a student house in the village. I can't imagine it's relevant to what happened last night, but it's worth asking questions about how they were received locally."

"What do you want us to do before then?" Rachael asked.

"Get hold of Gareth from community care and arrange a face-to-face with him. I was going to speak to him, but there's a chance I'm going to be summoned by Dewhurst for the initial press conference. Don't give Gareth too many details but ask him whether they have anyone in their care capable of doing something like this. And a list of recent releases."

"You think it's random, then?" Abbie asked.

"It's too soon to tell, but we can't rule it out," Fiona said, even though she was praying it wasn't in case they struck again. "Ask him if he knows anyone with a serious issue with the university or students generally. When you're finished in Mickleburgh, assist Eddie and Andrew."

"Doing what?" Andrew asked.

Fiona turned her attention to DC Andrew Litton and DS Eddie Jordan. "I want you two at the university talking to friends of the victims. Concentrate first on Isabella's. She is studying English Literature. The victim's course details are in the file. See if they've upset anyone recently and what type of company they kept. Usual preliminaries until we can get a handle on this. Keep in contact with everyone and pass on any significant updates. The university has called about security. Until we know something more, reassure the students we don't think they are at additional risk, but they should be extra vigilant and contact us if they see or hear anything unusual."

Fiona and Humphries were preparing to leave when Fiona sensed Superintendent Ian Dewhurst approaching her desk. He was the last person she wanted to see, but she forced a smile and turned to face him.

Dewhurst rocked up and down on the balls of his feet with his hands clasped behind his back. Ignoring Humphries, he spoke directly to Fiona. "That was a nasty business last night. Let's hope it was some kind of personal student vendetta, and you quickly get to the bottom of it. I don't like the idea of that type of lunatic roaming the area."

"I don't think anyone does, sir," Fiona said. "I have a team on its way to the university, and we're just leaving to visit the student who survived the attack."

"That's unfortunate as I was hoping you would join me in a press conference this morning. Well, I suppose it is early days, and all they will be looking for is a general reassurance that we are doing everything we can to catch the person responsible and keep our community safe."

Fiona nodded along, relieved Dewhurst wasn't insisting she attend. She wouldn't be so lucky avoiding subsequent ones.

Dewhurst paused to look Fiona up and down. "You look tired and not dressed for a conference."

Fiona sucked in her cheeks before pointing out, "I didn't arrive home until after four o'clock this morning."

"I appreciate that," Dewhurst said. "As you know our new DCI is due to start next month. Until then, you continue to report directly to me."

Fiona nodded her agreement. The arrival of the new DCI would take some of the pressure off her - so long as they got along. "I look forward to meeting her, but meeting with the witness has to be my priority for now."

"I quite agree. It must have been a terrifying ordeal for the poor girl," Dewhurst said, shaking his head. "I believe I know her father."

Knowing how Dewhurst networked, Fiona silenced an inner groan. "Well, time is of the essence."

"Yes, yes, of course," Dewhurst said, showing no signs of moving away. "Indeed, I'm here to bring you some more good news. I have a new DC for you. Miss Kerry Vines. She'll be here tomorrow, or possibly the day after."

Fiona hurriedly hid her frown. The last thing she needed was a young recruit in need of training. She picked up her bag, nodded to Humphries, and said, "We should be leaving."

Dewhurst continued to block Fiona's exit. Humphries had stepped away, but he returned to Fiona's side in a show of support. Still rocking on his feet, Dewhurst said, "I take it from your expression you recognise the name. Yes, her father has done incredibly well for himself in the force, but he wants his daughter to be treated like any other young constable. I'll make the introductions tomorrow morning."

"I look forward to meeting her," Fiona lied, as Dewhurst finally moved out of the way, and she hurried towards the door.

In the corridor, Humphries said, "Oh goody, we're going to be joined by police royalty. Do you think he'll expect you to curtesy tomorrow morning?"

"I'm no more impressed about it than you are, but let's not worry about it now," Fiona said, marching along the corridor. It seemed Humphries had returned to his usual self, but the constable's background didn't interest her.

"You do know who her father is, don't you?"

"I've no idea, but I expect you're going to enlighten me."

"He's an Assistant Chief Constable in Dorset. It will be some sort of personal favour. I expect it was all agreed over cocktails," Humphries said.

Fiona clocked the information, saying nothing, deciding last night's wish for the return of the old Humphries had been hasty.

"Dewhurst giving us an experienced officer who has moved up the ranks by merit would be too much to ask for," Humphries continued. "And despite all the promises he'll make to the press this morning, he'll be complaining about our overtime within a week."

"It is what it is, and I don't have any say in the matter," Fiona said. "We're at the start of a potentially difficult case, and I don't want any unnecessary distractions. Chances are the others won't recognise the new constable's name any more than I did, and we won't tell them. I want you to be civil to her and treat her like everyone else."

"Just like dear Papa requested."

"That's that sorted. Now, can we focus on the case? The family will be distraught by what has happened."

"Sure. It might have reduced the house's value."

"Humphries! I'm warning you."

CHAPTER EIGHT

Fiona and Humphries found the Stainton family in a private side ward at the hospital. There hadn't been any press at the hospital entrance, so it seemed for now they were unaware of the girl's location. The officer stationed outside took their details and confirmed there had been no visitors other than the parents who were with their daughter. Fiona knocked before entering and waited to be invited inside. A young woman who introduced herself as Becky, the family liaison, opened the door

Isabella's father, who was tall and stern-looking, became overly concerned about the lack of chairs and said he would go to find some, while her mother perched anxiously on the edge of the bed. Isabella sat cross-legged in the middle of the bed, surrounded by discarded gift wrapping.

Fiona sat on the chair Isabella's father had vacated and asked her how she was feeling.

"Much better than before, but still a little groggy," Isabella replied. "They gave me something to calm me down and help me to sleep last night."

The smile Isabella had given when they entered was gone. Close up, Fiona could see her eyes were troubled, and she was trembling. The earlier Christmas morning imagery had been illusionary. "I know you've suffered a terrible ordeal, but we need to ask you about what you remember of last night."

Isabella gave an involuntary gulp and put her hand to her chest. "Daddy warned me you would, and I want you to catch that horrid man."

Twisting the bed sheet into a tight knot, her mother said, "We should wait until my husband returns. He shouldn't be long."

Fiona nodded her agreement and settled for chatting with Isabella about her course. As they talked, Isabella relaxed, and it was clear that university was more of a social activity than an intellectual one for her. She was scathing about her course and the lecturers, but had made some super chums.

She was relieved to see Humphries stand unnoticed beside Becky in the corner of the room, jotting down names and anything else that seemed relevant. He had expressed his views on adults who referred to their parents as Mummy and Daddy in the past, and it wasn't flattering. Fiona's gut feeling was that it indicated Isabella's immaturity as much as her class.

Isabella's father bustled in carrying two chairs. He positioned his chair alongside Fiona while Humphries edged his chair back out of sight. Isabella's mother remained on the edge of the bed, occasionally stroking her daughter's arm.

"Can you tell us about last night?" Fiona asked. Isabella's response was to lower her head, forcing Fiona to prompt, "What were you all doing before the intrusion?"

Isabella's mother reached for her daughter's hand and gripped it tightly. "Does she have to do this?"

"I appreciate it's difficult, but unfortunately, yes," Fiona said.

"It's okay, Mummy," Isabella said, raising her head with a determined look.

Her father nodded his approval. "Probably best you get it over and done with."

Isabella exchanged a quick smile with her father. "I was in the kitchen preparing my supper while the others were in the living room watching a film."

"You weren't sharing the pizza?" Fiona asked.

"I'm particular about what I eat," Isabella said. "I was going to join them later."

Isabella's response sounded cold and haughty, taking Fiona by surprise. It was possibly nothing more than a defence mechanism, but eating separately suggested a demarcation in the house. She was looking for any early clues to explain why she was spared and told herself not to read too much into their eating arrangements. "Did you hear the pizza being delivered?"

"Yes, that was a while before. Have you visited the house?" Isabella asked. When Fiona nodded, she said, "Then you'll know the kitchen window looks out over the front garden. I looked up when I heard him rev his motorbike, and I saw him drive away."

"That's helpful to know," Fiona said, hoping it also meant she had seen the intruder arrive. "Did you hear the doorbell when the pizza boy arrived?"

"I did, but I was busy on the other side of the kitchen, away from the window, looking through the cupboards."

"What happened next?" Fiona asked. "After the pizza had been delivered."

"I carried on cooking. I had turned my music up, but I think I heard a knock on the door. I remember thinking that the delivery guy had forgotten something, so I was surprised not to see his bike when I walked over to glance out the window. There wasn't a car either, so I reasoned either I had imagined hearing a noise at the door, or it was someone from the village. They occasionally come around to sell raffle tickets or to update us about local matters. As I'm the house owner, I thought it was me that they needed to see, so I turned the saucepans off and washed my hands."

Isabella paused. Her hands trembled while she carefully folded a piece of wrapping paper until it could fold no more. She looked to her father for support, but he was distracted by something on his phone screen.

Fiona gave the father a scathing glare before softening her look and catching Isabella's eye. "What happened next?"

Isabella looked back with vacant eyes. "I heard a popping sound, and the girls screamed."

"A popping sound?"

"It didn't register as a gunshot. It was too quiet and muffled. I assumed the sound had come from the film they were watching, and it had made them jump. Except Tilly continued to scream. I dried my hands and walked through to the living area."

"You heard your friend screaming and you didn't think to run away and hide?" Fiona asked. "Or run to her assistance?"

Isabella shook her head. "I thought it was odd, but it didn't occur to me that something serious could be happening. I mean, why would it? It was just a regular Friday night. I thought they were messing around, and the visitor was someone they knew. Can I stop for a glass of water?"

Isabella's mother jumped up to fill a glass from the jug on the side. Her father reached forward to pat her on the shoulder. "You're being incredibly brave."

Fiona waited while Isabella drank her water. She couldn't work her out and wondered if she was still in shock. She was recalling events in a deadpan way without embellishment. Besides seeming nervous when they first entered, there were no tears, and Isabella's lack of emotion was unsettling. It was possibly the drugs she'd been given to calm her, but something didn't feel right. Her mother didn't seem surprised by the lack of emotion. As for her father checking his phone instead of giving his daughter his full attention - she had no words.

Fiona had expected sobbing and questions from all of them. The father looked like he was in a board meeting, and the mother looked permanently scared of her shadow. There had been nothing in the medical records, but there was something seriously off about how the family interacted.

Isabella handed the glass back to her mother. "I'm ready to go on now."

"Take your time and describe what you saw when you walked into the room," Fiona said.

"The first person I noticed was Suzie crouched behind the sofa. She looked up at me with a look of terror on her face." Isabella shuddered. "That look she gave me kept coming back to me last night. The nurse said I woke up a few times screaming, but I can't remember. My head feels like it's stuffed with cotton wool."

"The effect of the drugs, I expect," Fiona said. "What happened after you saw your friend?"

"Then I heard the popping sound again. I was so sure it was on the television I looked up at the screen first. I guess I must have taken a step forward, although I'm not entirely sure. That's when I saw him. He was standing in front of Tilly, facing us. She was slumped over the arm of the sofa. He was dressed in black and had a balaclava on. All I could see was his eyes. They were black and so cold. He stared right through me, and I froze."

Isabella stopped talking and stared at the door behind Fiona. She wasn't blinking, but her eyes widened and narrowed as she looked directly ahead. Fiona felt guilty about her earlier observations. How was someone who had been through what Isabella had, supposed to behave? She chastised herself for not limiting herself to making observations. She was drawing conclusions when she was too tired to think straight.

"Can't we leave it there for another time?" Isabella's mother pleaded. "You could come back tomorrow."

"Hopefully, we won't be here tomorrow," her father said. "We'll all be back home and working hard to put this dreadful chapter behind us and get on with our lives."

"What about my lectures and my end-of-year exams?" Isabella asked.

"I'll speak to the university and arrange something."

Fiona turned to look at Isabella's father. His bored expression was completely out of place. "I'm afraid we would like Isabella to stay in the area. At least until we complete our initial enquiries."

"You can't expect her to stay in that house! As soon as you've all finished in there, it will be professionally cleaned and put up for sale," Isabella's father said.

"Is there anywhere else you could stay?" Fiona asked.

"We could book into a hotel for a few days, but I have work commitments."

"Maybe, your wife and daughter could stay behind," Fiona said.

"We could stay at the Birstall Lido," Isabella's mother said. "There was an article about it in one of my magazines the other week."

"You and Daddy would find it much too hip and hate it,"

Isabella said. "It's all vegan and helping refugees. The chef is from Syria."

"Well, maybe somewhere else more suitable in Clifton," her mother said.

"Let us know when you've decided," Fiona said. "Are you okay to carry on, Isabella?" Fiona asked.

Isabella nodded. When she spoke again, it was monotone, delivered as if she was repeating a memorised list. "He was holding a pistol with a long end. It looked like a toy. I don't think I moved. I think I just stood there, watching him. He walked straight in front of me, raised the gun and shot Suzie. I watched her crumple to the floor. When I looked up, he was standing directly in front of me. He looked me all over with those black eyes, and I thought this is it. I'm next. Weirdly, I didn't panic. It was like it was all happening in a dream, to someone else. I would wake up, and it would all be okay. He moved closer, and I could smell his rancid breath. Then he turned and walked away. I think that was when I started screaming. After I heard the front door close behind him."

"Did the attacker say anything at any point?" Fiona asked. "Before walking away, maybe?"

Isabella hesitated for a fraction of a second before shaking her head. "No."

"Can you remember anything else about the intruder? Were they tall, thin?"

"A few inches taller than me, so over six feet. And he was chunky. Not skinny, but not fat." Isabella pointed at Humphries. "His sort of build."

"And you said their eyes were black. Would you say the person was white-skinned?" Fiona asked.

"I couldn't tell you. He was dressed in black and wore gloves."

"You've referred to the person as male throughout. Are you sure it was a man?"

"Definitely a man."

"How are you so sure if the person didn't speak and was covered from head to foot?"

"I could just tell. You can, can't you? It was a man."

"Can you think of anyone who might have had a serious grudge against any of you? Had any of you had any recent problems at the university? Or with an ex or a stalker, maybe? Anything at all, really, that might help us find who did this?"

"No, nobody," Isabella said, shaking her head. "I've never mixed with that type of person."

"What do you mean by 'that type of person'?" Fiona asked.

Isabella hesitated for a beat. "Someone who carries a gun and wanders into random houses to shoot everyone, to start with."

"Can we leave it there for today?" Isabella's father asked. "I can tell my daughter is becoming tired and tetchy. The doctor said she needs to be calm and rested."

"We can leave it there for today, but we will have to speak to you all again." Fiona handed her card to each of them. "If you think of anything else that might be relevant, please get in touch with me. And let me know where in the area you decide to stay."

CHAPTER NINE

Fiona and Humphries stopped in the hospital café to grab a couple of drinks and a snack. Settled in a quiet table in the corner, Fiona asked, "What did you make of them?"

"Upper-middle-class idiots who think they are special."

"Can we get past the class issue? What did you think of their reactions as a family?"

"All part of the same thing," Humphries said. "I tried to give them the benefit of the doubt, but they weren't concerned about the fate of the other students. Not one of them asked about the other families and how they were coping. Cold. They don't care about anyone except themselves."

"That was my first impression, but I don't think it was all down to class. I agree that the only time Isabella showed any emotion was when she considered her own safety, and she didn't appear upset about the death of her friends. But we don't know how much of her performance was due to a combination of delayed shock, a defence mechanism and whatever sedatives she's been given. We can't draw any sweeping conclusions about her so soon after the attack."

"I appreciate there may be an element of delayed shock, but there is something very wrong about the whole family. Even I'm prepared to say it was more than a sense of privilege and superiority," Humphries said. "I felt a physical chill in that room. Isabella is one cold fish."

"I understand your reaction. It's similar to my first impression, but I will reserve judgment until we see how she reacts in the coming days and weeks," Fiona said. "Put yourself in her position. Do you honestly know how you would react?"

"Not exactly, but I would be gutted about my friends and asking about their families. I certainly wouldn't concern myself with commenting on where my parents chose to stay. Did you hear what she said about the hotel, or were you in a different room? That told me the type of person she is."

"Maybe, but that doesn't alter the fact she's been severely traumatised, and we can't rely too much on that first interview," Fiona said.

"It's probably the most unguarded and unfiltered one we're going to get."

"Consciously guarded, possibly, but that's not giving us the complete picture of what's going on in her head," Fiona said. "Anyway, big picture. Do you think she's capable of shooting her housemates and then making up a story about a masked intruder?"

"Do I think she's a psychopath?" Humphries asked. "She appears to have plenty of the recognised traits. And I didn't buy that stuff about hearing a popping sound and thinking it was a film track! Sorry, but you don't stop to dry your hands when you hear a friend screaming. You drop everything and run in one direction or the other."

"Some people are more screamy than others."

"What's that supposed to mean?"

"I'm not saying I believe her account, only that we shouldn't judge her too harshly until we have a better picture. It's far too vague, for one thing. When we reinterview her, we'll ask for more precise details," Fiona said. "Interesting she said she thought she heard a noise at the door. Didn't the report say the lock was bumped?"

"It did." Humphries rolled his eyes. "Maybe that was the TV as well."

"Does she look like she knows how to bump a lock? And where the bodies were found, suggests they were taken by surprise in the living room by someone entering from the hallway," Fiona said. "She said she was in the kitchen, and Tracey's report says someone had been cooking."

"Turning up her music while her friends were watching television in the adjacent room is at best rude," Humphries said. "Or she didn't want her delicate ears to hear what she knew was coming."

"I suspect she was excluded from the pizza evening, and I doubt she was going to join them," Fiona said. "But if I had arranged for someone to burst in and kill my housemates, I would arrange to be elsewhere. And where's her motive?"

"We all mess up our diary from time to time."

"You're so full of bull sometimes." Fiona shook her head, but the comment lifted an otherwise bleak and depressing conversation.

"They might not have been excluding her," Humphries said. "Tina won't let me order takeaway pizza. She says they're bad for you and contain double the calories you should eat daily. Isabella could have been telling the truth about the meal if she cares about what she eats. She looks like the type to swing from one faddy diet to the next. That's about the only thing she said that I half-believed."

Fiona gave Humphries a surprised look. It was a fair comment, but this was Humphries who regularly ordered a full English breakfast with all the trimmings. "I'm going to call the liaison officer to make it clear I want a close eye kept on the family, so they don't disappear anywhere. Do we know what the father does? I'll hazard a guess that the mother is a stay-at-home housewife."

"A lady who lunches," Humphries replied, reaching for his phone. "The father is listed as a businessman and consultant. No details as to what field he's in."

Fiona finished her call to Becky and checked for any other messages. "No developments of any note. Once we've finished our coffee, we'll head out to the university to see how Andrew and Eddie are getting along. The last message from them says they're moving to the Veterinary School. I'll quickly check they're still there."

CHAPTER TEN

Fiona parked on a narrow side street and walked over to meet Eddie, who was waiting outside the veterinary school building. "Hi, how did you get on with Isabella's college friends?"

"Isabella wasn't exactly popular. Only a handful were prepared to admit to a friendship, and the two we most want to see are having a jolly in London today, so we moved on to the other students' friends," Eddie said. "Andrew is inside with someone you're going to want to talk with. Harry's best friend for the last three years, George. According to him, Harry hated Isabella. She was the worst landlady ever and had just given them all less than a week to get out of the house."

"That is interesting," Fiona said. "Did Isabella's friends know about it?"

"If they did, they didn't mention it," Eddie said. "A small group think she is great, but most of the students on her course thought her a stuck-up snob living on a different planet," Eddie said. "But as far as any of them know, nobody hated her enough to want to break in and kill her. She was aloof and condescending, but they viewed her more as a figure of fun than a serious annoyance."

"They didn't though," Humphries said. "They broke in to kill her tenants who she wanted to leave and made a point of eating separately."

"The eating separately ties in with what we've learned," Eddie said. "Although people hadn't heard anything about an eviction, it was common knowledge that Isabella and her tenants didn't

54

get along."

"Is it possible she wanted to get rid of them, and one of her friends decided to do her a favour?" Humphries asked.

Eddie pulled a face. "Not any of the giggly, superficial ones we've interviewed."

"First impressions can be deceptive," Humphries muttered.

"It's a bit of a leap," Fiona said. "It's not that unusual for living arrangements to break down at university. The normal reaction is to arrange different accommodation, not to shoot each other."

"And there was nothing normal about the family," Humphries said. "Maybe that's the way they deal with peasants."

Fiona narrowed her eyes at Humphries. "Shall we go in and see what George has to say?"

George and Andrew stood up from their chairs in the small lobby area when they walked in. Andrew introduced Fiona and Humphries before saying, "We have a couple of other students to speak with, so we'll leave you to it."

"Thanks," Fiona said. "After that, you may as well salvage what's left of your Saturday, but ring me if you hear anything significant. Otherwise, briefing first thing in the morning."

After Andrew and Eddie left, the three sat. "Thank you for agreeing to speak with us," Fiona said. "We understand Harry was a good friend."

"Yes, we met on our first day, nearly three years ago now, and hit it off straight away," George said, his voice filled with disbelief. "He was a real quiet and gentle guy. I can't get my head around what happened. It doesn't make any sense. He would have been a fantastic vet."

"What do you know about what happened?"

"Just what I've been told," George said. "Some crazy lunatic broke in and shot the lot of them. Well, all except the Ice Bitch."

"I take it that's your name for Isabella," Fiona said. "Did you know her as well?"

George looked disgusted at the suggestion. "I don't move in the correct circles. It wasn't just that she was ridiculously rich; she was a vile person inside and out. I didn't know her personally, but I heard all about her from Harry and the others. There was a room free at my place a few months back. I tried to persuade Harry to move then. But he wouldn't without Tilly. I'm freaking out with the idea that if I had managed to persuade him, he would be alive today."

"Don't blame yourself," Fiona said. "Would that be Tilly Feakes, a first-year student who also lived at the house?"

"Yes. I can't believe … She was always so full of life. Always laughing." George stopped to take a deep breath. "Sorry. All this. I just can't …"

"It's okay, take your time," Fiona said. She gave George a few moments to compose himself before asking, "Were Harry and Tilly a couple?"

"It was slowly moving in that direction. They would have been perfect together."

"Did you know the other students in the house?"

"Not as well as Harry and Tilly, but I've been out with them as a group a few times. They were all pretty sound."

"When you went out as a group, did that include Isabella?" Fiona asked.

"You're kidding, right? She wouldn't lower herself to mix socially with the likes of us. She made it very clear she owned that house, and the others were paying tenants. Soon to be ex-tenants. If only it had happened after they'd moved out."

"They were due to move out?" Humphries asked.

"Yes, although I don't know how soon. An argument blew up over a loaf of sourdough, would you believe? And she said she wanted them out. To be fair, it had been brewing for months. My understanding is they were planning to stay put until after the exams and look for somewhere else for next year," George said. "She had no concept of other people's rights. She demanded they leave within the week. Typical of her, thinking she could click her fingers, and everyone else would jump to attention and do her bidding."

"So, just to be clear," Fiona said. "You're saying the five murdered students got along well with each other, but there was a rift with Isabella, and nobody in the house liked her?"

"That's a fair summary, yes," George said. "They were all easy to get along with. I'm not sure you could describe them as close friends, but there was no animosity between them. Harry was the most inoffensive person you could ever meet. He spent most of his time quietly studying."

"Do you know if any of the group had a falling out with anyone else recently?" When George shook his head, Fiona asked, "Any recent relationships that ended badly? Were any of them concerned about someone paying them unwanted attention?"

"No, nothing like that at all," George said. "Suzie was single and had been for some time. Martin and Simon had long-term partners at other universities. I think Suzie might have had a few one-night stands in the past, but nothing serious. Tilly probably had the widest circle of friends, but as far as I know, hasn't dated anyone since she arrived here. None of them were exactly party animals which is probably why they ended up living in the sticks with the Ice Bitch. Sorry, that's what they all called her. Or IB for short."

"Were any of them regular drug users?" Fiona asked. "Or into illegal activities of any kind?"

"Honestly, they were a bunch of boring squares who preferred walking in the countryside to partying. They were into hiking, volunteering and going to car boot sales. I can't imagine any of them doing anything that would warrant the attention of a violent gunman. It must have been a completely random attack. You hear about it happening in America all the time."

"How about causes? Were Harry or the others involved in any political groups or organisations?" Fiona asked.

"As far as I know, none of them were. They had their opinions but were armchair critics rather than activists. I'm certain none of them attended rallies or marches."

"How about online?" Humphries asked.

"That would be more their style, but I've never heard them passionately arguing about anything. They weren't that type," George said.

"Did Isabella threaten them with anything if they didn't leave?" Humphries asked.

"I see what you're getting at, but much as I dislike the IB, and it sticks in my throat that she survived, I can't imagine she was responsible in any way. Her only threat was that she would tell Daddy on them," George said, rolling his eyes. "She never leaves her safe little world of ponies and daddy's money. The only explanation is it was a random lunatic, and they were in the wrong place at the wrong time."

"Why do you think Isabella was spared?" Fiona asked.

George shrugged. "If the guy was after money, maybe she bought her way out? I could imagine her bargaining for her own life and not caring about what happened to the others."

"Okay, thanks for your time," Fiona said. "Take my card and call me if you think of anything else that might be relevant or if you hear something."

Humphries checked his phone after George left. "Rachael and Abbie have finished speaking to people in the village and are heading to the engineering block to speak to Martin and Simon's friends. Nobody in the village remembers seeing anything unusual last night, but we now have a possible motive for Isabella."

"We still need to see Tilly's and Suzie's friends, but we might as well wait to hear back from the others first. I suggest we head back to the station and see what we can dig up on the Stainton family. I want to speak to Isabella again tomorrow. And if possible, those two friends who have gone to London."

"Assuming it wasn't her, do you think George could be right? Could she have struck a financial bargain with the gunman?"

"It would be unusual, but then the whole scenario is strange," Fiona said. "And I noticed a slight hesitation when I asked Isabella if the gunman said anything to her."

"Initial reports have come back negative on Isabella," Humphries said, reading from his phone. "Just minor gun residue, which would be expected after being so close to the shootings."

"That tells us she hasn't recently fired a gun, but I think we'll find our answers to what happened somewhere in her background."

"It does seem too convenient that a masked gunman has gotten rid of her unwanted tenants for her," Humphries said.

"I understand your reasoning, and her reaction is odd, but I'm not necessarily saying she was responsible. Killing them is excessive when there were only a few weeks to the end of term, when they were going to move out anyway," Fiona said. "I'm more interested in discovering what set her apart from the others. Why kill them and leave her behind as a witness? That should be where we focus our energy when looking at her. Along with the remote possibility that she somehow bargained for her life."

"Should we be looking at ex-boyfriends and anyone else who has been obsessive about her in the past? It might not be someone connected to the university."

"Wouldn't she remember an ex-boyfriend's eyes?"

"Maybe she did, and she's not telling," Humphries replied. "Or it could be someone who has obsessed over her from afar and overheard her talking about her troublesome tenants."

"That possibility can be a strand in our investigation, but there could be other reasons why she wasn't killed with the others," Fiona said.

"Such as?"

"That's what we need to find out," Fiona said, "I can't help thinking that whether she remembers them or not, the killer is someone who has crossed Isabella's path. When we see her next, we'll ask her to think about the eyes and what about the intruder's movements convinced her he was a man. Maybe it will jog something in her memory."

"So where are we with the theory that the house was chosen randomly?" Humphries asked.

Fiona rubbed her eyes. Her lack of sleep from the night before was catching up with her, and she was finding it hard to think coherently. "It's still there. Gareth might have some insights for us. But I keep coming back to the same question. If it was random, why was Isabella excluded? We know she was in the room with the others because of the blood splatter and gun residue. While I won't dismiss it entirely, I can't visualise someone halfway through shooting a room of people stopping to discuss a financial deal."

"Depends what was on the table."

CHAPTER ELEVEN

Fiona could hardly keep her eyes open on her drive home. While thoughts of the murdered students and their families were never far away, she longed for the comfort of her duvet wrapped around her and sleep. Optimistically, she convinced herself that her exhaustion would keep nightmares related to the shooting at bay.

When she pulled up outside her house, her mind was focused on grabbing something quick to eat, heading upstairs and collapsing into bed. She wasn't sure she had the energy to undress. Everything could be thrown in the wash in the morning when she woke up, hopefully feeling fully refreshed.

She was halfway through the front door, achingly close to the calm relief of her bed, when her phone rang. Pulling it from her pocket and squinting at the screen took effort. If it didn't look urgent, she would ignore the call. Seeing it was Stefan, she accepted the call. A relaxing chat while she made herself a sandwich wouldn't be so hard.

"Hi, Fi, what did you think of the house?"

Fiona let her bag slip off her shoulder and drop to the floor in the hallway. She had forgotten about the earlier message. "I've just arrived home after a rotten day. I'm making a sandwich and crashing." She changed hands to open the kitchen door. "Can we talk about it tomorrow?"

"We could, but we might lose the house," Stefan said. "It's been priced for a quick sale."

Fiona turned on the phone's loudspeaker and propped it up on the counter while she pulled out the things she needed for her sandwich. "I have a new murder enquiry, so I wouldn't be able to drop everything for a viewing," Fiona said, hoping that would be an end to the matter. The location could be discussed another day when she had more energy.

"But what do you think?"

Buttering slices of bread, Fiona said, "It looked a bargain price, but it's way outside the area we agreed we would look at."

"But can you see how much more we can buy if we move out this way? The house is perfect. Think of all the privacy and space we would have. And it's not far from the beaches. We could have a different way of life."

"I don't want a different way of life, and it's too far away. Even if I was prepared to commute that far on regular days, what would I do the nights I'm on call?" Fiona asked. "It's just not practical."

"There are other stations, you know. Believe it or not, Wales has a police force. They would be desperate to have someone of your experience."

Fiona put down her knife and turned toward the phone. Her moving station had never been part of the equation. She hadn't even considered it as an option. "Sorry Stefan, I'm exhausted. I can't think about such a major change at the moment, let alone discuss it," Fiona said. "You've thrown this at me completely out of the blue. I love my work here."

"Sorry, you're right. We've never discussed it seriously, but we have talked about the advantages of living this way. You love exploring the area and all the castles when you stay. I admit I got carried away when I saw this house, but I thought you would love it as much as I do," Stefan said. "And I'm sorry you've had a bad day. I wish I was there with you now to support you when it's been a rough day. It's why I want us to move in together as soon as possible. That house was chain-free, and after seeing it I was so excited, I guess I got a bit ahead of myself."

"Wait! Hang on. You've been to see this house?" Fiona asked. "What happened to joint decisions?"

"Only because I know it's going to be snapped up quickly, and I realised you might not be able to get away quickly."

Feeling too tired to argue constructively, Fiona was at risk of crying with frustration. "I can't do this on two hours of sleep. I'll call you sometime tomorrow after I've slept and had time to think."

"Okay. I can hear you're tired and upset. Go and get some sleep, and we can talk tomorrow. If we lose the house, then maybe it wasn't meant to be. Love you."

"Love you too," Fiona said to end the call, although she wasn't sure she meant it. She slammed cheese, lettuce, tomato and cucumber inside a sandwich and took a big bite. She chewed and took another bite. She felt tired, hungry and angry. Love didn't come into it. She crammed the rest of the sandwich into her mouth and stamped her way up to bed.

CHAPTER TWELVE

Fiona woke feeling surprisingly refreshed and ready to start the day. Moments later, images from Isabella's living room came crashing in, followed closely by last night's conversation with Stefan. Today wasn't going to be the standard lazy Sunday that most people would be enjoying, but lying in bed and looking at the ceiling wouldn't help matters.

She threw off the duvet and swung herself out of bed, consoling herself with the thought it was a miracle she had slept free of intrusive thoughts and nightmares. She would need all the energy she could get over the coming days, and she doubted she would get such another good night of interrupted sleep.

Brushing her teeth, snatches of her conversation with Stefan resurfaced. She spat out her toothpaste, making excuses for him. He wouldn't have known about the shooting. She pulled herself up straight and brushed her hair. But he should have known she had no intention of moving station and setting up home miles away in Wales.

She was unable to push her personal problems back into their box at the back of her mind until she ran through the early morning briefing. The lack of progress soon fully occupied all her thoughts. They still had no clues as to why the students had been slaughtered or why one was left untouched.

Isabella was universally disliked outside her small friendship group. The consensus was she was a spoilt, snobby bitch and should have been the first to be shot, but not a killer. The murdered students were generally well-liked and described as being reserved and thoughtful. Everyone agreed none of them were the sort to have any contact with a violent gunman, let alone annoy one.

They needed to dig far deeper to explain events. One of the girls interviewed suggested they visit a local women's refuge where Suzie and Tilly regularly volunteered, and another suggested the homeless charity where Martin sometimes prepared meals. Fiona doubted either location held the answers but had sent Andrew and Eddie to the two centres. Rachael and Abbie had gone to speak to Suzie's and Tilly's friends. Once they had done that, she told them to go and spend the remainder of their weekend with their families.

Gareth from community care had been vague when Abbie and Rachael spoke to him, and Fiona planned to find the time to visit him. Despite his general mistrust of the police, he always jokingly flirted with her when they met, and she felt they had a good working relationship.

One of Gareth's comments to Abbie and Rachael circled her mind but failed to lodge anywhere. He had suggested survivor's guilt might explain a witness being left behind, and she wanted to pin him down on whether he was referring to a particular patient or talking generally.

Meanwhile, she was impatiently drumming her fingers, waiting for Dewhurst to appear with their new DC before she left with Humphries to reinterview Isabella. The delay was doubly frustrating as Dewhurst had arranged a meeting for them with the murdered students' parents for after lunch. As usual, he hadn't consulted her first. She would prefer to spend the time investigating so she could provide the family with answers rather than offer them empty platitudes. That was more Dewhurst's forte. But having dodged the initial press conference, she knew she wouldn't get away with it for a second time.

She had no doubt Dewhurst would spend his morning picking out a suit and practising his concerned look in the mirror, while she felt sick at the thought of how emotional and draining the meeting would be. Anything she could possibly say would be inadequate and there were people better able to say the right things to them. But Dewhurst had insisted she attend as the senior officer on the case. Local officers had informed them of the deaths, and they were travelling to Birstall to demand answers. He failed to appreciate that she had no answers for them and was petrified of saying the wrong thing.

After the meeting, she would have to quickly pull herself together as she had arranged to visit Isabella's two best friends, Camilla and Laura. Eddie briefly spoke to them before they left to watch a show in London and thought they were Isabella's closest friends. While she had been dismissive when Humphries suggested Isabella had employed a hitman, her survival and her detachment from her tenants' deaths worried away at her.

Humphries called across the office, "Tracey has just sent the final scene report," as Dewhurst walked in.

Fiona called back, "Let me know if there's anything substantially new in it," as she stepped forward to greet Dewhurst and her newest recruit. "Hello, Kerry, isn't it?"

"Well, I'll leave you two to get acquainted," Dewhurst said. "I have a busy day ahead of me. Don't forget the conference room at one o'clock."

"I won't," Fiona said to Dewhurst's disappearing back. She bit her lower lip to stop herself from taking her annoyance out on her newest recruit and forced a smile. "It's good to have you on board, Kerry, but you may have heard we are in the early stages of a multiple murder enquiry, so things are a little hectic. As it's a Sunday, I won't insist you work today. I'm sure you would prefer an extra day to get your bearings, and you can start properly tomorrow."

"I'm already unpacked and don't know anyone in the area, so I'm happy to work today."

"I'm already late for a meeting. If you stay, I will have to leave you to your own devices for a couple of hours. I'll go through some things with you as soon as I return."

"No problem," Kerry said. "What can I do to help while you're gone?"

"Sorry to lumber you with it, but as you're asking, you see that stack of statements," Fiona said. "I've only glanced through a few that have been highlighted to me. If you could read through them and put them into some sort of order, that would be helpful. Make a note of anything that should be followed up, trends or anything going against the overall views. We've received access to their social media accounts. If you're finished with the statements, make a start on going through them. I'll let the desk sergeant know you're by yourself up here, but could you answer the phones? Fiona asked. "You can leave whenever you've had enough, but make sure he knows so he doesn't continue to transfer calls up here."

"Okay. I'll probably stay until you return."

"Here's my card. Contact me if you come across something that looks urgent. I'll be back as soon as I can."

Fiona grabbed her jacket from the back of her chair, called to Humphries and hurried from the room. She felt guilty about abandoning Kerry and had no idea how experienced she was, but what else could she do with her? She had chosen to stay when she'd been given the opportunity to have a free day. Seeing how she coped would at least give her some idea of her training and her strengths.

CHAPTER THIRTEEN

When Fiona returned to the station, she wasn't surprised by Kerry's absence. Wandering around alone would be more entertaining than organising statements in a stuffy office. She found a note on her desk from her, saying she had been called away by Dewhurst to go through some personnel details and to have her access to the computer system set up. That did surprise her as she assumed Dewhurst would be off playing golf, not hanging around the station waiting for the parents to arrive.

Putting the note to one side, she sat on a front desk in front of the whiteboard. Not much had come of Isabella's second interview. She was no closer to pinpointing what had set Isabella apart from the others. On their return journey, Humphries had crowed about being right about her callous lack of concern for the fate of her housemates being due to a sense of superiority, not delayed shock or medication. Fiona had argued hard for the girl, stressing her detachment could be a defence against the trauma. Seeing five people shot at close quarters and having the gun directed at you would mess with anyone's mind.

Humphries was missing the point anyway. So far, they didn't have a shred of evidence that Isabella was responsible for the shooting, directly or indirectly. Just that she didn't get along with her tenants and had argued over a loaf of sourdough. While glaring holes remained in her description of events, they didn't have enough to bring her in for formal questioning or insist on access to her bank records. It might be that Isabella would give voluntary access but that would have to wait until she received advice from her father. Her reaction was odd, but killing someone involved passion, not cold indifference.

Fiona remembered her early twenties and tried to imagine herself in Isabella's place. Back then, she might have called her father for advice. Her feelings of insecurity about everything from her body shape to her abilities to cope, which surfaced in her teens, had peaked around her early twenties. She had felt awkward and inadequate inside, but that wasn't the image she portrayed. While she had been naturally shy and introspective, she had somehow fooled people into thinking she was quietly confident and capable. Accepting how good she had been at hiding her true feelings, she felt more convinced that they were no closer to seeing the real Isabella.

On the surface, Isabella had appeared more concerned about what to wear for her Spa afternoon with her mother than the brutal slaying of her housemates. A chilling lack of emotion, even if there had been friction in the house. If it was a true reflection, but was it? Isabella was selfish and snobby, but Fiona was far from agreeing with Humphries that she was a psychopath even though she didn't think she was telling them the whole truth about that evening.

It didn't help that some of Isabella's claims directly contradicted other people's recollections. Most notably, she insisted that there had been no massive bust-up with her tenants, referring to it as more of a mutual agreement to go their separate ways.

Isabella claimed not to have a recently jilted partner or a stalker, but if she was as self-obsessed as she seemed, would she have noticed if she did? Somebody unhinged who desperately wanted to please her, was a potential explanation for the shootings. She had pressed Isabella hard on the possibility, but she had completely denied the suggestion.

If Isabella wasn't in some way responsible, what had five unassuming, shy students done to deserve their fate in the eyes of the killer? So far, all their enquiries had led to one big blank. And if they found an answer, would it explain why Isabella wasn't shot with the others? Isabella had ridiculed the idea when Humphries suggested that she had offered money in return for being spared. To be fair to Isabella, Fiona couldn't see anyone popping down their gun while they wrote down their bank details either.

The other possibility was even more bizarre. Someone had randomly chosen that house on a whim, wiped all those young lives out without a second thought, and disappeared into the night without a trace. And Isabella had been left alive because of something as arbitrary as he liked the colour of her hair or had run out of bullets. Somebody who was that unhinged wasn't going to shrug and return to their day job and loving family. They would go out on another killing spree. And another until they were caught.

She doubted she would find anything her team hadn't already highlighted in the statements as they were all experienced officers, but reading through them would give her additional insights into the victims before meeting their parents. She had started reading when Humphries interrupted her with a decent coffee and a chocolate brownie.

"Thought you might need a treat before your meeting."

"Thanks. I'm dreading it," Fiona said, savouring her first sip of coffee.

"Yeah, rather you than me," Humphries said.

"Anyway, what are you still doing here?" Fiona asked. "I said you could go home."

"And leave you alone to have all the fun," Humphries said, sitting beside Fiona. "Tina's parents are visiting today, so I may as well be here. I just passed the new girl in the corridor. She's very smiley."

"I don't think that's a crime yet."

"Give it a week, and I'm sure you'll have that smile wiped off her face and she'll be as downtrodden as the rest of us," Humphries said. "What are you doing?"

"Reading through friends' statements before the meeting."

"I'm off to get another one for your collection. One of Simon's friends. He wasn't around yesterday."

"Come back with the name of a violent thug with firearms experience and severe mental health problems who was last seen in Mickleburgh," Fiona said. "Preferably one that the group publicly ridiculed last week while Isabella defended him."

"I'll do my best."

"If you don't fancy a day with your in-laws, be back here by three, ready to interview Camilla and Laura with me."

"They sound scarier than the disturbed gunman." Humphries stood and headed for the door. "I'll see you later."

Fiona tried to enjoy her brownie while she flicked through the statements. Next to the victims' names the same descriptive words and phrases repeated themselves. Kind, introverted around strangers, loyal and generous friend, preferred staying in than socialising, loved the countryside and nature, concerned about the environment and social inequality, studious, community-minded and caring. Involved in local voluntary work but didn't protest their beliefs or call attention to themselves in any way.

Fiona pushed the statements away in frustration. If the statements were to be believed, she couldn't imagine any of them picking a fight with a stranger, and the only people they would upset would be climate change deniers and flat-earthers.

The only recent disagreement they had was with Isabella. According to one of the statements, there was no mutual agreement about leaving the house, and it would be a nightmare for them to find somewhere else to stay so close to exams. It was a shouting match that came close to blows, with things being thrown around the kitchen. Fiona sighed. She would have to speak to Isabella again.

CHAPTER FOURTEEN

Fiona looked down as she followed Dewhurst into the conference room. She was seething that he had given her a dressing down on not adequately supervising Kerry rather than asking for an update on the murders. His priorities never ceased to amaze her.

She busied herself settling into her chair to listen to his speech before looking up. She was expecting to see a row of angry faces. In some ways, that would have been easier to deal with, although she anticipated anger would come later.

Seeing the broken people sitting in small groups was harrowing. Their eyes reflected more than sorrow. Their hopes and dreams were shattered by overwhelming grief. With tears streaming down their faces, their eyes asked why. Why our beautiful sons and daughters? Fiona shifted her attention to Dewhurst, knowing she didn't have an answer.

She cringed listening to Dewhurst's empty, generalised spiel about being tough on crime and ensuring justice would prevail. When he finished, he had the gall to step back and pause as though waiting for applause. Accepting none was forthcoming, he invited questions, sweeping his arm across to indicate they should be directed at Fiona. A woman to the right of the room stood and introduced herself as Harry's mum.

Feeling sick inside and trying not to look like a frightened hare caught in headlights, Fiona readied herself as best she could, expecting her wrath to be directed at her. When the woman spoke, Fiona was lost for words.

"I know we are all hurting, but it's important we try to understand why the man behaved so violently and remember he was somebody's son, too." Speaking through tears, her voice croaked, but her conviction was strong.

Fiona held her breath, expecting an eruption of anger. Instead, there came mumbles of agreement. It was clear where the students' personality traits flowed from. Like their children, these were gentle, considerate people. She hoped their anger, when it came, wouldn't turn to hate and bitterness.

Dewhurst faded into the background, referring all questions about the investigation to Fiona. Fiona stood to give her inadequate replies, which amounted to 'we're in the early stages, but we're doing all we can.' The parents sniffed and sobbed, but all were polite and understanding. Their respect and restraint floored and humbled Fiona. But it also gave her renewed determination to bring them some justice. Answers, at least.

When the question session was over, Dewhurst excused himself while Fiona stayed to speak to every family individually, promising she and her team would do all that was humanly possible to find the person responsible. Harry's and Tilly's mothers gripped her hand in response and said, "Don't let this happen to another family."

Every parent had an endearing story to tell about their child. Their pride and love were embroidered into their accounts. Each tale found a new way through Fiona's defences. She could sometimes distance herself from cases, but this one was finding its way into her soul.

Afterwards, Fiona went to the nearest place to find solitude: the ladies' toilets. She locked herself in a cubicle and sat down to ponder the quiet dignity she had just witnessed - the silent majority of good people who never liked to make a fuss, the ones who grinned and bore their own pain while helping others, the ones who still gave her faith in human nature and a reason to continue with the job. She thumped the wall bruising her knuckles, unlocked the door and went to collect Humphries for the interview with Isabella's two best friends.

CHAPTER FIFTEEN

Fiona and Humphries were buzzed up to Camilla's third-floor flat overlooking one of Birtstall's many parks. Camilla greeted them at the door wearing grey trousers and a flowing, linen button-down shirt. She led them through a high-ceiling room with a beautiful open fireplace to a large veranda. Laura lounged in a chair, wearing a long beige skirt and knee-high mauve suede boots. Two decorated cocktails sat on the table, and both girls wore sunglasses.

Fiona took in the scene and ignored the available chairs. "Shall we step inside?" She was relieved when they followed her inside without an argument. Better still, they pushed their sunglasses to the top of their heads, although the polished floors and startling white sofas gave them an excuse to continue wearing them. Glancing around the room, Fiona was surprised there could be so many shades of white.

Laura draped herself over one of the sofas, but Camilla remained standing. "Can I get you both a drink?"

"We're fine, thank you. Come and sit down," Fiona said. "I'm sure you know why we're here."

"Yes, that ghastly incident at poor Isabella's country cottage," Camilla said. She sat primly on an opposing sofa, staring intently at Fiona. "One can only imagine the horror. We were so relieved to learn Isabella was unharmed."

"An anomaly we're struggling to understand," Fiona said through gritted teeth.

"Certain types of people attract unpleasantness," Laura said.

"What do you mean by that?" Fiona asked. "Do you have some information about the victims that would help us find the responsible person?"

Laura sipped her cocktail. "I was referring to the world they inhabit generally. If you indiscriminately mix with all sorts, you're going to come across undesirables. In a large city, one must apply filters. The current trend of being hip and authentic is dangerously naïve. I'm sure Isabella has learnt from the experience."

Fiona was pleased she hadn't accepted a drink, as she would probably be choking on it or - worse - pouring the contents over Laura's perfectly styled hair. She didn't dare risk a glance at Humphries to see how he was taking it. Badly, she assumed, and it would be better if she quickly moved things along without expressing her feelings. "Did you know the victims or anything about them?"

"I had no direct contact with them, but Isabella told us what they were like."

"What did she say about them?"

"She said they were rather uncouth and didn't appreciate how lucky they were to be living with her in Mickleburgh. It wouldn't be my first choice, but it was rather quaint. And far better than the cramped bedsits they would be living in otherwise. Some people don't know how to be grateful."

"Isn't that the truth," Humphries muttered.

"Did Isabella say anything more specific about them?" Fiona asked.

"No. They were non-entities," Laura said with a wave of her hand.

"What you're trying to say," Humphries said, "is they didn't have mummies and daddies as rich as yours, so that made them less important."

Laura gave Humphries a disapproving look. "No, I'm saying they didn't have the same background or contacts, so they mixed in the type of circles likely to attract violent consequences."

Fiona was sickened by the contrast between the two girls and the family members she had been speaking with and decided to let Humphries carry on. Playing nice was unlikely to get them anywhere, and if rattled, they might let something slip.

"Are you saying one or all of them were involved in violent crime?" Humphries asked, with his eyebrows at risk of floating somewhere above his head. "Drug smuggling, maybe?"

Laura folded her arms. "Not as far as I know, but I hardly knew them."

"Robbery or kidnapping?"

"No."

Camilla perched forward. "I think all Laura was trying to say was that it's possible one of Isabella's tenants inadvertently strayed into a world they didn't understand, and it led to that terrible event. She's not in any way suggesting they themselves were that type of person."

"Thank you for your clarification," Humphries said.

Fiona glanced away when she saw Camilla's smile of thanks, questioning how tone-deaf she must be not to hear the sarcasm dripping from every syllable.

Humphries narrowed his eyes at Camilla's smile. "So, you don't think the shooting happened because the other students were involved in criminal activity? Activity that involved firearms and murder. So bringing the situation on themselves."

Camilla frowned as she considered the possibility. "I don't think they could have been as they didn't have excessive money. Isabella said one of them, I can't remember which, was as poor as a church mouse."

"If they did, then they also put poor Isabella at risk," Laura said.

Humphries turned to Laura, his sarcasm becoming tinged with anger. "Or maybe these are things you would know more about? After all, you do have *excessive money*."

"Me? Now, you're being silly," Laura said.

"Am I? From where I'm standing, your dear friend wanted her terribly working-class tenants to move out. Next thing, a gunman bursts in and murders those *non-entities,* but for some inexplicable reason, he passes over Isabella. Do you see our problem?"

Laura clutched her necklace, and her eyes nearly popped out of her head. "O.M.Geeee. Are you being serious?"

"Should I contact Daddy's lawyer?" Camilla asked, equally wide-eyed.

"It would help if you could answer our questions with what you know rather than making wild assumptions," Fiona said, deciding it was time she stepped in. "As my colleague has said, leaving one person alive is odd. We haven't uncovered anything in the victims' backgrounds to explain why they were targeted, and we believe the gunman was connected to Isabella in some way."

"Goodness! That's equally unbelievable," Camilla said. "How would Isabella know a gunman?"

"I don't think she's even been pheasant shooting," Laura said.

That wasn't the type of gunman Fiona had in mind, but it was something to consider. "Does the university have a shooting club?"

"I've no idea, but I've never heard Isabella express any interest in shooting," Camilla said.

"There's a clay pigeon shooting club," Laura said. "Edward was a member."

"Edward?"

"Old boyfriend of mine. Ancient history."

"Did he know Isabella?" Fiona asked.

"No. He graduated last year, and I haven't heard from him since," Laura said.

"You don't really think Isabella could be responsible, do you?" Camilla asked. "She can be a little blunt and impatient at times, but something of this order and magnitude is not her style."

"So last season," Humphries said.

"One possibility we're considering is that the gunman was someone obsessed with Isabella," Fiona said. "We're thinking of a stalker or an ex-boyfriend, unable to accept the relationship was over. Was there anybody like that in her life?"

Camilla and Laura looked blank and shook their heads.

"Nobody at all?"

"Oliver likes her," Camilla said.

"Oh! But he's rather sweet and effeminate," Laura said. "And anyway, he broke his arm during a polo accident a couple of weeks ago. I saw him yesterday, and he still has the cast."

"Can you think of anyone else? Someone who always seems to be hanging around in the background. Or have you ever felt like you were being watched when you were with Isabella?"

Laura clutched her necklace again. "I won't be able to sleep tonight."

"Nobody springs to mind," Camilla said.

"Do either of you shoot?"

"Occasionally, I'll go pheasant shooting at home, but I'm a terrible shot," Camilla said.

"I hate winters in England. They're so damp and miserable," Laura said. "I stay in our ski chalet in Switzerland until it's all over."

"Where were you both last Friday night?" Fiona asked.

"That's easy," Laura said. "I was at Henrietta's hen do in the Lake District."

"It was my brother's birthday, so I went home for the day," Camilla said. "You can't seriously think either of us were responsible. That's preposterous."

"We need to check the whereabouts of everyone," Fiona said. "What do you know about Isabella asking her tenants to leave? Was it a violent disagreement?"

"Isabella said they were awful, and they hadn't been getting along for ages," Laura said.

"My understanding was that they were keen to leave rather than Isabella forcing them out," Camilla said.

"Just before their end-of-year exams? That seems rather unlikely," Humphries said.

"We only know what Isabella told us," Laura said, shrinking back in her chair away from Humphries. "Maybe she gave them a little extra push, but our understanding was that it wasn't a big issue."

"For Isabella, maybe," Humphries said.

"As far as you're aware, there wasn't a major argument in the kitchen about it?" Fiona asked.

"If there were, that's the first we've heard about it," Camilla said.

"Do you know all of Isabella's friends? Did any of them give you grounds for concern?" Fiona asked.

"We were her only close friends. We called ourselves The Three Musketeers. If she wasn't doing something with us, she rode her horse or went home," Laura said. "And we certainly don't know any crazy gunmen."

"We'll leave it there for now," Fiona said. "We will be checking your whereabouts on Friday. Please don't leave Birstall again without telling us, as we may need to speak to you again."

Driving away, Humphries asked, "Are they worth seeing again?"

"We'll check their alibis, but probably not," Fiona replied. "I don't think they're clever enough to lie, and I doubt they have any additional information."

"I agree. They wouldn't find their way out of a paper bag without Daddy's money. Scary to think they'll probably end up with highly paid jobs, responsible for making important decisions that affect everyone or breeding the next generation of chinless wonders. No wonder the country is in the state it's in."

"Interesting though your socio commentaries are, none of it is helping us discover who murdered five students for no apparent reason," Fiona said. "Somewhere along the line, we're missing something, and I'm convinced Isabella holds that missing piece of information," Fiona said.

"Or it was a completely random attack," Humphries said.

"Even so, why chose that house and why leave Isabella behind as a witness? It doesn't make sense. There must be a reason."

CHAPTER SIXTEEN

Ryan Slater had no idea why he had been called to the manager's office on Monday afternoon, but it was beyond annoying. He had a difficult client to placate before he could leave for home, and he didn't want to be late again. He huffed his annoyance as he got up to walk through the open-plan office to the mini-Hitler's office. The guy even had a silly little moustache.

Normally, there was good-natured jeering when someone was summoned to the inner lair, so he was surprised to see several people look away as he walked through the desks. Maybe he was being over-sensitive and imagining it as he was tired and stressed. Before he knocked on McNab's door, he noticed the blinds were drawn. That was always a bad sign.

"Come in and close the door behind you."

Ryan closed the door and sat in the vacant chair, facing the firing squad. The head of personnel sat alongside McNab, and he wondered which of his team members had messed up. Jill, probably. She was undoubtedly the thickest person he had ever met. It didn't help that she didn't realise she was so stupid and liked the sound of her own voice. He was a good manager, but he could be a great one if he only had the staff.

McNab steepled his fingers and looked serious. "Before we start, do you have anything to say?"

Ryan forced a wide smile, meeting McNab's stare square on. "I don't know why I'm here, so I don't know what you're expecting me to say."

"Some messaging via the company's internal system has come

to light. We found its tone shocking."

"Oh, yes," Ryan said, thinking McNab was referring to the rocket he had put up the team a couple of weeks ago to ensure they got off their lazy backsides and hit their monthly targets. In his defence, it had worked. "Occasionally, a short, sharp rap on the knuckles is needed to get things back on track. I'll be careful with my use of language in the future."

"I'm referring to your league of - I'll use your terminology - operators I would most like to shag and those who would need a bag over their head."

Ryan's face turned red, and he started sweating. "Those were private messages," he stuttered.

"They were on the company system," McNab said. "And yes, I have read your disparaging comments about my abilities."

"Sir, they were taken out of context." Sweat was pouring down Ryan's back, and he felt sick. Those messages were clearly only meant for the recipients, all of whom he trusted. How had they somehow reached McNab? He struggled to find his voice, fighting a heady mix of anger and embarrassment. "Nothing was meant by it. I've always had the greatest respect for you."

"I've read the entire exchange," McNab said. "What's more concerning are the suggestions that we as a company are involved in fixing industry prices and setting lower expectations and standards across the industry."

"That was after the talk we …"

"Such behaviour would never be company policy, and you'll not find any reference to it in our professional standards."

"Okay. Heard and understood," Ryan said, realising McNab was covering his own sorry arse.

"I don't think you do fully understand, Ryan. These damaging statements have been widely viewed, and the company can not allow itself to be tainted by such attitudes. In the circumstances, I have no option other than to let you go. When you leave here, I ask you to clear your desk of personal items, and you will be escorted from the building."

Ryan jumped to his feet. "But, sir, this is totally unfair. How about the invasion of my privacy? Those messages were never intended to be circulated. Who leaked them? They are the ones who should be punished."

"Sit down, Ryan. They were posted on a company system, and have you given any thought to the women you have upset and degraded with your depraved comments?"

"Those comments were foolish, I admit. They were only meant to be light-hearted fun, but now you've brought them to my attention, I understand how they could be deeply upsetting. I will apologise to everyone involved and explain they were never to be taken seriously and don't reflect the deep respect ..."

"Save it, Ryan. The attitudes behind what you consider to be a bit of fun can not be tolerated in a modern, forward-looking organisation. Don't make this any more difficult than it needs to be. I think we can all agree it is time we parted company."

"But I have a mortgage and a family to support."

"I'm sure you'll find alternative employment," McNab said. "Will you be leaving voluntarily, or do I need to take firmer action?"

"No, it's okay. I'm leaving." Ryan's pinched face turned even whiter when he was met by a security guard outside McNab's office. He felt the eyes of the office watching him as he packed up his few things. They could all rot in hell. They would soon regret their treachery without him to cover for their mistakes. The rotten sods were all in it together, but who was the ringleader? He had nearly stuffed all his belongings into his briefcase when his phone rang. Seeing it was his wife, he thought it better he replied while he technically was still in the office. "Hi Ann, is it important? I'm busy with a client. Can it wait?"

"Not really. I have just seen the most fantastic deal on a holiday in Barbados. The deal will be gone in two hours. Should I go ahead and book?"

"No!"

"Come on, Ryan. We've been talking about going there for years. Now is our chance for the holiday of a lifetime at a fantastic price. It's an offer too good to miss."

"Things that look too good to be true often are," Ryan said, running a shaky hand through his hair. "Look, I'll be home in less than two hours. We can talk about it before making the final decision. Okay?"

"The price goes up every hour. We need to get in now to lock in the price."

Ryan tried to keep his voice steady, but he could feel the panic rising in his chest. "Hold off until I arrive home. I've got to go. I'll see you in a bit."

He threw the last of his belongings in his briefcase and endured the indignity of being hurried back through the office and down the stairs to the entrance by security. He hadn't even been allowed to say a final goodbye.

He contained his anger at the unfairness until he pulled over around the corner from the underground car park. He shouted in frustration and thumped his car door, ignoring the strange looks from passersby. His knuckles stung, and it had done nothing to improve his mood. He needed to get home quickly to stop Ann from booking the blasted holiday, but first, he wanted to know which traitor had shared his private messages.

He called both numbers for his closest friend at work, but Jim didn't answer either. He knew he was in the office, so assumed he was on a call. Maybe he could work it out if he read back through the messages. Whoever it was would have been careful with what they said or not responded at all. When he saw it, he kicked out at the door and thumped the steering wheel.

Not believing it at first, he rechecked. There was no denying it. Only one person hadn't joined in or commented. The person who would be promoted to replace him. How could he have been so blind? Bloody Jim had probably been planning it for months. Winding him up and encouraging him in person but not saying a word in the group chat.

He threw his phone on the passenger seat and started the engine. The warning light for low fuel came on to add salt to the wound. It had flashed a couple of times on his way into the office, but he had been running late and had ignored it. Running out of petrol halfway home would be the perfect finishing touch to his afternoon. And if he didn't arrive home in time, Ann would book the dream holiday they couldn't afford. It would have been a struggle if he hadn't lost his job, and who knows how long it would take him to find another. Sighing, he accepted he would need to stop at the first garage he passed.

He was nearly out of town when the slow-moving traffic abruptly stopped. The occasional flash to remind him he was low on fuel was now a constant, pulsating warning that he couldn't switch off. He swore at the delivery lorry that was blocking the lane. The oncoming traffic streamed past as Ryan felt his stress levels hitting the roof. He shouted at the petrol warning light, reminding him that his idling engine was using up the last dregs of the fuel, "I bloody know." Finally, the delivery driver came out of a newsagent, giving an apologetic wave before climbing up into his cab.

CHAPTER SEVENTEEN

By the time Ryan joined the queues for the petrol pumps, his car was running on fumes. Typically, his line was the slowest. Nobody was using the quickest option of paying at the pump and moving out of the way for the next customer. They were all leaving their vehicles blocking the pumps while they trundled into the kiosk. He could see them through the window, wandering around the aisles, wondering what chocolate to buy. He groaned when he reached the pump and read the sign saying all purchases had to be made in the shop.

He filled the car tank and shuffled along with the others waiting to pay inside. No wonder the queues had been so long. One young boy served customers from all eight pumps. Ryan checked his watch and was horrified to see that almost an hour had passed since he had spoken to Ann. He had told her to wait until he arrived home, but unless he rang her, she would be tempted to go ahead and book before the price went up. When he tried her number, it was busy. He hoped that meant she was chatting with a friend. He knew from the bills those chats went on for hours. If it prevented her from booking the holiday, for once he wouldn't complain. He refused to entertain the idea that the phone was engaged because she was booking the holiday.

Looking at his feet, he shuffled forward with the queue. Only two people were in front of him, and he silently prayed they would be quick. His head shot up when he overheard the conversation at the till.

"Sorry, madam. This card has been declined."

"It must be a mistake. Try it again."

"Sorry, it's been declined again due to insufficient funds."

"That can't be right," the woman said, turning red. She rummaged in her handbag and pulled out another card. "Here, try this one."

Ryan sighed as loudly as he could and looked up at the ceiling, praying the second card would work and the stupid woman would stop holding everyone up.

"Sorry, it's been declined as well."

The woman became flustered and started to cry. "There should be plenty of money in the accounts. My husband was only paid yesterday."

"Maybe the money hasn't cleared yet," the young man behind her said helpfully.

"Thank you. Yes, that's probably what has happened." The woman wiped her tears and waved to the three children watching from a dusty estate car parked at the pumps. She turned to the counter and said, "I don't know what to do."

"Check you have money in your account before filling up your car with petrol!" Ryan shouted, which caused more tears.

The young man in front turned around and gave Ryan an angry look while the boy behind the counter said, "You'll have to fill out an inability to pay form. I'll go and find them."

"I don't believe this!" Ryan shouted. "I'm a busy man, and I've already been waiting hours because your machines aren't working. Now you expect me to wait even longer because this foolish woman can't pay for her petrol. She probably already knew there was no money in the account before she filled up. I bet it was a full tank as well. She probably does it all the time."

"This has never happened to me before," the woman said before bursting into tears.

"Oh, please," Ryan said, rolling his eyes. "Where did you go to acting school?"

"It's the truth," the woman sobbed as the young man tried to console her.

The young boy behind the counter said, "Umm. I can't see the forms. I'll have to go out the back to find them."

"What! At least serve customers who aren't trying to rip you off first. You know, the ones that actually have some money to pay with." Jabbing his finger in the woman's direction, Ryan said, "She caused the problem. She's the one who should have to wait."

"I'm so sorry," the woman sobbed. "I don't mind waiting, but can I go out and check on my children in the car?"

"Oh yes," Ryan said. "Do you think we were all born yesterday? You're going to drive away without paying. How often do you do this? Once a week? Daily? What sort of way is that to drag your miserable children up?"

The young man gave Ryan a filthy look before stepping up to the counter. "I'll pay for the petrol. How much is it?"

"Oh, thank you. That's so kind. If you give me your details, I will reimburse you as soon as I've spoken to my husband."

"I bet she hasn't even got a husband." Ryan turned to the man in a baseball cap waiting behind him and nodded toward the young man paying for the petrol. "There's one born every minute. So long as people continue to be so gullible, more people will try this on. It's the same with street beggars. They would soon disappear if people didn't give them any money."

The man shrugged and looked away.

"Oh, brilliant, another one who falls for every fake bleeding heart story," Ryan said. "I'll tell you what. I've had an atrocious day. Can you pay for my petrol, and I'll just walk out of here? That's how being a freeloader works, isn't it?"

The man in the baseball cap glared at Ryan and clenched his fists, so he turned his back on him to wait his turn to pay.

The man in front finished paying for the petrol and walked up to Ryan. "Why don't you shut up and go and pay for your petrol?"

Ryan gave the still sobbing woman a disparaging look and said, "At last."

Before escorting the woman away, the man said, "None of us know what's around the corner, but I hope I'm there the day you need a helping hand."

Ryan paid for his petrol in silence and set off for home. He was about to insert his house key when his front door was flung open, and his two sons came tumbling out. "Dad! Dad! Guess what? We're going to Barbados!"

"Go and wait in your rooms. I need to speak to your mother."

CHAPTER EIGHTEEN

Fiona made herself comfortable on her sofa before returning Stefan's calls. Five postmortems in one day had taken their toll on her. Even if it hadn't been a ridiculously hard day, she would have waited until now to make the call.

Some of her anger about him viewing a house without her had dimmed, and she'd had time to think. The surprise engagement had spooked her, but she didn't want to lose Stefan. Her day had left her emotionally drained but had also reminded her how fragile life was. She wanted to live with him more than ever, only not miles away in Wales. She understood the difference in house prices but needed to be here in case of emergencies. Stefan worked cold cases and could keep regular hours, so it made sense for him to be the one with the longer commute. Her parents' health was fading, and she needed to live close to them.

"Hi, I thought you were never going to call," Stefan said when he answered. "I thought I had scared you away."

Quietening the butterflies in her stomach brought on by Stefan's voice, Fiona said, "Of course you didn't. It's been hectic at work."

"I saw the report on the students being shot. I'm so sorry about springing the house on you. I didn't realise," Stefan said.

"It looked quaint, but …" Fiona started.

"Don't worry about it. There will be other houses. I'm more worried about you. How are you coping?"

"Fine. Frustrated more than anything. We're getting nowhere fast."

"Wasn't there a witness left behind?"

"Yes. Oh, can I put you on hold for a minute? I've another call. I'll be right back."

Fiona took the other call and stood after the initial shock. She sat on the corner of her coffee table to listen to the details. Confirmation of her worst fear twisted her stomach into a tight knot. The thought that her choosing to focus on Isabella had caused unnecessary delay tightened the band around her stomach. "I'm on my way."

She took a deep breath before speaking to Stefan. "Sorry, I'm going to have to go. I'll call you later."

Her voice shook when she called Humphries. "There's been another one."

"What do you mean, another one?"

"An insurance manager was having supper at home with his family when a masked gunman broke in. He shot his wife and two sons but left him unharmed. It sounds like the same man."

"We're sure he's a man now?"

"Apparently, he spoke to the father."

"Okay, I can be ready to leave in five minutes. Where was this?"

"In Tilbury, but we're heading to the station to speak to the father. He is cooperating fully as he wants to be quickly eliminated from enquiries so we can focus on finding the gunman."

"I'll cycle in and meet you there."

"Okay. I'll see you in the incident room in about fifteen minutes."

CHAPTER NINETEEN

Fiona drove to the station on autopilot, trying to make logical sense of the shootings. If it wasn't personal, why would someone slaughter entire households, minus one? Was it due to some bizarre confidence that he wouldn't be caught despite leaving a witness at each scene? How did he single the survivor out, or was it sheer luck? Isabella was the furthest from the living room entrance. Was that the only reason she was alive? And how was he selecting the houses?

Isabella's house was set back and partially shielded from the lane by a lawn and mature shrubs. Most houses on Ashburton Road in Tilbury opened straight onto the pavement with their garages on the side, but a few were set back behind front gardens. She would prefer to prepare the lines of investigation for an early morning briefing rather than view the scene tonight, but she could get an idea from Google Maps.

Humphries was waiting for her in the incident room, already logged onto a computer screen. She joined him at the desk. "Has anything new come in?"

"I'm just looking at the preliminaries. The boys were only eight and eleven. What had they ever done to deserve this? We've got to get this guy off the street before he attacks again."

"Agreed," Fiona said. Humphries looked as upset about the shooting as she felt. Her earlier decisions on the case handling continued to accuse her. She should have looked deeper into the possibility that Isabella's home was selected randomly. How much time had she wasted having everyone pick through the minutest details of the students' lives? Hours looking for the magical, elusive answer to why Isabella had been spared, in the hope that would be the key to solving the case. Had her stubbornness in not widening the investigation led to the death of two innocent children?

She felt sick at the thought of three more deaths. Deaths she could have prevented as head of the investigation if she'd made the right decisions. Despite hours of work, they were no closer to knowing who was responsible. She couldn't recall a case where she had felt so out of her depth. There again, she'd never dealt with the random slaughter of households before. There was always a logical reason somewhere - a deep hatred or a betrayal, hidden in the everyday details.

But what if this case was the exception to the rule? She had to start from a different position if there was no reason for the victims' selection. The question was, where? "Have you an image of the front of the house?"

Fiona looked at the image Humphries brought up. It showed the detached house was slightly set back from the road by a gravelled area, and the front door was obscured by the family campervan parked there. "He's choosing houses where the front door is screened from the road."

"That doesn't narrow it down much."

"There should be numerous cameras in that area, street and door cameras. We need all of it collected and gone through," Fiona said.

"Street camera footage has already been requested, and we can ask the neighbours tomorrow morning for anything they have."

"We need to get a dedicated phone line and a social media request out tonight. If it's not been done already, I'll arrange it straight after the interview," Fiona said. "Do you know which room the father is in?"

"Yes, he's in the family room and ready whenever we are. I said we would ring down to say we were on our way."

CHAPTER TWENTY

When Fiona and Humphries entered the room, Ryan quickly stood. He was of average build and height, in his mid to late forties, with slightly thinning hair. His glasses magnified his red-rimmed eyes, and he looked every inch of a downtrodden office worker in an insurance company. It was difficult to see what he could have in common with Isabella other than witnessing a terrible crime.

"Please sit," Fiona said as she indicated the chairs and nodded to the liaison officer she recognised. "We're so sorry to hear about your family."

Humphries sat beside Fiona. "You have our deepest condolences, and we're going all out to catch this person."

With a haunted look, Ryan said, "It won't bring them back, but I want him caught and punished. I hope when he is, you throw away the keys. It's a shame we don't have the death penalty anymore." Ryan took off his glasses and wiped the lenses with a cloth from his pocket. "I'll do everything and anything I can to help you."

"Thank you. It's appreciated," Fiona said. "I know it will be painful, but it will help us if you tell us about your evening in as much detail as possible."

Ryan nodded and replaced his glasses. "Until a few hours ago, I thought I was having the worst day of my life, but nothing compares to this."

"What happened?" Fiona asked.

"It doesn't seem important now. Do you need to know?"

"Things that seem unimportant at the time can prove to be relevant," Fiona said. "Why don't you give me a quick summary to start?"

"I lost my job and had a meltdown in a garage on the way home over a poor woman who couldn't pay for her petrol," Ryan said. "While it was totally insignificant in the scheme of things, what the young man said to me will stick with me forever. As it turned out, it was rather prophetic."

"What did he say?"

"That nobody knows what's around the corner, and he hoped he would be around when I needed a helping hand. I expect I'm reading far too much into it, but when taken with what the gunman said, it's more than a little creepy. It's like he had a premonition."

"What did the gunman say?"

"Look at what you've done."

"Anything else?" Fiona asked, trying to understand why the gunman was blaming Ryan. The statement suggested that he knew Ryan, and she wondered if there was a connection to his dismissal from work.

"No, just that."

"Did you recognise the voice? Could it have been someone you know? A work colleague, perhaps?"

"I don't think so."

"And those were his exact words? Look at what you've done." Ryan nodded, and Fiona asked, "What do you think he meant by them?"

Ryan shrugged. "That it was somehow my fault. I don't know. A stupid mind game? He was trying to make me think that I had pulled the trigger when I hadn't. Nothing made sense in that room, so why should what he said?"

"What happened after he spoke to you?"

"He turned as calmly as you like and left. I wish now I had done something to stop him from leaving. He didn't even run. He walked out of the house like he had all the time in the world. Like he knew I would be too much of a coward to do anything,"

Ryan said. "What would it matter if I was shot? He'd already destroyed my life. I have nothing left except a determination to see him punished." Ryan's voice caught on an involuntary sob. "As it was, I froze and did nothing. I just sat there like a useless lump. Nothing like the big man I was in the garage."

"You behaved differently in the garage?"

"I was stressed and started shouting my big mouth off." Ryan dropped his head to his hands. "I wish I could rewind the clock. It's almost like the guy in the garage knew something dreadful would happen."

Intrigued by how Ryan was connecting the garage altercation with the shooting, Fiona asked, "Do you know the name of the garage?" As she jotted down the name, she asked, "Could the man in the garage and the gunman in your house be the same person?"

"I wondered that, but no. The guy in the garage was well-spoken with blue eyes. I remember thinking he was probably a student at the university. The eyes of the gunman were black and lifeless. And he had a broad local accent."

Fiona shared a look with Humphries, before asking, "Can you remember anything else about the man in the garage? Would you recognise him again if you saw him?"

"I think so. He was in his late twenties, and although he was dressed casually in jeans and a sweatshirt, they were good quality. I noticed his shoes. They weren't trainers, but proper leather brogues. He had short dark hair, was average height and a healthy weight. Possibly a regular gym goer. He had that confidence about him that comes with money."

"What time were you in the garage?"

"I was impatient to get home and constantly checked the time," Ryan said. "I was there from four o'clock until half past."

"Do you want me to get hold of the security footage?" Humphries asked.

Fiona looked at the liaison officer. "Could you ask someone to request it as soon as possible?"

"Sure. I'll be back in a minute."

Fiona returned her attention to Ryan. "How would you describe the man who broke into your house?"

"He was dressed in black and wearing a balaclava, so I can't describe his features. He was above average height and well-built. Not fat, but well covered. It might have been muscle, I couldn't tell. I noticed when he left that he had a slight limp. He seemed to be dragging his right leg." Ryan shook his head. "It reminded me of the actor John Shaw. Crazy what images the mind will conjure up at the weirdest of times."

"Would you say he was white?"

"I honestly couldn't say. He had a strong Birstall accent, if that helps. And it was slow. Almost a drawl. I know you can't tell much from a few words, but he didn't seem that bright. Not backwards, but not the sharpest tool in the box."

"And his clothes?"

"Black trainers, black jeans, nylon black bomber jacket and a black balaclava. Nothing fancy. It was all plain and cheap looking."

"Anything else of note?"

"It was his eyes that I remember the most. Empty and vacant are the only words I can think of to describe them. And so incredibly dark."

The liaison officer slipped back into the room and nodded to Fiona to indicate the security tapes had been requested. After nodding her thanks, Fiona asked Ryan, "Can you talk us through your evening before the shooting?"

"There had been an incident at work, and they sacked me. So, when I returned home to find Ann had booked a holiday that we couldn't afford, we argued."

"Can we go back a bit?" Fiona asked. "It must have been a serious incident at work for them to dismiss you."

"I would have had a case for unfair dismissal if they had," Ryan said. "No, they suggested I leave voluntarily after someone I considered a friend set me up. It turns out he was only after my job."

"What did he do?"

"I had made some fairly stupid comments about work colleagues and general company practices in what I thought was a private chat. He leaked those messages to the boss. It didn't help that I had made some derogatory comments about him."

"I'll need the names of your boss, your friend, and other people involved in the chat."

"I'm happy to provide them, but none of them were in my kitchen this evening. I've worked alongside them for years and would recognise their voices and eyes," Ryan said. He rubbed the back of his neck and added. "It breaks my heart to think that during the last hours I spent with my family, we weren't speaking to each other. What an idiot I was." Ryan covered his face with his hands and shook his head. "Stupid. Stupid. Stupid. What did any of it matter anyway."

"Would you like to take a moment?" Fiona asked.

Ryan wearily lowered his hands and swiped away a stray tear with his forefinger from behind his glasses. "No, I can continue. You need to get this monster off the streets as quickly as possible."

"Okay, so you argued about a holiday when you arrived home."

"Yes. I sent the boys upstairs. Ann was livid when I explained why we couldn't afford the holiday she had booked. I offered to go and explain to the boys that we wouldn't be going to Barbados. I wish I had left that for another night. When I went upstairs, Ann started banging about in the kitchen. The boys were angry and disappointed, and they blamed me. I was still trying to reason with them and saying that we would go another time when Ann called us down for supper. We filed into the kitchen, took our seats and ate in silence.

"We were almost done when the gunman appeared in the kitchen doorway. Ann saw him first as she was facing that direction. Up until then, I hadn't noticed anything. I turned around in my seat to see what had caught her attention. It was as I was turning that he fired. Bang. Bang. Bang. One after the other. I don't think I had moved from my seat when he looked right at me and said, 'Look at what you've done.' I instinctively turned toward the table and saw ... What I saw ... I jumped back. I remember my chair went skidding across the floor. When I looked to the doorway, he was limping away. It was as if he had never been there at all. I crumpled to the floor, put my head in between my knees and howled. I don't know how long I was like that before I realised that I had to call for help. The next thing I clearly remember is one of your colleagues leading me out of the room."

"Thank you, Ryan. I appreciate how difficult this must be for you," Fiona said. "I just have a couple more questions this evening. Even though you were eating in silence, you had no inkling that someone had entered your house. Is that correct?"

"I should have said the television was on in the kitchen. Not that anyone was watching it. But yes, I didn't know he was there until I looked around after seeing the startled expression on Ann's face."

"Do you normally leave the front door unlocked?"

"No. It locks automatically," Ryan said. "It's possible in the circumstances that I didn't shut it behind me, but I think I did."

"Does anyone else have keys to your house?"

"Nobody, as far as I know."

"The intruder shot your family in quick succession and then spoke to you. Was he pointing the gun at you?"

Ryan closed his eyes and swallowed as he remembered the scene. "No, he lowered the gun to his side when he spoke. I had no coherent thoughts in my brain at the time other than I expected to be dead shortly. I remember my ears were ringing from the gunshots. I shut my eyes to wait for the inevitable. It took a while for my brain to register I was still alive, and he was leaving. I don't think I'll ever come to terms with what happened to my family."

"Sorry to stop you there, Ryan," Fiona said. "Earlier, you said you looked back at your family after he spoke?"

Ryan rubbed his hands up and down his face, dislodging his glasses. Righting them, he said, "He spoke, and then I closed my eyes. When nothing happened, I opened them and looked at my family. I had the crazy thought that they would all be sitting there like before, as though nothing had happened. Then I jumped back from the table."

"Can you think of anyone who would want to harm your family in this way?"

"Nobody. I don't …no. It doesn't make sense."

"We'll be contacting your employers and colleagues. Will that be a problem?"

"My ex-employers and colleagues," Ryan said. "Go ahead. It's hardly important to me now. I have a family to bury."

"Do you know Isabella Stainton?"

Ryan looked blank and shook his head.

"Martin Kelley? Simon Marlow? Harry Benningfield? Tilly Feakes? Suzie Blackford? Do any of these names mean anything to you?" Fiona asked.

Ryan shook his head at each name. "Are those the students that were killed a few days ago?"

Fiona nodded. "Have you heard any of those names or visited Mickleburgh before?"

"Over the years, I've been for a few meals in the pub in the village, but I don't know anyone who lives there."

"Okay, we'll leave it there for tonight, but we will keep you updated. Here's my card if you think of anything else that might be relevant."

CHAPTER TWENTY-ONE

In the corridor, Fiona stopped and turned to Humphries. "Did I get everything wrong on this one?"

"How do you mean?"

"By concentrating on the students and not accepting the house was chosen randomly, I've wasted a lot of time."

"Hey, don't be so hasty. We still need to check for a possible connection between Ryan and the students."

"Right now, the only connection I can see is that Ryan and Isabella recently argued with someone, but I expect that's true for most of the population," Fiona said. "In Isabella's case, it was in the privacy of her home, and the people she argued with are dead. Following that logic, the garage owner or Ryan's work colleagues and boss should be the victims, not his family."

"It sounds like Ryan upset a lot of people recently. Maybe he upset the same person as the students did," Humphries suggested.

"It's worth checking, but do you really believe that, or are you just trying to make me feel better?"

"A bit of both," Humphries said. "But it's possible."

"Thanks for trying, but it's not working," Fiona said. "At least Ryan lived in a built-up area, so we should see what the guy looks like. Maybe we'll get really lucky and see him get into his car with the registration plate on full display. And pigs might fly."

"Always the optimist. You never know," Humphries said. "We

should have much more to go with the second scene. We had nothing after the first shooting. No cameras or witnesses other than Isabella."

Fiona rubbed her tired eyes. "You look as exhausted as I feel. I'll check on the possibility of a dedicated phone line, but there's not much more we can do tonight if the garage and street footage have already been requested. Hopefully, it will come in overnight, and we can start going through it first thing in the morning."

"At least I managed to spend a few hours with Tina before being called back out."

"How are things going between you?" Fiona asked.

"Fine. The usual ups and downs," Humphries said. "Everything good with you and Stefan?"

Fiona stopped at the station's rear exit doors. "I've just remembered I was on the phone to him when the call came through. It's too late to ring him back now. I'll ring him in the morning."

Humphries opened the door and stepped outside, pulling his coat around himself. "At least he understands how our job works."

"There is that, I suppose," Fiona said, following Humphries outside. "Another bonus. It looks like the press has given up for the night. They'll be here in spades when news of the second shooting hits."

Humphries looked down at his phone. "It's already all over social media. We had better get out of here before an angry mob carrying pitchforks arrives for us."

"Don't joke. They could be waiting for us around the corner," Fiona said, heading towards her car.

Humphries walked in the opposite direction to collect his bike, calling across the car park, "Get some sleep and don't beat yourself up over the case. We've done all we could, and we'll have some decent leads tomorrow."

Fiona stopped herself from saying, 'But it wasn't enough,' and waved. "See you tomorrow."

CHAPTER TWENTY-TWO

Fiona ran the gauntlet of the press outside the station and hurried upstairs. She opened the operations room door to hear numerous telephone conversations and keyboards clicking. Pulling off her coat, she saw that Humphries was free. "Was all the camera footage sent over last night?"

"Abbie and Rachael are going through what came in and I'm chasing for the last of it. An appeal has already gone out for local doorbell cams."

"While you chase up those cameras, I'll call Tracey to see if she can confirm how he gained access. Ryan was fairly sure he closed the door but said he didn't hear anything."

"Lock bumping doesn't make much sound. If they were at the back of the house with a television on, they might not have heard it," Humphries said. "Ryan admits he came home agitated, and he wasn't sure. It's just as likely he didn't properly close it behind himself when his sons accosted him."

"That suggests the shooter was casually walking along the street trying unlocked doors, and I don't even want to think about that possibility. My brain constantly returns to the same conclusion. There must be a connection between Ryan's family and the students. We need to eliminate that possibility before concentrating solely on the random stranger theory." Fiona rubbed her temples with her fingertips. "Did you check whether the garage footage arrived? If they didn't and there's likely to be a delay, we could go around to collect it as we'll want to speak to the boy working behind the counter and identify the man who spoke to Ryan."

After calling Tracey, Fiona called across the room, "You were right. The lock was bumped. A skill mastered by many."

"Including engineer students," Humphries said. "Come and look at this. While you've been speaking with Tracey, I've looked at the garage's tapes, which alternate between the shop and the forecourt,"

"Tell me you have the registration plate of the guy he argued with," Fiona said, walking over to Humphries.

"Oh, way better than that. His name, address and the fact he's a mature student studying civil engineering alongside Simon Marlow. Eddie took a statement from him."

Hearing his name, Eddie wandered over. "What was that?"

Humphries pointed to his frozen screen. "Do you remember interviewing this guy in connection with the first shooting?"

Eddie squinted at the screen as other people ended their calls when they could and crowded around the desk to hear what was happening.

"Vaguely," Eddie said. "He was on one of the courses with another of the students. I don't think he was able to add much. If I remember correctly, he wasn't a close friend."

"He was also the guy in the garage who told Ryan to watch his back only hours before his family were gunned down."

"A big step from a few cross words," Eddie said.

"Play the tape," Fiona said. "Let's see what happens next."

As more people crowded around to watch, the tape moved from inside the shop to the forecourt and the cars pulling away.

"He waited for him to leave and followed him out," Abbie said.

"It's a definite connection between the two shootings," Andrew said. "It's about time we had a break."

"Okay, let's not get ahead of ourselves," Fiona said. "Ryan doubted the person in the garage was the person who killed his family. His voice, eyes and build were wrong."

"He had a brief encounter with him at the garage before

witnessing his family being slaughtered. How accurate are you expecting him to be?" Humphries asked.

"He was adamant about the eyes," Fiona said.

"Ever heard of tinted eye contacts and the mind filling in the details?" Humphries asked.

"Do we know anything else about the student?" Fiona asked.

"I can only work miracles one at a time," Humphries replied.

"If he's the gunman, we know he's armed and highly dangerous. If we decide to bring him in, I want an armed response team involved," Fiona said. "I'll check on availability while you see what more you can find out about him."

Straightening up from watching the tape, Rachael asked, "Do you think it's him?"

"I'm not entirely convinced, but if there's even the slightest possibility that this student is our man, I want him off the streets today," Fiona said. "What's his name?"

"Julian Thume," Humphries said.

"Gather all the available information on him and check his lecture timetable," Fiona said. "I would prefer not to drag him out of a packed lecture hall. If he has lectures, two of you go out there and watch from a safe distance where he goes afterwards."

A sheepish Kerry walked in as they drifted away from the desk. "Sorry, I'm late. My alarm didn't go off."

Fiona thought she could smell alcohol on her breath, and she looked hungover. Another time, she would pick her up on it, but getting Julien Thume off the streets was her priority, so it would have to wait until later. "Don't make a habit of it. I'll be giving a briefing on a new development shortly, and there's a stack of video footage for you to help to review."

CHAPTER TWENTY-THREE

Driving to meet the armed team at the address, Fiona looked across at Humphries when he finally put his phone away. "Anything new we should know about him?"

"Nothing that would raise any flags," Humphries said, stifling a yawn.

"Sorry, am I keeping you awake?" Fiona shook her head. "I was running around making phone calls as information came in. Could you summarise everything we know?"

"The second of three children in a stable family, no mental health issues and expected to graduate with a first. He's never been in trouble with the police. Outside of his studies, he plays tennis and is on the university football team. According to his social media profile, he has a steady girlfriend, a wide circle of friends and an active social life."

"Any recent events that could have caused him to flip? Any obvious changes in his behaviour?"

"Nothing obvious," Humphries said.

"Where's he from?"

"Somerset."

"Our guy has a Birstall accent," Fiona said, indicating to turn as alarm bells rang in her head. Despite his connection to both incidents, Julien didn't sound like a likely suspect. She'd only agreed to bring him in after they discovered he had accused Simon of stealing one of his designs the previous academic year.

"An accent is easy to fake, and the Somerset accent isn't that different. It could explain the drawl that Ryan referred to," Humphries said.

Fiona frowned. "I'm starting to have doubts and think we may have jumped the gun. Maybe I should cancel the armed response guys before they leave. Have you got him up on any social media profiles?" Fiona groaned after glancing across at the images Humphries showed her. "He's got startling blue eyes, like Ryan said. They stand out a mile in all those images. We're still going to pay him a visit, but I'm going to cancel the backup. We don't need it."

"I agree his profile doesn't obviously fit, but in this case, I would prefer to be wrong than sorry."

"Fair comment, but I don't think it's him, and you're not the one who has to justify the expense."

"Is my life worth so little?" Humphries grumbled while Fiona made the call.

Fiona sighed and put her phone away. "Too late. They left shortly after Andrew confirmed Julien had cycled home from his lectures. They're probably there already."

"Did you get anything else from Tracey when you called her earlier?"

"The scene was similar to last time, and the evidence supports what Ryan told us. The gunman walked directly to the kitchen, shot the family and walked out," Fiona said. "They're concentrating on the front door, hoping he left some traces there. The scene was even more harrowing to process with two children involved."

"Hang on," Humphries said. "Is it possible he knew the layout of the two houses?"

Fiona tapped the steering wheel. "Good thinking. Isabella's father bought the house recently. We need to find out when Ryan bought his home and which estate agent they used. It will also be worth checking whether workmen have been in the houses recently."

"Looks like we're here," Humphries said as Fiona turned into a narrow residential street with police vans parked about halfway down. "How are you operating on so little sleep? They won't let us anywhere near the place until it's been thoroughly checked, so I'm going to take a quick nap."

"Seriously?" Fiona parked behind the van. Counting the house numbers, she looked up at the three-storey terraced townhouse. "Lights are on, and Andrew saw him go in, so we know he's there. How many students are registered to the address?"

"Three, but that doesn't always mean much."

"I'll let them know we're here." Fiona left the car to walk over to the officers grouped around the back of one of the vans. As she approached, she felt increasingly guilty for wasting their time.

An officer reached for her warrant card without speaking. He examined it closely before handing it back. "We're ready to go. If you could reverse your car down the street and wait inside it, we'll confirm when the property is secure."

Fiona didn't appreciate being treated as an inconvenient intrusion, but his attitude made her feel less concerned if it turned out that she had overreacted by calling them in. She returned to reverse her car and watch them get into position. "Did you never fancy that?"

"No. There is too much reliance on brawn and fancy equipment. I prefer to use my little grey cells," Humphries said, pushing back the car seat to make himself more comfortable. "How about you? It's open to women."

"Never fancied it," Fiona said. While Humphries closed his eyes in the reclined seat, Fiona gave a running commentary. "It all looks very quiet. Too quiet. Oh, they're going in. Doesn't look like they've met any resistance. I can't hear anything or see any movement from inside, but we had better wait until they give us the all-clear. They'll check the rooms for firearms before they let us anywhere near."

"Wake me up when they do," Humphries said without opening his eyes. "Good job it's a pleasantly warm day."

Half an hour later, Fiona nudged him awake. "Looks like we can go in." She opened the car door to get out and speak to the officer walking down the street towards them. He confirmed what Fiona had expected. They met with little resistance, and no firearms were found in the property. Fiona thanked him and apologised for calling them out unnecessarily.

Inside, Fiona and Humphries found five students, three male and two female, sitting on the sofas in the living room with confused expressions. "Which one of you is Julien Thume?"

Julien stood and said, "That's me. How can I help you?"

"We have some questions we would like to ask you, and it would be easier if you come to the station with us," Fiona said. While she read him his rights, a girl stood beside him and clasped his hand.

Julien politely waited for Fiona to finish. "Sure, I've no problem coming with you, but what am I supposed to have done?"

"We'll discuss that at the station."

The girl wrapped herself around Julien. "Jules? What's happening?"

Julien stepped away from the girl, releasing her arms from behind his back. "There's obviously been some silly mistake, and I'll be back soon. You may as well wait here with the others. Hopefully. I'll join you later." Julien looked over at the other students. "Okay if she stays here to wait?"

CHAPTER TWENTY-FOUR

In the interview room, Humphries read Julian his rights again and asked him if he wanted legal representation.

"Am I under arrest?"

"No, you're currently helping us with our enquiries," Humphries said. "If that changes, we will let you know."

"Can you clarify what I'm supposed to have done, because I'm not aware of what it might be."

"We'll start with your visit to Oldbury Hill Garage yesterday afternoon," Fiona said.

"Oh, that," Julian said, relaxing. "Why is the garage taking action? I paid for her petrol." He fumbled in his pocket for his phone. "The transaction should be on here somewhere."

Fiona quickly looked at the screen, noting the time he had paid for the petrol. "Can you tell us what happened?"

"There's not much I can say. The woman's card wasn't working. I thought at first it was a problem with the garage's machine. A massive queue of people was already waiting as their pay-at-the-pump function was down. She started crying, and the lad behind the counter couldn't find the form she was supposed to fill out, so I stepped forward and offered to pay for the petrol. I told her not to worry, but she insisted she would pay me back. I haven't heard from her yet, so maybe she won't."

"That was very good of you to pay for a stranger's petrol," Fiona said.

"I had the money in my account, and she was getting upset," Julien said. "She had young children waiting for her in the car, so I thought I would help her out. Doing good deeds, karma and all that. I felt good about helping someone, but I didn't expect all this trouble."

"The garage camera shows you having words with the man standing behind you," Fiona said.

"Oh, that bad-tempered bully. Is he the one making a fuss? I can't see why it has anything to do with him. If I want to help someone, that's up to me."

"Why do you call him a bully?"

"Because he is. He could see the woman was upset, but he carried on spouting stuff about her being a fraud and accused her of filling up her car when she knew she couldn't pay for it. Hardly the milk of human kindness," Julien said. "He was being a complete jerk."

"Can you remember what you said to him as you were leaving?"

"I can't remember exactly, but it was something along the lines of he might need someone's help one day."

"You said that you hoped you were around when he needed a helping hand and that nobody knows what's around the corner," Fiona said. "What did you mean by that?"

"Just that. What comes around goes around. I've always believed in karma," Julien said. "His attitude had wound me up and I wanted to make the point we all make mistakes and need help now and again."

"It wasn't a threat?"

"Goodness, no. It was a throw-away comment. His attitude was the pits, but I didn't really wish him any harm. Well, maybe I did a bit. I admit I was hoping there was a fault in the garage's system and his card would be declined. It would have served him right for being so obnoxious to the poor woman."

"Is that why you waited for him on the forecourt?"

"What? No, I didn't. I drove away without giving him a second thought," Julian said, starting to look worried again. "If something happened to him outside of the garage, it had nothing to do with me. I didn't see anything kicking off, so it must have happened after I left. I was the only person who said something but everyone in the line thought he was being a pain."

"Everyone? Are you sure about that?"

"Doesn't everything show up on their cameras?"

"Their cameras show you arguing with him inside the shop, outside waiting for him to leave, and then you driving off the forecourt behind him."

"I waited to see the woman get into her car, and then I joined the queue of traffic to leave. I have no idea who I was behind."

"Did you see the man leave the shop and walk to his car?"

"Yes. I've admitted I felt disappointed his card wasn't declined, but I didn't watch him all the way to his car."

"The cameras tell a different story," Fiona said. "They show you following him."

"There are only two options after you pull out from the garage. Right or left. It's possible we went the same way, but I wasn't following him. I wasn't even aware I was behind him until you just told me."

"We'll be looking at all the cameras in that area," Fiona said. "How far did you follow him?"

"I wasn't following him," Julian said. "I drove to my girlfriend's house to pick her up."

"After following the gentleman home to see where he lived."

"No. Absolutely not. I drove straight to my girlfriend's house on Sopworth Road. She'll confirm when I arrived. It was about ten minutes after I left the garage."

After jotting down Julian's girlfriend's address and telephone number, Fiona asked, "When we look, that's the direction we'll see your car take? There won't be any diversions on the way? You're sure of that?"

"One hundred per cent."

"How did you spend the rest of the evening?"

"I hung out with my girlfriend and her housemates for a couple of hours. Then we went to the Elephant and Castle pub on

Station Road and met up with some of my friends, and then we went back to my place."

Fiona studied Julien for a while with the sinking feeling he was telling the truth. He was a decent person who had done someone a favour. That left them back at square one unless they could find another connection between Ryan and Isabella.

A new thought entered her mind and disappeared along a tangent. Ryan had just been fired; maybe he had been unstable for a while. Could the students living with Isabella have been a practice run to provide him with the cover to kill his family and get away with it? It was extreme as a theory, but so was killing a man's family because he had been annoying in a petrol station. She forced her attention back to Julien. "How well did you know Simon Marlow?"

"Not that well. I'm not sure anyone did. He was quiet and kept himself to himself, but he always seemed pleasant," Julien said. "What happened to him doesn't make any sense. Either he was in the wrong place at the wrong time, or it was a case of mistaken identity. That's what everyone thinks and what I told the copper the other day."

Fiona creased her brow. "We understood you had a major disagreement with him last year. You accused him of stealing one of your designs."

"Oh, that," Julien said. "It was all resolved amicably. He showed me his research notes, proving it was a coincidence that our minds were on the same track. When we looked a little closer, it was clear some elements were very different."

"Where were you last Friday night?"

"The night they were shot? Is that the real reason you've brought me in?" Julien asked, his calmness shifting to agitation. "I've already told you. I was in the Rising Sun pub with a large group of people, including my girlfriend. A local Country and Western singer was playing. Rhiannon Paige."

"Then where did you go?"

"Nowhere. I'd had a skinful. I staggered home with my girlfriend and a couple of my housemates, then crashed until

Saturday lunchtime. Ask anyone."

"We will," Fiona said. "After your accusations against Simon, did you have much contact with him?"

"Not much. Like I said, he kept himself to himself and didn't socialise much, but we were good after the misunderstanding was resolved. We occasionally had the odd chat when I saw him in lectures."

"Okay." Fiona looked sceptical, but she closed her pad and ended the interview. "We're going to check the traffic footage now."

"And what about me? Am I free to leave?" Julien asked.

"If the footage confirms what you say, then yes."

"You still haven't said why I'm here. Did something happen to that guy in the garage?"

"You could say that."

A cross look ran across Julien's face. "Seriously? You drag me in here, and that's all you're going to say?"

Knowing news of the second shooting was already circulating on social media, Fiona said, "A masked man broke into the man's house and shot his wife and two children in front of him."

Julien's face turned white, and he sprung from his chair. "Christ! That's terrible." He paced and raised an arm to rub the back of his neck. "I saw a report about it, but I didn't know it was him. He was bang out of order in the garage, but nobody deserves that. I'm so sorry. You didn't really think I could have …?"

"We invited you in here to help with our enquiries because of the incident in the garage. We haven't decided if it has any bearing on what happened."

Julien raised his hands, palms forward. "I'm always happy to assist the police, but I have no idea what happened after he left the garage." He dropped heavily to his chair and ran his hands through his hair. "Was it the same person who shot Simon and his friends? Oh, God. It was, wasn't it?"

"It's too soon to speculate about what might have happened," Fiona said. "Thank you very much for coming in to talk with us.

We'll return once we've reviewed the tapes."

CHAPTER TWENTY-FIVE

"What do you think?" Humphries asked as he walked alongside Fiona to the operations room. "He had a reason to hold a grudge against Simon."

"His alibis and the street cameras need to be checked, but my gut tells me he's telling the truth. Nothing untoward was found at the house, and you said nothing of concern turned up in his records," Fiona said. "We're looking for someone with major issues. Something must have led up to these shootings. They haven't happened out of the blue."

Humphries opened the operations room door. "Or something has triggered a childhood trauma."

"Or he's recently moved to the area," Fiona said. "Which reminds me, I want to have a word with Gareth to see if someone new to the area or a recent release has the type of background we're looking for."

Rachael handed Fiona a report. "Julien's record is squeaky clean, and he has no legal access to firearms. Eddie has gone back through the statements, and several students confirm he was at a gig on Friday night. He called a couple of them to double confirm he was where he said he was that night."

"Sightings of his car after leaving the garage?"

"Andrew and Abbie are going through them now."

The door opened behind them, and Dewhurst swept into the room. "DI Williams! My office, now."

With her back to him, Fiona pulled an annoyed face and looked to the ceiling.

"Now!" Dewhurst repeated before leaving the room.

Fiona turned to Humphries. "It's probably about calling out the armed response team unnecessarily. I don't know how long I'll be, but if the footage shows Julien driving to his girlfriend's house, we haven't enough to hold him. Check his alibi for last night and see whether anyone in the pub remembers him being in there. If everything checks out, release him."

Fiona took a deep breath and stood up straight before knocking on Dewhurst's door. She sat opposite him after being called in. He was leaning over his desk, playing with an elastic band. Fiona didn't mind a quick dressing down, but she didn't want her time wasted. "Sir. You wanted to see me."

Dewhurst put the elastic band to one side. "I hear you have a suspect in the cells. One that required an armed escort," His head shot up, and his eyes bored into Fiona's. "Why wasn't I told about it?"

"I did try to call you earlier, but your phone was unavailable, sir," Fiona said.

Dewhurst picked up his phone to check his call history. "Well? Is he our man?"

"A few details are being checked, but I very much doubt it," Fiona said. "And he was never under arrest or armed escort. He came in to answer some questions."

"Then why am I going to receive an expense for the armed response team."

"In the circumstances, I thought it a prudent precaution for them to check the property, sir," Fiona said.

"I'm sure you will detail your reasons in your report," Dewhurst said. "But it won't help the situation with the press if they've heard wind of it. I have a meeting with them in ten minutes, and you can join me to explain the present state of play, as you've clearly not been keeping me fully informed."

Ten minutes later, Fiona followed Dewhurst into the conference room, where they were met by flashing camera lights. Predictably, they somehow knew they had brought someone in for questioning, and Dewhurst left her to field their questions. The only positive was that they were so focused on asking questions about Julien that they didn't press hard for details on the enquiry's lack of progress generally. Dewhurst called an end to the meeting before they realised their oversight and ushered Fiona out of the room.

CHAPTER TWENTY-SIX

The press numbers outside had doubled when Fiona arrived at the station the following morning. Having successfully dodged them, Dewhurst intercepted her in the reception area. "The press is braying for progress. Can I tell them we have another suspect up our sleeve?"

Fiona shook her head. "Sorry, sir."

Dewhurst's face dropped. "Have you anything useful to tell me?"

"We're going through camera footage from outside Ryan's house and following up on every lead," Fiona said.

"That's a no, then." Dewhurst frowned. "The new DCI is unable to join us earlier. Should I try to draft in a more experienced officer to oversee the case?"

"That's your decision, sir, but you may as well wait to see what the camera footage throws up," Fiona said.

"Keep me properly informed," Dewhurst said before spinning on his heels and marching away.

Fiona reached the operation room and unbuttoned her coat when Rachael told her that there was some camera footage she would want to see straight away. Although she was still wearing her coat, a shiver ran down Fiona's spine when she watched the grainy image. A stocky man, wearing dark clothes and a baseball cap pulled down low to cover his face, casually walked up the path towards Ryan's house at the correct time. A few minutes later, he re-emerged from behind the campervan and walked away in the direction he had come. Due to the camera angle and the positioning of his cap, there was no clear view of his face, but his overall appearance matched Isabella's and Ryan's descriptions, and he did have a slight limp.

She looked up when she heard the door opening. "Morning. Have you seen this?"

Humphries placed his cycling helmet on a desk and watched the footage while Fiona flicked through the overnight reports. After watching it twice, he asked, "Then where does he go?"

Looking up from the report she was reading, Fiona said, "According to the reports, he's seen moments later at the end of the street and then disappears. As no cars head either way along the street at a corresponding time, it's assumed he carried on walking, but he hasn't been picked up on any more cameras yet."

Humphries squinted at the second piece of film showing the end of the street. "I know that area. There's a shortcut across a piece of wasteland that used to be a garage and a pub. The garage building was demolished ages ago, but a bunch of NIMBYs continually delay the development of the site because they claim the pub should be a listed building and not knocked down. I doubt they care about a historic building, but they don't want new housing there."

"If he walked across there, where would he come out?" Fiona asked.

"Eventually at the main dual carriageway that links Tilbury to Sapperton," Humphries said. "If he stayed on foot, he would have to go through the underpass first. I'm sure there are cameras at either end, but they're often broken by the kids that hang around there after dark. If he parked his car alongside the dual carriageway, it might have been picked up on one of the cameras. If it wasn't, it will be impossible to pick him out from the other vehicles on the road at that time of the evening."

"Check the cameras. I'll organise a couple of constables to include the underpass on their evening shift. Some of the kids might have seen him."

"And if we can't get any clear visuals of him?" Humphries asked. "What then? Do we think these are random attacks, or are we concentrating on finding a connection between Isabella and Ryan?"

"The two aren't mutually exclusive," Fiona said. "A request to enhance the images has been made, and they will be circulated. Hopefully, someone will recognise him and come forward." She turned away from the screen and perched on the edge of the desk. "I had a crazy idea last night. Can I run it by you?"

Humphries pulled out a chair to sit. "Go ahead."

"Preliminary investigations show Ryan was in financial trouble, and things weren't going well in his marriage or at work. He also increased his wife's life insurance last year." Fiona paused before continuing, "What if he killed his family? What if he shot the students a few days before so we would assume it was a serial killer and not ask too many questions?"

Humphries ran a hand through his hair. "That's a bit left field. What about the guy we've just watched entering and leaving his house?"

"Because of the positioning of the tree and the parked campervan, we haven't though, have we? We've seen him approach the house and leave shortly afterwards. What if Ryan arranged for something to be delivered, knowing we would waste time looking for the delivery guy?"

"Either way, we need to trace him," Humphries said. "If you're correct, why did Ryan go all the way out to Mickleburgh to choose his victims? What's the connection there?"

"I checked while you were watching the video, and Ryan's company insures Isabella's house. He had access to the house plans and knew its location."

"Have you checked to see if his car registration plate was picked up in the area?"

"Next on my to-do list, but what do you think? It neatly explains why a witness was left behind when nothing else has," Fiona said.

Humphries pulled a series of faces while he considered the

suggestion. "It's possible, I suppose. Will you share this theory with the rest of the team?"

"How crazy does it make me sound?"

Humphries shrugged. "Like I said, it's left field but remotely possible."

"Then I think I should share it as one of several possibilities."

Fiona updated her team before assigning their duties. "Eddie and Andrew, I want you to pick apart every aspect of Ryan's life. Start with his employers. Why was he sacked, and what was his state of mind when he left the office that day? Then move on to family, friends and neighbours. Highlight any areas where he could have encountered any of the students."

"On the face of it, it seems unlikely," Eddie said. "Any suggestions on where their paths might have crossed?"

"We already know that Ryan's company insured Isabella's house, and whatever connects them could lead us to the killer. Check whether she ever made a claim on the policy." Fiona hesitated before adding, "We can't rule out the possibility that the first attack was part of an elaborate plan whereby Ryan could slaughter his family and still be considered the victim." Looking out at a row of faces stunned into silence, Fiona added, "It's one of several possibilities."

"Does this mean we're focussing all our attention on Ryan and the second shooting?" Abbie asked.

"The location of his house means we have more to go on from cameras and witnesses."

"Viewing him as a potential suspect, I meant."

"Not necessarily. It's one possibility. I thought I made that clear. If he's innocent, we still need to discover what links him to the students," Fiona said. "Kerry, how are you getting along with the students' social media profiles?"

"I've nearly finished, but I've not found anything so far. None of them were high users, so it shouldn't take me much longer."

"When you've finished, can you review the garage footage to see if anyone else was paying Ryan any special attention? Julian said he wasn't the only person annoyed by his callous attitude towards the woman. When you've done that, start on Ryan's social media accounts. Pay special attention to any interests he shared with the students."

"Will do."

"Can everyone note all the possible contact points between the two households as you come across them?"

After nods of agreement, Fiona asked if anyone had anything to add.

Kerry's hand shot up. "There is one thing." Kerry dropped her hand, looked around and shyly said, "Tilly was messaging a friend the afternoon of her murder. She said she couldn't leave because a workman was in the house. He was mending the radiators by the sound of it. Should I try to find him?"

"Yes, it's possible he saw something when he was in the area. Also, ask him whether he recently did any work for Ryan," Fiona said. "Before you all go,
 can you think of any similarities between the households?"

"They lived on the outskirts but commuted to Birstall most days," Rachael suggested.

"Unfortunately, so do thousands of others," Humphries said.

"Then, no. Nothing springs to mind," Abbie said to a murmur of agreement.

"Their paths could have crossed anywhere," Fiona said. "Clubs, gyms, supermarkets? I'm going with Humphries to see Isabella again. After seeing her, we'll show Gareth the footage of the man outside Ryan's house in the hope that he recognises him. If it turns out he's someone known to community services, I will let you all know. As always, if anything significant comes up, let me know."

"Are we discounting the possibility the choice of households was completely random?" Abbie asked.

"Nothing is entirely random. No matter how insignificant, something links the two households," Fiona said. "If and when we receive an identification of the man outside Ryan's house, I'll reassess our approach. Unless you hear differently, we'll have a briefing back here at five o'clock."

Walking through reception, Fiona's path was blocked by a woman who had been crying.

"Are you here to see me? Only they said someone would be down to speak to me about an hour ago."

Cursing her good manners, Fiona said, "I'm on my way out, but I'll go up to the desk to ask for you." At the desk, she said, "Sykes, that lady says she's been waiting an hour to be seen. What's going on?"

"Half the station is out on calls, and the other half have called in sick. I can't find anyone."

"What's she in here about?"

"To report her missing son."

"I'll call a constable down to speak to her, but that means there will be no one in our section to take calls for a short while. The constable I have in mind is new and won't know where the interview rooms are, so you'll have to show her." Fiona walked away from the desk to make her call so Sykes couldn't object. Kerry confirmed she would come down straight away. Fiona passed the message on to the woman and ran out the door toward her car, where Humphries was waiting before anyone else held her up.

CHAPTER TWENTY-SEVEN

Kerry watched the others leave the room before logging in to review the social media files. She was relieved rather than bothered about being abandoned in an empty room. She found fitting in with the tightly knit group hard and felt like a complete outsider. She had always struggled to make friends, and while she was comfortable in a one-to-one situation, she could only speak in a crowded room of strangers with the help of a drink or three. Without alcohol's assistance, she could never think of anything remotely interesting or entertaining to say.

She was flicking through Tilly's account but was nursing a hangover and found concentrating hard. She could see the victims' faces on the whiteboard whenever she looked up. Knowing what had happened to them, she avoided looking at them closely. Scrolling through happy pictures of them at social events was challenging.

She hadn't looked at the crime scene reports for the same reason. The news reports about the event were bad enough. Thinking about how frightened the students and Ryan's sons would have been in their final moments brought a lump to her throat. She smiled and shook her head at her mother's frequent warning that her imagination would be the death of her.

She was startled from reminiscing when a phone on the far side of the room rang. Even though she was alone, she pointlessly looked around, hoping someone else would answer it or it would stop ringing. On a plus note, nobody would see how nervous she was about answering the call.

She logged out of the computer system and hurried down to take the statement. She had no idea what it was about. DI Williams hadn't said, and she hadn't thought to ask. She had fought hard against her father for this placement as far away from him as possible, and she was keen to make a good impression through her work. So far that hadn't been possible, but maybe she could turn things around with the statement.

She had a good relationship with her parents, and she would always appreciate the start in life they had given her and their unwavering support. But she wanted to stand on her own record, not on who her father happened to be. She hoped out here that nobody would know who he was, let alone her connection to him. If she could also get a handle on her drinking, that would be the icing on the cake.

On her way down the stairs, it occurred to her she couldn't remember where the interview rooms were. Superintendent Dewhurst had given her a whistle-stop tour of the station on her first day, but all she could remember was they were somewhere on the second floor. She understood now why her father had been vague about whether he liked him. He was pompous, and his constant false smile had been off-putting. She would make a final judgement after she had seen a bit more of him, but on first impressions, she felt that he was someone to avoid as much as possible. She had the sneaky suspicion that so did the rest of the station.

The desk sergeant reminded her of her kindly grandfather, although today, he looked harassed. She quickly smiled at the woman, who she assumed was waiting for her, and turned to the desk. "Hello, I'm here to interview Miss Claydon. Could you tell me where the interview rooms are, as I'm new?"

"Second floor, right down the end. Interview room three is available. I'll take you if ..." Sykes was interrupted by the desk phone. "Sorry, I'll just answer this."

"Thank you. I'm sure we'll find it," Kerry said, turning to the woman who was now standing behind her. Kerry beamed her brightest smile, and said, "Hello, Miss Claydon. Sorry you've had to wait so long. I'll take you to the interview room now. Are you happy to take the stairs?"

"Yes, it will add to my daily steps. Call me Angie. Everyone else does."

Kerry smiled at Angie, noticing she had been crying. She toned her smile down as she had lost count of the times people had moaned at her for her inappropriate reactions. She couldn't help it. Grinning manically like the Cheshire Cat was her stock reaction to feeling nervous and out of her depth. It seemed she always got it wrong and was also regularly told not to look so bored and miserable in social situations. Leading the way to the doors, to fill the silence and make Angie feel more relaxed, she asked, "Have you come a long way today?"

"A short bus ride. I live out at Sapperton."

"I'm new to the area. Is that where the shopping centre is?"

"Yes, I live a short drive from the big supermarket."

Hearing Angie's laboured breathing behind her, Kerry slowed down on the steps. She was enthusiastic about staying fit. As she wasn't one for socialising or having hobbies outside of work, she spent some of her free time running, cycling, or at the gym. She figured the exercise would counterbalance her drinking and keep her healthy.

Walking along the corridor, she tried to read the door name plates without it looking obvious and was relieved to see the sign for the interview rooms. She led Angie inside number three and invited her to make herself comfortable. She couldn't offer her a drink as they hadn't passed a drinks machine in the corridor, and she couldn't remember where one was. Thankfully, a statement pad and pen were already on the table, as she hadn't thought to bring anything with her.

CHAPTER TWENTY-EIGHT

Kerry waited for Angie to finish adjusting her sitting position and settle. "How can I help you, Angie?"

Angie smoothed down her knee-length skirt for the hundredth time and sat up straight. "I want to report my son as missing. He went to work the other day but didn't come home. I thought maybe he had made up with Shelby. When she finally returned my calls, she said she hadn't seen him and hung up. I called his manager this morning, but he said he hadn't seen him either. He reassured me he was probably out on a call, but he rang me back an hour later to say Will hadn't turned up. It's not like him to be so unreliable. He's a good boy. Something must have happened to him."

Kerry looked up from making notes and smiled. "There's no need to rush. You can relax and take your time."

Angie pulled a wad of tissues from her coat pocket and blew her nose. "I thought you were busy?"

"We are, but it's important we have all the correct details." Kerry smiled again. "Can I take his full name for the report?"

"It's William Jackson, but he goes by the name Will these days. And that's his father's name. We're divorced."

"And where does Will work?"

"He's a qualified electrician, but he works for Hobbs Letting Agency as an odd-job man. I've told him he should make more of himself, but he likes the variety of the jobs they send him out on. He likes chatting to all the different people and sorting out their problems for them. Everyone loves him. Some evenings, he struggles with his supper, he's been given that many biscuits and cups of tea."

"He sounds lovely," Kerry said. "How old is Will?"

"He'll be thirty in a few months. I was going to arrange a little surprise for him because he needs cheering up."

"Why's that?"

"His marriage broke down recently, and he's been so down in the dumps and hardly leaving his room other than to go to work. That's why he moved back in with me. He's got a beautiful little boy. He reminds me of somebody else from long ago." Angie paused to dab her eyes. "Will absolutely dotes on him. He's due to stay over this weekend, and Will wouldn't let him down. I know he wouldn't. He's the only thing he really cares about."

"When did the marriage break down, Angie?" Kerry asked, starting to worry if there was a suicide risk.

"About four months ago. Maybe a little less."

"Have you contacted his wife?"

"Yes, but she didn't care. Shelby said she hadn't seen him and hung up."

"Shelby? Is that his wife?"

Angie sucked in her cheeks. "I suppose you could call the little madam that."

"Okay. I'll need her contact details," Kerry said.

After reeling off the details, Angie said, "It won't do you no good. He won't be there. I've since found out that she's moved her new bloke in. Probably the only reason she agreed to Will having Noah for the weekend. She hasn't made things easy for him."

"Do you know when the new partner moved in?"

"She told Will it was recent, but I wouldn't be surprised if he moved in the day Will left."

"Has Will ever disappeared before without telling anyone?" Kerry asked.

"Not like this, never. He wouldn't go off without telling me.

He knows how I worry, and we've always been close since the accident."

"Accident?"

"He was in a serious car accident when he was a teenager. At first, they didn't know if he would survive, and then it was a battle to save his leg. He was in hospital for months. He had to learn to walk again. It still causes him trouble now. He's regularly on strong painkillers, and I can tell when he's tired as his limp gets worse. More noticeable, like."

"Do you know the name of his doctor?" As Kerry wrote down the details, she decided Will Jackson was a high suicide risk. She looked up when she heard Angie sobbing. "Try not to worry, Angie. With everything going on in his life right now, he might have needed a few days alone to think things through, but you said he has Noah's visit to look forward to. When you return home, could you check to see if he has taken his painkillers with him?"

Drying her eyes, Angie shook her head. "I know my son. He would have told me if he was moving out to a new place. He knows he's all I have now."

"I appreciate that, but it's worth checking his medication and letting me know what you find. It might help to set your mind at rest. Have you called his friends and the local hospital?"

"Yes. Nothing."

"Okay, we'll contact them again. Could you give me his friends' names?"

"He's a bit of a loner, and I can only think of two. He spends a lot of time in his room playing games on his computer."

Kerry took the two names and Will's social media accounts before asking, "Did you bring a photograph of Will with you?"

Angie fished through her bag and produced three snapshots. Highlighting one, she said, "This is the best likeness."

Kerry looked at the smiling face of a slightly overweight man with a young-looking open face and dark hair. "How recent is this?"

"It was taken a few days ago when we heard Noah was going to be able to stay the weekend with us," Angie said. "It was the first time in ages I've seen a smile on his face. That's why I took the picture. You will find him, won't you? I can't sleep at night for worrying about what might have happened to him."

"We'll do everything we can to find Will," Kerry said. "Can you think of any places he might have gone?"

"No. I would be checking them if I did."

Kerry put down her pen and gave another bright smile. "Before you go, I'll give you the number for family support. They are available around the clock if you need to speak to someone. It might be worth asking your doctor for something to help you sleep. I will register Will as missing and circulate his details."

"Will you do a television appeal? Or is that only for important people?"

"We'll start with a social media appeal and contact some of the people and organisations we've discussed. We'll let you know what we discover and whether there are other steps we can take," Kerry said. "Meanwhile, could you check his medication for me once you arrive home?"

"Thank you, I will." Angie fussed with her purse's clasp and stood. "Do you think Noah will still be able to stay this weekend?"

Kerry stood and pushed her chair in, noting it was the first time Angie had looked hopeful. Happy even. "I don't know. That's something you need to discuss with his mother."

CHAPTER TWENTY-NINE

After seeing Angie out, Kerry returned upstairs to enter Will's details on the missing person database. She was torn between reviewing the social media accounts and garage footage as DI Williams had asked or concentrating on Will's disappearance. Because of the marriage situation, his disappearance should be classed as medium risk, if not higher. Without the murder enquiries, she would be informing her of the case, but she doubted her phone call would be welcome right now. Weighing up the risks of immediate harm, she decided the answer was obvious.

She looked up the details of the local hospitals and was relieved to be told no one fitting Will's description had been brought in. Next, she rang Will's employers. His supervisor confirmed he hadn't turned up for work as expected, which was unusual as he was generally reliable if something of a loner. "I didn't want to upset his mother further, but he hasn't turned up for jobs for a few days." He went on to say he had no previous inkling that Will had marital problems, but that was typical of Will. He was a good worker, and customers liked him because he was respectful and polite, but he was also a man of few words. He promised to speak to some people who might know where he was and get back to her if he discovered anything.

Kerry leaned back in her chair, chewing a pen. It was clear the whole station was overstretched. DI Williams would be back soon, and she would ask her if she should make the follow-up enquiries about Will or pass the case on to someone else. She hoped it would be the former. Working alone on her own case rather than being thrust into the group investigation would give her time to find her feet.

The short delay in waiting for a decision wouldn't make much difference as Will had already been missing for several days, so she turned her attention to the remaining social media accounts, trying not to think the worst about what had happened to Will. She scrolled through the accounts while her mind wandered. People only put on social media what they want others to see. The exaggerated whirlwind of fun social activities made her feel worse about her hermit status, while finding Will before he did something stupid could make a real difference.

Kerry logged out and decided to review the students' earlier statements, looking out for any connections to Ryan and his family. Her second read reconfirmed that the victims were shy, peaceful, uncomplicated, and caring, while Isabella was rude, entitled and spiteful. Even Isabella's friends admitted she could occasionally be thoughtless and tactless, although they insisted that she wasn't a cruel person. But she found nothing to indicate where their lives might have intersected with Ryan's.

If the opinions were correct, it seemed unfair that Isabella and Ryan were the ones to survive. But then, since when was life fair?

CHAPTER THIRTY

Fiona shrugged off her coat and put it on the back of the chair. Seeing Kerry working at a desk reminded her of the woman in reception when they left. She quickly checked for any urgent messages and wandered over to her, "How did the missing person interview go?"

Kerry jumped up from her chair, "I was going to talk to you about that, Ma'am. Would now be a good time?"

"As good as any, but there's no need to call me ma'am," Fiona said, hoping she didn't sound too weary. She noticed Humphries skulking off to the coffee machine and wished she had grabbed a coffee before coming over to speak to Kerry. Her enthusiasm as she related how her interview had gone was draining. Maybe she had spent too much time with Humphries and his gruff sarcasm.

"I understand how busy you are with the murder enquiry, but so is everyone else, and I'm concerned for his safety," Kerry continued. "Because of the recent break-up with his wife, I think he should be classed as vulnerable. Could I interview his ex-partner and arrange a media request for any sightings of him?"

"Have you handled cases of missing persons before?" Fiona asked. She needed all hands on deck with the murder enquiry, but supervising an inexperienced officer took up more time than it saved. Maybe a side project to keep her occupied until she found time to devote to her would be a good thing.

"Yes, I've done a few."

"You really should have someone assisting you, but we're stretched as it is. Go ahead with the preliminary investigations and media request, then report back to me. I'll see if I can find someone to help you, but don't hold your breath," Fiona said. "Once you've set the ball rolling, the murder investigation has to be your priority. I would still like you to sit in on the briefings. That way, when he's found, you'll already be up to speed on the case. Do you think you'll be able to handle that?"

"Yes," Kerry replied with a wide smile. "I've already entered his details into the database and spoken to his employer. It's only really his wife I would need to see urgently."

Fiona nodded her agreement. "Have you finished reviewing the students' social media accounts?"

"They don't add anything," Kerry said. "I've read back through the statements trying to find a link between the students and Ryan but couldn't find anything to link them. No wonder people assume a random lunatic is responsible for the two shootings."

"We don't make assumptions," Fiona said. "I'm guessing you didn't look at the garage footage."

"Sorry."

"Review it as soon as you've spoken to the missing person's wife."

"Thank you, Ma'am," Kerry said enthusiastically. Suppressing her grin, she said, "I'll find the time to watch the video later."

"Fiona."

"Fiona," Kerry repeated, grinning.

CHAPTER THIRTY-ONE

It took Kerry a while to understand how the back-to-front housing estate in Sapperton worked. Shelby lived on a council estate built in the sixties before everyone had a car, and it was assumed that residents, particularly women, would walk or use public transport to get around. The front doors opened to a footpath that linked all the houses and led across a park to the main shopping area. After circling the area twice, Kerry discovered that to access the houses by car, she had to take a different road that ran along the back gardens. Visiting a stranger's home through their rear garden seemed odd, but she assumed the residents thought it normal.

Shelby was fake-tan-orange all over and wore an inch of makeup. She clattered through the kitchen in her stilettoes and welcomed Kerry into her cluttered lounge, talking constantly. Brightly coloured toys littered the floor, but she had sent her little boy, Noah next door so they could talk. And could Shelby talk! By the time Kerry was seated, her brain was filled with bus timetables, the cost of food, the new nail bar that had opened along the road and the trials of working in a newsagent.

While Shelby continued to talk about her new diet based on fasting, Kerry pulled out her notepad and pen. "Can we talk about Will?"

Shelby was momentarily silenced, and she narrowed her eyes. "Have you spoken to his mother?"

"Yes, she came into the station to report him as missing."

Shelby folded her arms and stared at a point above Kerry's head. "I'm nowhere near as bad as she says. There's being overprotective, but she's something else. The sun doesn't shine out of Will, and he doesn't pooh gold nuggets. If she …"

"It's Will I want to ask you about," Kerry said. "How he was the last time you saw him, who his friends are, and where he goes. That's all I'm interested in."

"I told him about Joe moving in the last time I saw him, so he wasn't happy." Shelby gave a long, drawn-out sigh. "But that's hardly my fault. He has to move on the same as I have. Life is what you make it. That's what my mum always says. That and if you don't ask, you don't get. I want to make something of my life. I work hard, and I deserve better."

"I'm sure you do, but have you spoken to Will since?" Kerry asked, tapping her pen on her notepad.

"Yeah, the other day. I said he could have Noah for the weekend. Now Angie says he's disappeared, I don't know what to do. I've planned to go away for a few days and can't decide whether I should cancel. My mum would have Noah on Friday night and probably Sunday, but she always goes out for a drink with her friends on a Saturday night. What do you think? Should I cancel or wait to see if he turns up?"

"That's a decision for you, I'm afraid," Kerry said. "How did Will sound when you spoke to him?"

"Normal. He was looking forward to having Noah to stay. I knew he wouldn't mind as he doesn't have a social life. I expect his mother would take over if he had to go out. If he did, it would be more likely because of a work emergency somewhere. A burst pipe or something along those lines."

Kerry wondered if Will didn't talk much because he never got the chance to get a word in edgeways at home between Angie and Shelby. "When you were together, did he go out much?"

"Only when I forced him to. He doesn't have any friends. He'll chat with a couple of people from school or where he works if he sees them, but he doesn't have people he can call up for a chat.

And he's always been weird about getting into cars. He doesn't like to be driven and always insists on driving. His car is a pile of old junk. It was in the garage as often as parked out back, so that was limiting. I like to look my best when I go out, so I can't walk around in the wind and rain."

"Was his reluctance to be a passenger because of the accident?"

"Possibly." Shelby showed her nails to Kerry. "I just had them done at the new place. What do you think?"

"Very nice," Kerry said after a cursory glance. "Can you think of where Will might have gone?"

"No. He usually runs off to his mum if life isn't going his way. Now, that's an odd relationship. It explains a lot of things."

Determined not to be pushed off track, Kerry asked, "When you were together, did Will ever suffer from depression or disappear by himself for a few days?"

"He was never the life and soul, but I don't think he was ever depressed. What did he have to be depressed about? Although, I wished he would disappear sometimes. He went to work and came home. The only other place he went was to see his mum. Or she came here, looking down her nose at me."

"How was he when your relationship started to fail?" Kerry asked. "I assume it wasn't an overnight thing."

Shelby hugged her arms around herself. "It was in a way for him."

"In what way?"

"Will isn't a bad person, and I hope you find him, but him and me, we were never a real thing."

"How do you mean?"

Shelby looked out the bay window onto the pathway. She was still for the first time since Kerry arrived. "I was a kid, barely sixteen. Will was older. I became pregnant and was scared and excited at the same time. Will wanted to do the right thing, and I wanted to get away from home. Thought the grass was greener - the usual stuff. We bumped along, and things were fine until I met Joe and realised what being in love was like. I'm sorry if I hurt Will, but I want to be with Joe. If Will was more normal, he would have realised a long time ago that I didn't love him. We didn't do things as a couple. I ignored him mostly, like my mum did my dad. If I knew where he was, I would tell you. I don't hate him. I don't feel anything for him. I never did. There, are you satisfied? Will you go and tell his mum what a horrid person I am?"

"Of course I won't. I'm only interested in finding Will. Thanks for being so honest about your relationship," Kerry said. "Before I go, could you explain what you mean by Will not being normal?"

"He's not crazy or anything. He's just not really there most of the time. I never knew what he was thinking. It was all going on inside, hidden from sight. There's probably a posh word for it, but I don't know it. My mate next door thinks he's autistic. He does like his routines and has set ideas on how people should behave, but he's not good with numbers, so I don't think he is. I think his mum has more to do with how he is. I hope he's safe and well somewhere, and if I do happen to see him, I'll let you know. I can't help you any more than that."

Kerry left feeling more worried about Will. Shelby may have considered it a loveless marriage, but that didn't mean Will had. He would have been devastated when Shelby told him about her new boyfriend if he had genuine feelings for her. Especially if she had been as brutally honest with him and said she had never felt anything for him. He could easily decide his life wasn't worth living without friends to turn to for support. She hoped she could find him before he did something stupid.

CHAPTER THIRTY-TWO

When Kerry returned to the station, she was disappointed to find the operations room empty. She was increasingly concerned about Will's welfare and wanted to talk to Fiona about what more she could do to find him. While waiting for Fiona to return, she decided to watch the garage footage as promised. She also remembered she had been asked to call Isabella's father to ask about the workman visiting the house. She rang his number, and his secretary told her that he was in a meeting, but she would ask him to call her back later. Kerry thanked the secretary and settled down to watch the garage tape but was interrupted by a phone call. "Hello, DC Kerry Vines."

"Oh, hello, luv. This is Angie, Will's mum."

"Oh, yes, hello Angie. I've spoken to Will's wife and passed his details to all our patrol cars, so they're all keeping an eye out for him. He's also on the national database, so people all around the country are looking out for him."

"Ah, yes. That's what I'm calling about. I'm afraid I've wasted your time. I've just heard from Will. He says he's fine and I'm not to worry. You were right. With his marriage collapsing and everything else going on, he felt he had to get away for a bit. He says he'll come back as soon as he feels ready. I'm so sorry to have wasted your time, but can you let everyone know he's not missing."

"No need to be sorry, Angie. That's excellent news," Kerry said.

"I'm relieved he's okay."

"So, will you let everyone know he's no longer missing," Angie asked. "Or do I need to do something?"

"I'll let everyone know, so you don't need to worry. I hope he sorts himself out quickly and he comes home soon," Kerry said. "Did he take his medication with him?"

After a short hesitation, Angie said, "Yes, so we know he's looking after his health and thinking straight, so nobody needs to be worrying about him."

Kerry ended the call feeling less reassured as she updated all the records to show that Will was no longer missing. She remained worried about his state of mind but tried to convince herself that if he had taken the trouble to contact his mother, he probably wouldn't do anything stupid.

She turned her attention to the garage footage, only to be disturbed by Superintendent Dewhurst, who wanted to know how she was settling in. She explained she was busy, but he insisted she join him in his office for a coffee and a chat.

CHAPTER THIRTY-THREE

Fiona and Humphries found Isabella lounging in her hotel room in a dressing gown and slippers. She invited them in and asked, "Has something happened?"

"There have been a few developments," Fiona said, thinking she must be the only person in the area who hadn't heard about the second shooting. "Where are your parents?"

"Mummy's downstairs having her hair done, and Daddy's gone to work today. Do you need to speak to them?"

"No, it is you we've come to see. We want to go over the evening of the attack again."

"Really? Again? I don't see what more I can possibly say," Isabella pouted. "I had hoped you had come to say you had caught him, not bother me with trivialities when I'm recovering from trauma."

Isabella had been through a horrific experience, but Fiona was finding it harder to sympathise with her. "I think there may be some omissions in your earlier account. Could you run through it again?"

"If I must," Isabella said, flopping onto a bed. "Do you mind if I paint my toenails while we talk?"

"Yes, I would mind," Fiona said. "I would like to have your full attention."

Isabella sighed and pouted again. "He came in, shot my tenants, looked at me and then walked out. What more are you expecting me to say?"

"And nothing else happened?"

"Like did he do a song and dance routine?" Isabella asked. "Then the answer is no."

"Did he speak to you?" Fiona asked.

Isabella looked like she was sucking lemons. "He might have mumbled something intelligible."

"What did he say to you?"

"I just told you it was intelligible. It sounded like, 'Look at what you've done.' But that doesn't make any sense, so I assumed I had misheard him," Isabella said. "Funny enough, I wasn't going to call him back to repeat himself."

"Assuming you heard correctly, what do you think he meant by it?"

"I have absolutely no idea," Isabella said, folding her arms. "I hadn't done anything. He is obviously crazy. He's totally off his rocker if you ask me."

"Why didn't you tell us this before?"

"Because it sounds so crazy, and I can't imagine how it would help you find him," Isabella said. "And if you must know, I'm not totally sure he did speak to me, or if I imagined it because of the drugs they gave me at the hospital."

"It didn't occur to you that it might provide vital clues?" Humphries asked.

Isabella feigned a look of boredom and looked down her nose at Humphries. "The only thing it could possibly tell you is that he's a fruit loop, and I thought you were supposed to be detectives. I think most people could have reached that conclusion without any additional help."

Fiona felt on edge, wanting to shake some sense into Isabella. She thought it best she didn't spend more time than necessary in her company in case she did. She leaned forward, forcing Isabella to look directly at her. "Did you recognise the voice?"

"No. It sounded local. Someone from Birstall. I don't have any friends from Birstall."

"Was it a broad Birstall accent?"

"Yes. It was very working class, and he sounded uneducated," Isabella said.

"Are you sure you've never heard that voice before?" Fiona held up her hands to stop Isabella from replying immediately. "Please take your time to think about it."

"I'm sure. He's not the sort of person I would mix with."

Humphries gave Isabella a withering look that went straight over her head. "Clearly."

"Have you remembered anything else about him?" Fiona asked. "Did he walk okay?"

"I guess. He didn't get down on all fours and leap around like an ape. He turned and walked out normally like nothing had happened."

"Did he move around easily?"

"What is this? He walked around like everyone else does. He didn't beat his chest or make animal noises. He simply walked," Isabella said. "How long do we have to stay here? Mummy is getting on my nerves, and I'm bored."

"We'll let you know in a few days," Fiona said. She pulled out her phone with the video of the man seen outside Ryan's house. "Do you recognise this man?"

Isabella glanced at the video and rolled her eyes. "How could anyone recognise that blur?"

"Look at it again," Fiona said. "Could this have been the gunman?"

Isabella took the phone and watched the video again before handing it back. "He's the right build, but I can't be sure. Haven't you a clearer picture?"

Fiona showed Isabella a picture of Ryan with his face blanked out. "How about this man?"

Isabella shook her head. "Far too skinny."

"When we spoke before, you said you had reached a mutual agreement with your tenants about them moving out. We've been told by several people that wasn't the case. There was a major argument in the kitchen over it, and things were thrown. Which is it?"

"Goodness, I don't think dropping a loaf of ghastly sliced bread on the table constitutes a violent incident."

"But was there a bitter argument that day?" Humphries asked.

"It did get a little heated, but it had all blown over by that evening. They were excited about finding a new place together, and I was relieved to know they were going. I felt we had reached a happy resolution."

"Who knew about the argument?" Humphries asked.

"I've no idea. I don't think I bothered to mention it to anyone. Why would I? It was a storm in a teacup as far as I was concerned," Isabella said. "I suppose they may have exaggerated our frank discussion to some of their friends."

"Was there anyone else in the house at the time?" Fiona asked.

"No … oh, yes. There was a workman. A complete waste of Daddy's money. Tilly complained about her radiator not working and the hot water not always coming on in one of the upstairs bathrooms. Hardly an issue coming into summer, but she kept going on about it, so I finally telephoned Daddy, and he said he would sort it. Does that make me sound like a bad landlord? It was being dealt with although there was no urgent need."

"Have you got his name?"

"The workman? No, why should I?"

"Did you speak to him?"

"The workman? No, I had lectures all day. I left Tilly to deal with him, as it was her who had been complaining."

"How would you describe him?"

"Like a workman. He wore blue overalls and was crawling around on the floor looking at the radiator. I didn't pay him any attention."

"Thank you for your time. We'll see ourselves out," Fiona said.

Outside, Humphries asked, "Is it worth following up on the workman?"

"Kerry should have already," Fiona replied.

CHAPTER THIRTY-FOUR

Fiona and Humphries met Gareth in a local gym run by two ex-offenders he had worked with in the past. As soon as he saw them, he climbed off the exercise bike, draped a towel around his neck and walked over to greet them. "I thought I would be seeing you after the second shooting. I assume you still haven't got a suspect, so it must be a crazy or an ex-offender."

"Where did you hear we don't have a suspect?" Humphries asked.

"I watch the news like everyone else," Gareth replied. "I told the other two that I would let you know if I heard anything, but I haven't."

"We have some footage of a person outside the house of the latest shooting," Fiona said, pulling her phone from her pocket. "Could you have a look at it and say whether you recognise them?"

Gareth watched the video twice before shaking his head. "Sorry. It doesn't remind me of anyone."

"Are you sure?" Humphries asked.

"I would like to see this person off the street as much as you do," Gareth said. "No, I don't recognise him. Anything else?"

"There is something else," Fiona said, taking her phone back. "You said something to my officer about how the shooter could be suffering from survivor's guilt. I wondered what you meant by that and whether you were thinking about someone in particular?"

After a moment's confusion, Gareth smiled. "I think they got the wrong end of the stick. I was talking about the unharmed student. It could seriously mess her up and send her along the wrong path. I've seen it several times in people I've helped."

"You weren't suggesting the gunman has survivor's guilt, and that's why he left a witness behind?"

"I wasn't, but it's possible."

"Are you currently dealing with someone who would fit that description?" Fiona asked.

"If I was, I wouldn't give you a name without something more, but I can tell you it's not the person you've just shown me," Gareth said. "Since you've mentioned it, I would say he may be leaving a witness behind, so they suffer like he did, but it's a bit like sexual abuse. Not all children who are abused grow up to become abusers, but yes, some do."

Fiona stared directly at Gareth. "Are you currently dealing with someone who could be responsible for these shootings?"

Gareth stared back with equal intensity. "No. In this case, if I were, I would tell you. Local people are scared. They think it might be their family next."

Fiona held his stare for a few seconds before breaking eye contact. Gareth was fiercely defensive of his charges, but she believed him. "If anything leads to you changing your opinion, will you let me know?"

"You have my word."

◆ ◆ ◆

When Fiona approached the incident room, she was surprised to see Kerry coming from upstairs. In a friendly voice, she asked, "Where have you been?"

"For a coffee with superintendent Dewhurst, Ma'am."

Hoping Kerry couldn't hear Humphries mutterings about cosy little power chats, Fiona asked, "Did you contact the workman who worked on Isabella's radiators?"

"Not yet. I called Mr Stainton for his details, and I'm waiting for him to call back."

Fiona opened the door to the incident room. "Chase him. The workman, who I suspect is a plumber, was in the house when the students were arguing with Isabella. It will be interesting to hear an unbiased first-hand account."

"Will do, Ma'am."

"Thanks, but stop calling me Ma'am. Call me Fiona like everyone else." Fiona shrugged off her coat and put it on the back of the chair. Remembering their last conversation, she said, "Did you interview the missing person's wife?"

"I was going to talk to you about that. Would now be a good time?"

"As good as any," Fiona said, with a sinking sense of deja vu. She noticed Humphries had skulked off to the coffee machine again.

"The thing is," Kerry continued. "His mother has since rung me to say she had heard from him, and everything is fine, and I've updated all the records to say he's been found."

"So, what's the problem?" Fiona asked.

"I understand how busy we are with the murder enquiry, but I'm still concerned for his safety. Because of the recent break-up with his wife, I think he could be classed as vulnerable. Have I done the right thing, closing everything down on her word?"

"I see. We are ridiculously busy, and if his mother has told you that he's no longer missing, that should be an end to it. If it would make you feel better, you could call his mother in a few days to check whether he's returned home."

"Yes, I'll do that," Kerry replied with a wide smile. "It will set my mind at rest."

Fiona nodded her agreement, pleased the matter had been resolved. "Have you reviewed the garage tapes and pulled off the registration plates?"

"Not yet. I was going to make a start, but Superintendent Dewhurst asked me to join him for a coffee. I said I was busy, but he insisted."

"Yes, he can be persuasive," Fiona said. "Review the tapes as soon as you can. We'll be having a briefing shortly once everyone returns, so it will probably have to be tomorrow morning."

"Thank you, Ma'am," Kerry said enthusiastically. Suppressing her grin, she said, "I'll look at them first thing tomorrow."

"Fiona."

"Fiona."

CHAPTER THIRTY-FIVE

Humphries brought a morning coffee over to Fiona, who was staring at the whiteboard. "Penny for them?"

Fiona gratefully took the coffee. "The guy leaving Ryan's house completely disappeared after reaching the end of the road. None of the cameras picked him up further along, and the teenagers who hang out in the underpass say they didn't see him."

"Nothing on the dual carriageway either?"

Fiona shook her head. "Either he got lucky or knew where to park his car away from the cameras on the dual carriageway."

"It suggests he's local to know about that and the shortcut."

"If we can't identify him, it doesn't matter where he comes from. Nothing came in overnight in response to the media posting his picture. Hardly surprising, considering how blurred it is, but I was hoping for something. As it is, we're left with trying to find something that connects Isabella or one of the other students to Ryan and his family."

"Because you don't want to accept the alternative? That someone out there is randomly selecting households for annihilation."

"Partly," Fiona admitted.

"Do you totally trust Gareth?" Humphries asked. "Are you sure he doesn't know someone who fits the bill? I noticed he watched the video clip of the man outside Ryan's house twice."

"I think he genuinely believes he doesn't know the suspect, but he could be wrong," Fiona said. "We could force the issue and make him hand over possible names, but I don't want to go down that road yet."

"What's the situation with investigating Ryan as a suspect?"

"Reports are still coming in, but like with Isabella, there's no evidence of him recently handling a firearm. The match run on unknown fingerprints at the two houses came back negative."

"Have Eddie and Andrew uncovered anything more on him?"

"They're working on discovering why his colleague leaked the messages that got him the sack. And speaking to friends and other colleagues about his recent state of mind to see if there could be a motive, but I'm not holding my breath. He doesn't have a record, and there has never been any suggestion of marital violence. People have described him as short-tempered, but it's a massive leap from being impatient to gunning down his entire family. While he has overstretched himself financially, it's nothing a spot of belt-tightening wouldn't clear in time. So far, there's nothing to suggest an affair or a hankering for a different life, and Isabella said he was far thinner than the gunman."

"So, all in all, it's not sounding too promising."

"Let's wait and see if everything checks out," Fiona said.

"If there's no evidence against Ryan and no connection between him and the students, are you sure we should be ruling out a random attacker?"

"Let me make this clear - I'm not," Fiona said. "I'm saying we need to look at why these two households were chosen. There must be something connecting them that explains why they were selected. It could be something minor that they have in common."

"Don't say that in front of Isabella. She would be appalled by the suggestion she breathed the same air as an insurance worker."

Fiona put her coffee to one side and walked closer to the board. "Why does he leave one person unharmed? And why Isabella and Ryan? Why not one of the others?"

"Could that be random as well?" Humphries asked.

"I don't think so," Fiona said. "Isabella was furthest from the gunman while Ryan was closest. Depending on your definition, they could be described as the head of the household, but that suggests the killer knew them. Ryan could be an obvious guess, but how did he know Isabella owned the house?"

"Do you think the connection is between Isabella and Ryan rather than between, say, his wife and one of the students?"

"Not necessarily, but I'm wondering if we have been looking at it the wrong way around. The opposite way to the killer, anyway. Isabella said she didn't hear or see a car arriving, but he would have needed some form of transport to get to Mickleburgh. If he's parking it some distance away, where he knows a camera won't pick it up, he's thought this through and is trying to avoid being seen. Which is odd when he's leaving a random witness behind."

"So?" Humphries asked.

"We don't know much about Ryan's wife and children, but we do know the students killed were a good bunch of kids, while people thought Ryan was bad-tempered and Isabella a spoilt brat. What if they were always the intended victims? He wanted them to suffer for what they had done."

"It fits with the comment about how they should look at what they've done."

"I've had a thought." Fiona pulled out her phone to ring Ryan. "Have you had any work done on your house recently? A plumber, maybe?" Her face fell as she listened to the reply. "No, it was just a thought. Before you go, did your family regularly order pizzas from one of the local companies?"

"It was worth a shot," Humphries said, uncharacteristically sympathetic when Fiona ended her call.

"That's my point. We could be searching for something that seems irrelevant on the face of it," Fiona said. "We've already received voluntary access to Isabella's bank accounts. Do we have Ryan's?"

"Yes, access was granted a few hours ago," Humphries said.

"Okay, they need to be gone through. We know who insured Isabella's house. Do we know who insured her car?"

"We can find out," Humphries said.

Fiona and Humphries looked around when Kerry came over.

"Has Isabella's father returned your call yet?" Fiona asked.

"No. I've left another message saying it's urgent," Kerry said. "I rang Will's mother to ask how she was. She repeated that he took his medication with him. I told her that was a good sign, but I'm not so sure it is."

"Try not to worry about it," Fiona replied, struggling to hide her irritation at Kerry's obsession with the missing thirty-year-old with an overprotective mother who wasn't even missing. "Can you concentrate on the murder enquiry? Have you reviewed the garage tapes yet?"

"I'll make a start on them."

Humphries watched Kerry return to her desk with a look of disdain on his face. "A merry little ray of sunshine, isn't she? A right little Pollyanna. I wonder if those rose-tinted glasses come free with private education?"

"Humphries! Leave it. I don't want that sort of attitude in the team."

Humphries shrugged and turned to face the whiteboard. He turned when he heard the door opening and waved Eddie and Andrew over.

"Have you anything new for us?" Fiona asked.

"Possibly," Eddie replied. "According to Ryan's boss, he's been showing signs of stress for a while. Sacking him was the culmination of months of missed deadlines, a bad attitude and misunderstanding company policy and instructions. He feels guilty about sacking him instead of trying to get to the bottom of the problem, as until the last few months, Ryan was considered a good manager who had been with the company for years. But it does suggest something was seriously bothering him. Maybe he did snap."

"Did you speak to the people he managed?"

"Yes, and they said something similar," Andrew said. "He's been short-tempered and abrasive for several months. One of the women who worked for him overheard him arguing aggressively with his wife over her expenditure. And the guy who has taken over his role thought his marriage was strained."

"That's the same person who leaked the messages that led to Ryan's dismissal?"

"Yes," Andrew said. "But the company insisted the messages were the final straw rather than the direct cause of his dismissal. I felt his friend had assessed the situation and has been waiting in the wings for the final push for a while."

"How did the two men get along?"

"They were considered to be friends."

"Some friend," Humphries said. "He sounds like a nasty backstabber to me. Has he an alibi for the shootings?"

"Yes. He and his wife were having dinner at the golf club with the manager."

"Cosy," Humphries said.

"Maybe, but it means he's not our murder suspect," Fiona said. "Anything in Ryan's medical notes?"

"He's not been to see his GP in years. His last company medical was two years ago, and no problems were noted then."

Humphries looked at Fiona. "We know he argued with his wife that night about her going ahead and booking an expensive holiday to Barbados and possibly realised his best friend just stabbed him in the back. Maybe Eddie is right about him finally snapping."

"No, that explanation doesn't fit," Fiona said. "If he's responsible, he's been planning this. The attack on the students was to throw us off the scent. That was why he had to leave a witness behind to say his intruder behaved the same way. Otherwise, he would have had to shoot himself and miraculously survive."

"But why a household of students?" Eddie asked. "He could have found an easier target. An older couple would be less likely to put up a fight and a more obvious choice."

"Maybe they weren't the first choice, but he found both their neighbours were out. One at a play, the other visiting family abroad," Humphries suggested. "Or maybe, as it was a Friday night, he didn't expect them all to be in."

"Damn you, Humphries!"

"What have I done?"

"Your comment about the neighbours makes logical sense," Fiona said. She turned to Eddie and Andrew, "Can you re-interview Isabella's neighbour and check whether they knew Ryan? If I remember rightly, the other neighbour was visiting family abroad. See if they have a number she can be reached on and ask her the same thing."

"Sure, but if it was Ryan, wouldn't he have wanted to have no connection with the first victims?" Andrew said.

"No obvious connection," Fiona agreed. "But he would have needed some knowledge of who they were, so they must have crossed paths somewhere along the line. Think laterally and dig a little deeper."

After Andrew and Eddie left, Fiona called Kerry over. "Leave what you're doing for now. I want you to go through Ryan's and the students' bank accounts with a fine tooth comb to look for casual connections. I'm talking supermarket shops, cinema or theatre visits, gyms or clothes shops - anything and everything that could have put them in close proximity to one another. Okay? Number one priority for the rest of the day. Even if Dewhurst does pay you a visit."

CHAPTER THIRTY-SIX

Fiona and Humphries drove to the address where Ryan said he was staying. As they crawled along in heavy traffic, Humphries said, "Are you sure you don't want me to call ahead to check he's in? I would hate this to be a wasted journey. Plus, we will have to drive back in all this traffic."

"No, I want an element of surprise, and we're nearly there."

"It would probably be just as quick to pull over and walk the rest of the way," Humphries complained.

"It's not like you to be so impatient," Fiona said. "Anything up?"

Humphries quickly shook his head. "No, it's just this case. The students and Ryan's kids." He fell silent until Fiona pulled over a short distance from the terraced townhouse. "Let's hope he's in."

Fiona rang the bell twice, but there was no sign of movement from inside the house. Humphries resisted commenting until they had returned to Fiona's car. "What now?"

"Call the station to see if anything new has been dug up about him," Fiona said. She settled into her seat and watched the residential street of small, terraced houses, only a few streets away from the bustle of shops, pubs and bus links. She guessed that the house would only have two or three bedrooms and a small backyard based on the size of the house. It looked like the type of place students or first-time buyers would live. Without averting her eyes, she sat up straight and gave Humphries a nudge. "What do we have here?"

Humphries looked up and quickly put his phone away. "To my inexperienced eye, it looks like a grieving widow walking hand in hand with an attractive young lady at least ten years his junior. And laughing at something she said and kissing her at the front door."

"Aren't you pleased we didn't call ahead?" Fiona opened her car door when the couple disappeared inside. "Hurry up. I would prefer to interview him while he still has his clothes on."

They knocked on the front door a third time and stood back to wait. They heard the clatter of shoes on wooden flooring, and a woman in her early to mid-thirties opened the door. Smoothing her ruffled hair, she smiled, and asked, "Can I help you?"

Fiona showed her warrant card. "We're here to see Ryan. We understand he's staying with you. Is he in?"

The woman shouted over her shoulder, "Ryan! The police are here to see you." She stepped out onto the pavement instead of stepping back to let them pass. "Is there any news?"

Fiona had no interest in seeing Ryan partly undressed, so she allowed herself to be drawn into the delay tactics without giving anything away. "Our initial investigations have thrown up a few things we need to clarify with Ryan."

"I see. It's such a shocking thing to happen. You will be gentle with Ryan, won't you? I'm giving him all the moral support I can, but I'm worried about him. He's very vulnerable after what's happened."

Ryan appeared behind the woman and pulled the door open wide. "Hello again. Is it okay if they come in, Em?"

"Of course. Take them through to the living room. I'll make myself scarce upstairs."

"Don't feel you have to our account," Humphries said, following Ryan and Fiona along the narrow corridor. "Not if you think he needs your moral support."

Em hesitated, clearly unsure if Humphries was making a point, smiled, and said, "I'll ask Ryan what he wants me to do."

Once they were all seated and it was agreed that Em was staying, Fiona asked Ryan how he was.

"Getting by, I suppose. Living each day an hour at a time," Ryan said. "I'm trying not to dwell on things, but as soon as I let my guard down, my mind takes me right back there."

"It will take time," Fiona said. "I'm surprised your family liaison officer isn't with you."

"I spoke with her earlier and said I wanted some privacy to spend time with my brother and his wife. Em has provided me with somewhere to stay and been so supportive, that it didn't seem fair to have someone else here all the time."

"Have they said when you'll be able to return home?" Humphries asked.

"No, but to be honest, I don't know how I'm going to feel about that. I don't think I could bring myself to walk through the front door. I might put the place up for sale without ever stepping foot inside."

"I've said he can stay here for as long as he needs," Em said. "Everything is very raw and he's not in the right place to be making major decisions."

"That's very kind of you," Fiona said. "How long have you known each other?"

Ryan and Em looked at each other before Ryan said, "It would be about five years now. Since Em joined the company. We hit it off straight away and have been friends ever since."

"Did you meet Ryan's family, Em?" Fiona asked.

"I briefly met his wife at a couple of office events. I didn't know her well, but what happened has hit us all hard at work," Em said. "The whole thing is upsetting for everyone. It's been a real wake-up call to how we take things for granted when nothing's promised in life."

"I appreciate that," Fiona said. "Do you see much of each other outside of work?"

"Rarely. Our friendship has always been based around the office," Ryan said. "And now, of course …"

"It's one of those strange anomalies of modern life. We spend most of our waking hours with work colleagues. I expect you find that," Em said with a suggestive smile.

"Before we go any further, I'm going to tell you that we saw you walking up the street together," Fiona said. "Do you want to make any comment?"

Ryan blushed and looked embarrassed. "It's not what you think. We've been friends for a long time, and I'm going through a very difficult time. Em has been there for me."

"We're not doing anything wrong," Em said defiantly.

"How long has the affair been going on for?" Humphries asked.

Ryan spun around to face Humphries. "We're not having an affair. You're jumping to conclusions. Em has been comforting me through this incredibly trying time. She's been trying to keep my mind off things and cheer me up. That's not a crime, is it?"

"Let me put this another way," Humphries said. "Were the two of you meeting up outside of work before the death of your family?"

"No, and I object to you asking," Ryan said.

"We will be checking," Humphries said.

"We've met up for a coffee on occasion," Em said. "But nothing like you are suggesting. We're good friends. Nothing more."

"Hoping to be more," Humphries said.

"Okay, we'll move on to what we came to talk to you about today," Fiona said. "Having spoken to your manager and colleagues, we understand you've been showing signs of stress for several months. Any reason for that, Ryan?"

"Signs of stress? That's nonsense," Ryan said. "Who said that, and what am I supposed to have done?"

"It was a universal opinion," Fiona said. "People thought you'd been more bad-tempered recently and made some poor decisions. From overheard conversations, they thought you might be having money or marital difficulties. Would that be true?"

"No. My marriage was fine, and I had no money problems until they decided to sack me unfairly without warning."

"No financial problems at all?" Fiona queried. "A lot of people are struggling at the moment."

"Well, yes. I have a mortgage, and the shopping and heating bills have been shooting through the roof, but we've been keeping our heads above water. We've had to make slight adjustments here and there to limit our spending, but nothing serious. Ann was talking about going back to work part-time. So, we were bucking the trend and thinking our financial position was going to improve."

"Was Ann happy about returning to work?" Fiona asked.

"She was excited by the prospect," Ryan said. "She never wanted to give up, but we were struggling with finding decent childcare, and at the time, it seemed the easier option. She always intended to return as soon as the boys were older."

"How about the bad temper and poor judgement?" Humphries asked.

"Again. Absolute nonsense. Tell them, Em. You work on the same floor. Would you say I've been bad-tempered recently?"

"No more than usual," Em replied.

Ryan's head swung around to face Em. "What do you mean? Why would you say that?"

"Calm down, Ryan. I don't mean anything. You've always been driven and impatient for results. There's no point in denying it. It's part of who you are, and I respect your passion for getting things done," Em said. "I'm saying I haven't seen any change in your behaviour. That's what they're getting at."

"And the poor judgment calls?" Humphries asked. "You had just been sacked."

"Outmanoeuvred more like. By a brown-nosing little snake," Ryan said. "I thought we were friends. I had no idea he was after my job. It's only now, when I think back, that I realise how he's been playing me for months to get his own way."

Fiona pulled out her phone. "As part of our investigation, we've obtained some footage of a man outside your property. It's from a neighbour's security camera, so it is not very clear, but could you take a look at the image and see whether you recognise him?"

Ryan took his time looking at the screen with Em looking over his shoulder. "It could be him. He's about the right build, but like you say it's very fuzzy."

Taking back her phone, Fiona asked, "Did anyone deliver

anything to your house just before the shooting?"

Ryan shook his head. "I don't think so, but I spent the evening arguing with my wife or upstairs trying to explain things to my sons."

"I know it's still very raw, but can you talk us through the events of the night of the shooting again?" Fiona asked.

"Really? Does he have to?" Em asked.

"If you don't mind, Ryan," Fiona said.

Ryan gave an identical account of the evening as he had given in the station, at times close to tears. Fiona wasn't sure whether they were due to grief or anger, but she thanked him at the end and confirmed they were leaving. She turned in the doorway. "All the time we've been here, you haven't asked how the investigation is going. Do you want us to catch who did this?"

Ryan threw his hands up in angry frustration. "Of course I do. But it won't bring my family back. I'll still be burying them in a couple of weeks."

CHAPTER THIRTY-SEVEN

Fiona arrived at the station early to make up for leaving on time the night before. It was the first time in weeks she hadn't left hours after she was supposed to. Leaving late had become so normalised that last night, she had felt like she was playing truant, and guilt had followed her all the way to her father's nursing home.

Instead of jumping straight into the overnight reports and preparing for the morning's briefing, she took advantage of the quiet stillness of the empty room to ponder the case generally. While she felt a possible affair gave additional grounds for linking Ryan to both shootings, with so little evidence against him, she had to consider the possibility he wasn't responsible. And if he wasn't responsible, they needed to discover who was and get them off the streets.

The image of the man outside Ryan's house hadn't led to a single credible lead. All it had done was assist the local press and social media to whip up a frenzy of concern. Advising people to be vigilant and keep their doors locked was one thing, but the element of racial speculation was disheartening. It was impossible to tell from their grainy images, but certain factions insisted it was of a non-white person and magically decided it was an immigrant. Apart from stoking racial tensions, it was a dangerous assumption to make.

With nothing else to anchor the case, she was at a loss

for how to proceed other than continuing to search for a connection between the victims. She positioned herself in front of the whiteboard with a coffee, hoping for some inspiration. Her thought process was disturbed by the noisy arrival of Humphries.

Humphries joined her at the board. "Couldn't sleep either? I woke up in a cold sweat last night and couldn't shake the thought that if this guy randomly targets households in the area, it could be any of us next."

"That's a reassuring thought to start my day with," Fiona said. "After we discovered the relationship with Em, I thought you were convinced it was Ryan. Why the nightmares?"

"Maybe I was just hoping we could pin everything on Ryan. I don't like the alternatives any more than you do," Humphries said. "I just remembered. Before I left last night, an additional report came in on the person seen outside Ryan's house."

"Why didn't you ring me? What did it say?"

"You looked exhausted, and I knew you were visiting your dad. It doesn't add anything, anyway. The only useful thing they've taken from the images is that the person was way over six feet tall. Although the timing is suspicious, we can't say for sure he was connected to what happened. Andrew went to Ryan's house to check on his way home, and some political leaflets were by the door. He's checking who was canvassing in the area and what time."

"Did you hear anything back from the others before you left?" When Humphries shook his head, Fiona said, "Let's hope one of them has something for us."

"And who knows, Kerry might finally meet her missing man," Humphries said.

"He's no longer missing." Fiona gave Humphries a stern look before turning her attention to the board. "What links them? What do they have in common?"

"I know one thing," Humphries said. Now that I've spent more time talking to Ryan, I think he's as difficult to warm to as Isabella. He's permanently on a short fuse, and I wouldn't like to work for him."

"I agree neither is instantly likeable, but we've met both of them after a traumatic experience."

"Friends and colleagues say they were the same before," Humphries said. "Anyway, how was your dad?"

"It wasn't one of his good days," Fiona said. "I know things are only going to get worse, and soon we'll be considering his bad days as the good ones, but it doesn't make it any easier."

"How's your mum coping?"

"On the surface, better than I expected. She carries on trying to jolly him along as though nothing has changed. She's continued with all her social outings, and she talks to him as if she believes he'll leave the home and join in with her soon."

"That's good, isn't it? Her maintaining a social life and staying upbeat."

Before Fiona could answer, the rest of the team started to arrive. Once everyone was in, she started the meeting. The meeting confirmed what Fiona already feared: The investigation was stuttering to a halt. She felt they were wandering around in circles and getting nowhere fast. The thought of failure coiled around her chest and tightened. She was the officer in charge but couldn't see a way forward without a break.

Nobody had anything to prove Ryan might have been responsible for the shootings, and with friends sceptical about an affair, they were lacking a solid motive. Work colleagues confirmed Ryan and Em got along well and often shared jokes, but they hadn't seen anything that suggested a romance. Em's best friend pointed out she had only recently split with her last boyfriend and was incapable of keeping a secret. While she had the sneaking suspicion Em liked Ryan, she was adamant that if something were going on between them, she would know about it.

There were still huge gaps in what they knew about Ryan's movements in the weeks leading up to the shooting and the cause of his recent moodiness. Although Ryan and Em had denied there was an issue, too many others said his mood had deteriorated recently to ignore it. She thought Kerry might benefit from some fieldwork, so she assigned her to help Eddie and Andrew's team piece together his last few weeks, while Abbie and Rachael pieced together the students' last few days. She asked everyone to continue cross-referencing in the search for something that could connect them. She was heading out to Ryan's ex-company with Humphries to interview Em without Ryan sitting next to her.

CHAPTER THIRTY-EIGHT

Ryan's ex-boss bent over backwards to be helpful, and he gave them his office for their interview. Em insisted she was not having an affair, and they had read more into what they had seen outside her house. She was still reeling from her recent break-up with a long-term boyfriend and wasn't even sure she was ready to walk straight into another relationship. She liked Ryan, and if something came of it, they would be taking it slow, but as far as she was concerned, she was currently doing no more than supporting a close friend. With nothing to suggest otherwise, they had to take Em at her word despite their suspicions.

Walking across the car park, Fiona and Humphries saw at the same time they had missed calls. They simultaneously returned their calls and came to a halt beside Fiona's car. Fiona finished her call first and looked across at Humphries. She couldn't catch his eye, but she could see the colour had drained from his face and assumed he was receiving the same news as her of another shooting with a witness left behind. When his hand holding the phone dropped, she asked, "Joe McLachlan?" When Humphries nodded, Fiona said, "Let's go."

Humphries rang the station to obtain more details as they sped towards Sapperton.

"We don't know for sure it's the same man yet," Fiona said, more to try to convince herself than Humphries. The attacks were becoming a regular occurrence, and she was at a complete loss as to how a bus driver and a single mother could be connected to Ryan or Isabella.

Humphries lowered his phone. "A man dressed in black and wearing a balaclava breaks in to shoot a man, leaving his partner unharmed, screaming hysterically. How can we think anything else?"

"Has the woman said anything yet?"

"They're trying to get something from her, but she's hysterical and not making any sense."

"My report said she was a single mother. Can we assume the children were at school? I haven't heard any mention of them."

Humphries was about to reply but was interrupted by his phone ringing. He wasn't saying anything, so Fiona concentrated on driving to the address. She would prepare herself for what they would likely see there when they arrived. She glanced across when she heard Humphries end his call and noticed his frown. "What is it?"

"It might not be the same person. A child has been snatched from the house."

Fiona slowed the breakneck speed of the car to merely reckless. "The child's father?"

"That's the first thought. They're trying to trace him now. Neighbours have said he left the house several weeks ago, and a day later, Joe moved in."

"Are there other children? Should we be going to the school to protect them?" Fiona asked.

"No, just the one child called Noah. So far, the only background information they have is from the neighbour. The mother is still too distraught to speak."

Knowing the housing layout, Fiona drove to the rear of the property and squeezed her car onto the pavement alongside the other police vehicles. When they walked through the rear garden gate, they could hear the screaming still coming from inside the house. They were asked to wait outside on the patio area until the scene of crime officer said they could enter. At least the screaming stopped while they waited. A clean-shaven man in scrubs neither of them recognised came to the door. Once it was established who they were and that it was his first week on the job, they were given protective clothing and led inside.

Pulling on the overall, Fiona asked, "What do we know so far?"

"Very little. It was the neighbour who first called the station. All we know is a masked man entered, shot the householder's boyfriend and snatched her son. She's stopped now, but you probably heard her screaming earlier."

"Would have been hard to miss," Humphries said, slipping protective covers over his shoes. "Did the neighbours see anything? There must have been people around this time of day."

"The neighbour who called it in heard a car speeding away. Officers are knocking on doors to see if anyone saw anything."

"And the little boy? Her son? Do we know anything about him?" Fiona asked.

"Only that the intruder has taken him."

"Can we speak to her?"

"Sure. That's what I've come out to tell you. She's a little calmer now, so hopefully, you'll get some sense from her. We also need her moved from the crime scene."

"Do you have her name?"

"Shelby Jackson."

Shelby was rocking forwards and backwards on a sofa in the living room. Her arms were tightly wrapped around her middle, and her face was a mess of mascara and orange foundation. A body covered with a sheet lay a short distance away on the floor. Fiona carefully stood to one side of the body and said Shelby's name, but didn't receive any response. Fiona stepped between the body and the sofa and gently touched Shelby's shoulder, repeating her name.

Shelby looked up through red-rimmed eyes. "Why? I loved him."

Fiona looked at the body and back at Shelby. "We need to talk about what happened and your little boy. Is there another room we can move to?"

"Noah? He shot Joe and took him."

"We know," Humphries said. "Let's go into another room and talk about him."

"I don't want to leave Joe all alone."

"Come on. He's gone," Humphries said. "You can't do anything more for him. Let's move into another room so we can talk about Noah."

Shelby continued sobbing, but she stood up. "We'll go into the kitchen."

"Good idea. I'll make you a cup of tea. How do you like it?" Humphries asked as he guided Shelby away from the sofa. She stopped to take one last look back before leaving the room.

Before following them out, Fiona picked up a framed photograph of a little boy she assumed was Noah. Once Shelby was seated and Humphries was fussing around preparing a pot of tea, she placed the picture on the table in front of Shelby. "We're so sorry about your partner, and we'll do everything we can to catch the person responsible. Our priority now is to find and bring your son home. Is this Noah?"

"Yes, that's my little Noah. Why did he shoot Joe and take him?"

"That's what we're hoping to find out," Fiona said. "Did you recognise the person who took Noah?"

"No. It all happened so fast. He burst in, shot Joe before any of us had a chance to move, grabbed Noah and was gone," Shelby said. "It was over in seconds."

"Did he speak to you, Shelby? What did he say, and did you recognise the voice?"

Shelby started sobbing again, vehemently shaking her head. "He didn't say anything. He shot Joe, grabbed Noah and left."

"Listen, Shelby, this is important. Did you recognise the man who took your son? Could it have been your husband?"

"Oh God! Someone needs to tell Will. He was due to have Noah this weekend. He'll be devastated when he hears. And that cow mother of his. She'll blame me and say it was all my fault."

"Will? Is that Noah's father?"

"Yes. Will Jackson. We're separated."

"Do you think it could have been Will who took Noah?"

"Will?" Shelby stopped to think. "He was tall, but Will? He never says boo to a goose. He can't even stand up to his mother. He just sits there and says nothing while she talks over him."

"But Will is tall, is he?"

"Yes. He's well over six feet. A bit of a gentle giant, really," Shelby said. "I suppose the intruder was the same shape as Will. But no. Will might be a bit soft in the head, but he wouldn't do something like this."

"Have you got a recent photograph of Will?"

"Somewhere in a drawer, there will be one. Should I go and look?"

Humphries placed a cup of tea in front of Shelby. "Drink this. Would you like me to go to look for you?"

Shelby nodded. "Top drawer of the dresser in the living room. There's a framed one of the three of us. I put it away when Joe moved in. It should still be there."

Humphries returned with the photograph and handed it to Fiona. After looking at it, over Shelby's continued sobbing, Fiona said, "We're going to leave now to find Noah."

"To find Noah," Shelby parroted.

"Yes. I'll send an officer in to sit with you."

"You're going to find Noah."

"Yes, we'll speak again soon, okay?" Fiona said, withdrawing from the room to find an officer to stay with Shelby.

Humphries was waiting for Fiona outside, holding his phone. "Guess what? Will Jackson isn't at work. He hasn't been in all week."

CHAPTER THIRTY-NINE

Abbie and Rachael were chatting by the whiteboard when Kerry slid unnoticed into the room. Everyone on the team seemed pleasant, but she still felt like an outsider, yet to prove herself. She had discovered that a recent complaint had been made about Ryan acting aggressively outside a nightclub in town, and Eddie had sent her to the station to find the file and any video footage. When she admitted she still hadn't watched the argument in the garage, Eddie suggested she also watched that. She had convinced herself on the drive back that it was an excuse to get rid of her, but at least it gave her something quiet to do by herself.

She requested the complaint file and pulled up the garage footage, but her mind was elsewhere on the missing person case. She remembered Angie saying Will was due to have his son over the weekend and wondered if she could call to see if he returned for that. She didn't know whether Will's boyish face with a look of hope in his eyes in Angie's photograph or Shelby's brutal honesty made her feel sorry for him, but she couldn't stop thinking about him. She firmly told herself there wasn't anything she could do to help him, and she should focus on the murder enquiries. She started by watching the garage footage.

She concentrated on watching Ryan and the man and woman standing in front of him. She didn't notice the man standing behind Ryan until he turned to speak with him. The man behind

Ryan in the queue was wearing a baseball cap and had the early sprouting of a beard, but she was sure she recognised him. She reversed that section of the tape and watched it again as she reached for her phone.

"Sorry, it's DC Kerry Vines again. It's incredibly important I speak to Mr Stainton now. Can you interrupt his meeting? Okay, thank you. If he doesn't call me in the next ten minutes, I'll be calling you again."

With the computer screen frozen, Kerry called Hobbs Letting Agency. "Hello again, it's DC Kerry Vines. I rang before to ask about one of your employees, Will Jackson. Does he work full-time for you, and do you know if he does other work alongside the jobs that you give him?"

Kerry ended the call feeling sick. She was about to get up to speak to Rachael when her phone rang. Her voice shook when she said, "Thank you for calling me back, Mr Stainton. Can you tell me the name of the man you employed to look at your daughter's radiators?"

Kerry swallowed hard and prepared herself to pass on what she'd learned when she realised Fiona and Humphries were standing over her desk. "I think I know who it is."

"Go on," Fiona said.

"I don't know why he's doing it, but his name is Will Jackson. He was the sole survivor of a car crash when he was a teenager. One of the victims was his younger brother, and it's why he limps. His relationship broke down four weeks ago, and he hasn't been seen since the shooting at Mickleburgh. He was employed to fix Isabella's radiators and stood behind Ryan in the garage. Oh God! I need to let his mother and wife know. Do you think they could be in danger?"

"It's a bit late for that," Humphries said. "If it's him, he's killed Shelby's boyfriend and taken their son."

"Noah. Oh, no. That's terrible," Kerry said. "I need to let his mother know."

"No, you need to calm down and pull yourself together," Humphries said. "Give me her address."

In a softer voice, Fiona said, "We're dealing with an extremely dangerous and disturbed man, and we'll be sending armed officers to his mother's house, so we don't want you to call her yet. Were there any sightings of him when he was reported missing, and is this a good likeness?"

Kerry looked at the photograph of Will with Shelby and Noah. "Yes, but he's growing a beard and wearing a baseball cap in the garage."

"Do you have his car details?" When Kerry nodded, Fiona said, "Get them and the images of him with a beard circulated to everyone. Stress he's armed and dangerous. They should report any sightings and follow him if it's safe to do so, but they shouldn't approach him. And call the others back in. There's no point in them wasting their time on Ryan."

"I'm doing it now," Kerry said, reaching for her phone.

CHAPTER FORTY

Fiona was agitated while waiting for a call from the armed response team and was tempted to drive around to Angie Claydon's house herself. "I can't stop thinking about the boy. He's little more than a baby. He hasn't even started his life yet."

"We don't know he's planning to harm his son," Humphries said. "We don't know anything yet." His grim expression suggested he didn't fully believe what he was saying and thought the same as Fiona.

"What sort of man would snatch his own son in that way? He must have been terrified seeing Joe being shot."

"A very sick one," Humphries said. "It seems like Gareth was right with his assumption of survivor's guilt. I've just read through Kerry's report on him. Probably due to his accident, he believes it is the survivor who suffers. Ryan and Isabella were the intended victims, not the people he shot. He wants them to struggle with the aftermath like he has."

"Thanks for the guide to mental health for dummies, but I can't sympathise with his childhood trauma right now. Children and adults are dead because of him. I know what you're going to say. It's down to society for not looking after people with mental health problems properly. Maybe I'll try to understand his reasoning later, but right now, I'm too angry," Fiona said. "We have to find him before he kills his son."

"Maybe he's taken him somewhere and doesn't plan to harm him."

"I'm not sure that I think that's a great improvement."

Humphries was interrupted by his phone ringing. "That was Shelby's liaison officer. They've explained that we think Will was responsible and she seems to have accepted it. She's much calmer and focused on finding her son. As it's not far from Angie's house, it might be worth popping back to talk to her again while we're waiting."

Crime scene officers were still working inside the house, and Shelby and the officer had moved to the garden when Fiona and Humphries arrived. They found them drinking tea on the small patio area where they had waited earlier. Next to them was a covered sandpit and an assortment of toy trucks and cars. Shelby started from her seat as soon as she saw them. "Any news?"

Fiona shook her head, and Shelby dropped back to her chair.

"Why would he take Noah? I said he could have him to stay this weekend. There was no need for him to hurt Joe. Why did he have to shoot him? It wasn't Joe's fault I fell in love with him."

Fiona and Humphries collected two folded chairs leaning against the small garden shed and joined Shelby around the patio table. "We don't know yet, but we're doing everything possible to find them," Fiona said. "Do you have a friend you could stay with? It might be a while before you are allowed back inside."

The liaison officer said, "A friend is coming to collect Shelby in about an hour when she finishes work."

"Do you think he'll bring Noah back on Sunday like we agreed?" Shelby asked. "He has Playgroup on Monday morning. He's doing really well there."

"Anything's possible, but it's unlikely," Fiona said and immediately regretted it when Shelby burst into tears.

Humphries looked down at the photograph in Shelby's hand. "Is that Noah?"

Shelby looked at the picture and smiled through her tears. "Yes, that's my little Noah in the park last weekend. We had such a lovely day feeding the ducks."

"Was that the three of you? You, Joe and Noah?" Fiona asked.

"Yes. We were like a proper little family," Shelby said. "That's all I've ever wanted."

"Did you go to the park with Will before?"

Shelby put the photograph down and wiped her eyes. "I know Will loved Noah in his own way, but he never had the time to do simple things like feeding the ducks. He wouldn't have seen the point."

"What sort of things did Will like to do?" Fiona asked. "Knowing that will help us to find them."

"I don't know," Shelby said, crying again. "We had agreed to Will having Noah for the weekend. He didn't need to barge his way in and take him. And then he … then he…"

"Okay, take your time," Fiona said as Shelby heaved more sobs. "Did Will tell you what he planned to do with Noah on the weekend?"

Shelby shook her head and cried louder. "Why did he kill Joe? Joe was kind and thoughtful. He understood that Will would always be Noah's dad and was okay with it. It was Joe who said that I should let him have Noah over to stay sometimes. I loved him, and he loved me."

Fiona shared a hopeless look with Humphries. It was too soon to press Shelby while she was in this state, but they needed answers fast if they were going to find Noah alive.

Shelby wiped her face and raised her head with a look of resolution. "It's Noah we should be thinking about now."

"Do you know what Will planned to do with Noah this weekend?" Fiona asked a second time.

"I don't know. I hadn't thought about it, but I assumed he would take him home to his mother. She couldn't stand me, but she was all smiles for Noah. She said he reminded her of the son she lost. Will's little brother. Have you checked her house?"

"We've people around there now," Fiona said. "Do you have any idea where Will might have taken him if not to his mother's home?"

"I can't think of anywhere else."

"Where you had your last holiday, maybe? Or another place

you enjoyed recently as a family."

"We went to Cornwall for a few days last year and Weymouth the year before, but we've never had a proper holiday as such. Will didn't like to go away for too long, and we couldn't afford it anyway. With Will, it never felt like we were a family. Not like it was with Joe. For a moment there, I dared to think that I had a future."

"You didn't with Will?" Fiona asked.

"We were three people who shared a house."

"Was there a place he liked to go to by himself?"

Shelby pushed the heels of her hands into her eye sockets, already blackened by mascara. "Sorry. There's only one place he used to return to, but I don't think he's been back there for a couple of years. The first time he took me there, I didn't know why it was so special to him. I thought it was romantic. A new farmer took it over and ploughed over the fields and blocked access. When Will ignored the signs, and the farmer found him there, he threw him off and destroyed his tent. He said he would set his dogs on him if he ever saw him there again. Will was always a bit of a coward, and as far as I know, he never went back afterwards."

"Where's this place, Shelby?" Fiona asked.

"I don't know if it has a name. It's above where his brother was killed in a car accident. On one side, there's a hill that slopes up the bank, and above it, there is a small wood. There used to be an old falling-down, bird-watcher hut by a river. Sometimes, he stayed in the hut; other times, he took a tent and camped out in the small clearing in front of it to stare down at the pond the car ended up in."

Humphries said, "I'll organise a team out there," and walked away towards the bottom of the garden.

"Thank you," Fiona said.

"I don't even know if the hut is still there," Shelby said. "The farmer could have pulled it down."

"We'll have someone out there checking the area shortly," Fiona said. "Is there anywhere else you think he might have gone?"

"No, that's it. The only other places he went were to his mother's or inside his mind."

"If you think of somewhere else later, here's my card," Fiona said, before being interrupted by her phone. She finished the call as Humphries returned.

"Was it about Noah?" Shelby asked.

"They haven't found them yet, but new information is coming in constantly," Fiona said. "We will keep you updated, and you'll be the first to know when we find them. We anticipate the media will arrive shortly. Officers will keep them away, but please don't be tempted to speak to them without clearing it with us first. We don't want them printing anything that could help Will while hindering our efforts to find them."

Shelby nodded, but her eyes had glazed over, and Fiona couldn't tell if she'd taken it in. The liaison officer leaned forward to say, "I'll stay here until Shelby's friend arrives and make sure they get off okay."

Leading Humphries away from Shelby's house, Fiona said, "We can go and see Angie now. He's not there."

"Has she heard from him?" Humphries asked before being interrupted by his phone. "Someone matching Will's description was seen sitting by the pond a few days ago."

"Okay. That's where we're headed. I'll send Rachael and Abbie out to visit Angie."

CHAPTER FORTY-ONE

Fiona and Humphries were delayed from leaving the house by Dewhurst insisting on a full update. When they approached the old accident spot they found several police cars and vans were already parked along the road from the pond. Fiona slowed down as they passed the pond, and a constable came over to speak to her through the car window. After initially trying to wave her on, he said she should drive the short distance to the village to park as it was too dangerous a corner for any more vehicles to pull in. To soften the requests, he promised that he would have arranged for someone senior to speak to them by the time they walked back.

Although frustrated by the further delay, Fiona was pleased to see three more police cars parked on the main street through the village and constables making door-to-door enquiries. "With the number of officers deployed, if he's here, we should find him," she said, getting out of the car. "Although knowing he's armed and surrounded by so many people is doing nothing for my nerves."

They started the walk back to the pond. With no pavement, they walked along the side of the road tight into the hedgerow. The few cars that passed were travelling slowly due to the police presence near the pond, but it wasn't a pleasant place to walk. On other days, with nothing to slow the traffic, it would be terrifying, especially with the overgrown hedges and a blind bend coming up.

"I'm not surprised they have the twenty-mile-an-hour limit

along here," Fiona said as cars passed by a hair's breadth away from them.

"It's rarely obeyed and remains a known accident black spot."

"Was the speed limit brought in before or after Will's accident?" Fiona asked.

"After I think, but there were several nasty accidents on the bend before," Humphries said. "And after."

They walked around the blind bend and saw the constable up ahead talking with an officer in full protective gear. "Looks like he was true to his word about arranging a senior officer," Fiona said, stepping forward to introduce herself.

"Officers have cleared the bank as safe, and it's now being checked for any recent signs of the suspect. The forward team has circled the birdwatchers hut and will shortly be closing in. So far, there have been no signs of recent activity."

"Can we go up there?" Fiona asked.

"The cleared bank area, yes, but no higher. They should be reporting back from inside the hut shortly, so your best bet is to wait down here for news."

Fiona and Humphries settled a short distance outside the cordoned-off pond to wait. Fiona pulled out her phone. "I may as well call Rachael while we wait to hear if they're up there."

"Put it on loudspeaker so I can hear," Humphries said. "I'm stuck here waiting the same as you. I don't want to listen to one side of a conversation as well."

"Hi, Rachael, are you with Angie?" Fiona asked.

"Yes. Hang on, I'll move outside so we can speak," Rachael said. "We've tried to explain to her what has happened, but she's not having any of it. Her lovely, gentle son would never do such a thing. We've got it all wrong, apparently. Abbie is trying to persuade her otherwise. She has more patience than me."

"At least she's safe," Fiona replied.

"What's happening at your end?" Rachael asked.

"We're not sure yet. We're still waiting to hear from the team circling the hut," Fiona replied. "I don't care how you do it, but you need to persuade Angie to tell you where her son might be staying in case it's not here. There were no sightings of him the day he was reported missing, so he must be holed up somewhere. A favourite place they liked to go to get away from everything or a holiday place maybe. The weather has been mild, so he could be sleeping rough. Or somewhere cheap where he could stay by himself with no questions asked. Or possibly an empty house."

"I'll ask, but she adamantly denies he is responsible for any of the shootings."

"Stress to her it's in his best interests that we find him quickly," Fiona said. "Shelby said she is very fond of Noah. Try working it from that angle. We're extremely concerned about Noah's welfare. We think there's a high risk that Will will harm him in his current state of mind. It might make her think differently."

"I'll try, but like she said, if she knew where he was, she wouldn't have reported him missing."

Humphries nudged Fiona's arm. "Someone's coming over."

"Keep me updated," Fiona said, ending the call and looking up. "Anything for us?"

"Possibly not what you want to hear. Someone has been camping there until fairly recently, but they've gone."

"Was it Will Jackson?" Humphries asked.

"Too soon to say. I've come over to tell you the area is clear for you to carry out your investigations. I'll leave a couple of officers in case he comes back, but otherwise, it's over to you."

"Was there anything to suggest when he was last there and whether he had a child with him?"

"Sorry, no. We've confirmed the area is clear and cordoned it off. The men wouldn't have been looking for anything else."

"Okay. Thanks for your help."

Giving the officer's back a willowing look, Humphries muttered, "Helpful. What do you want to do next?"

"As it doesn't sound like he's still in the area, we'll get the crime scene officers up there, and we'll return to the station. They'll be able to confirm whether he was staying there, but we need to concentrate on discovering where he headed after snatching

Noah. The cameras must have picked up something useful this time."

CHAPTER FORTY-TWO

Fiona and Humphries returned to the station to brief the team that were there and wait to hear if Will had been spotted after leaving Shelby's. Kerry hung back after the meeting to ask how Angie was.

"Rachael and Abbie have spent the last hour with her, trying to get some information about where Will might have gone, but should be back soon," Humphries said. "Why don't you ask them?"

"While you're waiting for them, I want you to help Andrew and Eddie to go through every inch of Will Jackson's life," Fiona said. "We need to find Will and Noah as quickly as possible. Every friend needs to be contacted, and every place he's ever visited needs to be noted. Every inch of road footage radiating from Shelby's home must be scrutinised."

After Kerry scuttled back to her desk, Fiona called across the room, "Are we tracking his bank accounts?"

"Yes, Eddie said. "The details have only just come through. I can see he has stayed in the area because he's used his card a few times, but nothing in the last twenty-four hours."

"Where?"

Eddie was frantically scrolling through the details. "Ah, here's something. He made a large payment in a camping shop in central Birstall last Saturday. Since then, it has been smaller payments. Looks like food and other essentials. All in the northern outskirts of Birstall."

"Get a map on the board and mark out the payments," Fiona

said. "Kerry, was his car registration picked up anywhere when he was reported missing?"

"No, but it was taken off the list as soon as Angie said she had heard from him," Kerry said.

"Is it possible he's using a different car?" Andrew asked.

"Ask all his friends if they've lent him a car. A hire car would show up on his bank account," Fiona said. "I take it there isn't anything there?"

"No," Eddie confirmed.

"Were there any genuine sightings of him when he was first reported missing?" Andrew asked Kerry.

"No, but he was only on the register for a few hours," Kerry said. "The amended description of the beard and baseball cap was only passed on recently."

"Now he has his son, how sure are we that he's still in our area?" Andrew asked.

"We're not. That's why we need to know what car he was driving," Fiona said. Looking around the room, she saw Kerry staring into space. "Kerry, start contacting his friends. Starting with where he worked. Find out if anyone has lent him a car recently."

Kerry picked up her phone. "Okay, okay. I'm doing it now. It shouldn't take me long, as he doesn't have many. Just a couple of guys he worked with and an old school friend."

"Don't forget to ask everyone if they have seen him driving something different recently," Fiona said. "If you get a registration number, send it out to the patrol cars. If it has been spotted anywhere, mark it on the map."

"Is it possible he's stealing cars to keep under the radar?" Humphries asked.

"Possibly, but we can't look into every car stolen in the area. We need to narrow down where he is. And where he's been."

Rachael and Abbie walked in and joined them. "One place he hasn't been is to see his mother," Rachael said. "An omission she is most put out by. Along with all the strangers in the house. She was returning from a food shop when everyone turned up. I'm not sure it's sunk in how much trouble her son is in."

"He was always such a good boy and took great care of her," Abbie said, rolling her eyes.

"Kerry, from talking to his mother and Shelby, did you have the impression Will was as close to his mother as she seems to think?" Fiona asked.

"Possibly. Shelby said he would run home to his mother if something bothered him, but there's animosity between the two women, so I don't know how much she exaggerates their bond," Kerry said. "Shelby thinks the abnormal closeness between them stems back to the car accident."

"I want to speak to Angie myself. Everyone else, I want to know everything about Will down to what brand of toothpaste he uses. If you speak to his friends, stress how dangerous he is, and they should call us immediately if he makes contact. If you have even the slightest hint they may be covering for him, follow it up."

"Angie received a note from Will," Kerry said.

"What note?" Fiona asked.

"I told you. That's why the missing person report was closed. Angie rang me to say she had received a note from Will saying he was okay but needed some time to himself," Kerry explained.

Fiona blushed, remembering Kerry had told her, but she hadn't taken much notice at the time. She looked to Rachael, who shrugged and said, "She didn't mention anything about a note."

"Right, I'm heading out to see her now."

"Fiona," Humphries said, pocketing his phone. "Cameras picked him up not far from Shelby's house. He got into a car and headed south. They've got the registration number. It wasn't his car."

"Make sure it's circulated to patrols in the area and keep me updated."

"Do you still want me to ring his friends?" Kerry asked.

"Yes, I want to know where that car came from. Run a check on the registration number to see if it came from one of them," Fiona said. "He's managed to avoid any sightings all week. That could be because no one was looking that hard, luck or because his friend has been shielding him."

Humphries handed a scribbled note to Kerry. "That's the car he left Shelby's in."

"Before I go, was there anything at all to suggest his mother might be in contact with him?" Fiona asked.

"My first reaction is no, definitely not," Rachael said before being interrupted by a ringing phone.

"She reported him missing, and she was genuinely upset that he hadn't come to her if he was in trouble," Abbie said.

"Could she be acting?"

"To be honest, I don't think she's bright enough to create such an elaborate bluff," Abbie said.

Fiona would have preferred confirmation from Rachael. She had worked with Abbie for several years, and while she was generally good with details, she was less good about people. In the past, she had leaked details of a case to a girlfriend who turned out to be a journalist and had spent time with a woman who had killed her sister without realising the danger she was in. Her relationship with Abbie was often strained, so Fiona thanked Abbie for her opinion and didn't wait for Rachael to complete her call before leaving.

CHAPTER FORTY-THREE

Angie's family liaison officer was closing the front garden gate behind her when Fiona and Humphries pulled up outside. Fiona quickly jumped from the car to speak to her before she left.

"Hi, Jane. How is Angie?"

Jane turned and walked over to the car. "As well as can be expected in the circumstances. She's struggling to understand how her son could have been so violent. She says it's completely out of character. I e-mailed my report in about twenty minutes ago and spoke to one of your officers. Kerry Vines? I believe she's already had some contact?"

They were interrupted by a reporter climbing out of a parked van and holding up a phone. Behind him, another pulled a camera from the back of the van. Fiona glared at them before ushering Jane back into the front garden.

"Yes, Kerry's new to our team, but she was involved when Angie first reported her son missing," Fiona said quietly. "I haven't seen the report yet, but I'll read it later. Do you have any initial thoughts or concerns about her reactions?"

"Maybe it will hit her later, but she's in total denial," Jane said, looking over her shoulder to check where the reporters were. Satisfied that Humphries was standing blocking the gateway, she continued, "That in itself isn't unusual in this type of case, but one thing seems at odds with what your constable said. She said Angie was very fond of her grandson and was emotional and tearful when she reported her son missing. She's shocked by the snatching of Noah, but I've not seen her shed any tears." Jane paused and shrugged. "Maybe it's part of her denial. She says Will would never harm Noah, and if he has him, he'll take good care of him. Maybe she genuinely believes that, but I think her overall reaction is too calm."

"Interesting," Fiona said. "Has she said or done anything to suggest she knows more than she is saying?"

"No, but then she's not saying much at all. I'm concerned about her generally. She's too detached. It could mean she's hiding something and is scared to let her guard down and say something incriminating, or it could mean she's inches away from a breakdown. I would prefer to stay with her, but I've another appointment I can't be late for."

"We'll be with her while, and I'll look out for anything worrying," Fiona said. Turning towards the house, a small Corsa car on the driveway caught her eye, and she called after Jane to stop. "Sorry to hold you up again. Have you been here all the time with Angie?"

Jane nodded. "Yes, but I do need to go now. I'll be back as soon as I can. Is there anything else?"

"Since the officers raced over here, has she ever been alone?"

"No," Jane replied, shaking her head. "Eddie and Andrew were here when I arrived, and I've not popped out for anything. And neither has she."

After Jane hurried away, Fiona wandered over to the car to peer through the driver's side window. She called Humphries over and, with her back to the reporters, pulled out her phone. "Rachael, you said when you arrived that Angie was returning from a shopping trip. I had the impression she was walking back from the shops."

"Yes, she was walking along the pavement carrying two bags of groceries," Rachael confirmed.

"It's just that I'm standing beside a Corsa parked on the driveway. Is it registered to her?"

"I presume it is, although I haven't checked. Do you want me to?"

"Yes, please," Fiona said. "When you were here, did you notice the car seat?"

"I assume you're referring to its position," Rachael said. "I asked her why she didn't take her car to the shops, and she said it was playing up. She had someone around to look at it a few days ago, and that's why the seat is set so far back. While they couldn't find a fault, she's convinced there's something wrong with it and preferred to walk to the shop to grab a few things rather than risk it breaking down on her."

Fiona and Humphries shared an unconvinced look before they stepped across to ring the front doorbell. While they were waiting for the door to be answered, Humphries said, "I'll check the distance to the local supermarket."

CHAPTER FORTY-FOUR

Fiona rang Angie's doorbell twice before lifting the letterbox flap to try to see inside. She caught a glimpse of a narrow hallway before the occupant's approach blocked her vision, and she quickly stepped back from the door.

"Okay, I'm coming." Angie opened the door as wide as the chain would allow and scowled through the narrow gap. "What do you want? If you're reporters, you can sling your hook. Bloody parasites. Haven't you anything better to do?"

Fiona held up her warrant card up to the small opening. "We're police officers."

"Don't you speak to one another? One of your lot has just this minute left."

"I'm the senior officer leading the case. We spoke briefly when you came to the station to report Will as missing. Can we come in?"

"If you must." Angie closed the door and took an age to release the door chain and reopen the door. "Come on in, then. Although I doubt that I can tell you something I haven't already said. Do you want to go into the kitchen or the front room?"

"Whichever you prefer."

Angie led them into a small living room with a bay window overlooking the front street. Once they were settled, Angie marched over to the curtains, pulled them shut, sat back, and asked, "How much longer will they be out there?"

"It's hard to tell," Fiona said.

Angie huffed and flopped down onto an armchair. "What more can I tell you?"

Noting that Angie hadn't asked whether they had found Will and Noah, Fiona asked, "How long have you lived here?"

"Here? Since I was married to Will's no-good father. That would be thirty-odd years now."

"Do you have any contact with Will's father?"

Angie laughed. "I haven't seen hide nor hair of him since he ran off with a barmaid over twenty years ago."

"He doesn't live in the area?"

"No idea. In all the years since I've never bumped into him, so I've assumed not," Angie said. "Lovely as it is to have a bit of a chit-chat, what is it you want to know?"

"How about Will? Was he in contact with his father?" Fiona asked.

Angie threw her head back and laughed, showing off a row of fillings and missing back teeth. "He wouldn't even recognise him. He would have been about five years old when his father left."

"You're quite sure he's never tried to make contact?"

"Absolutely. Will would have told me," Angie said. "He's never even bothered to ask questions. He's a good lad, like that. He knows who stuck around to bring him up. I've always taken good care of him. He knows that."

"You're very close with your son, I understand."

"Yes, we always have been, especially after ... Well, it was just the two of us."

"And he always tells you everything that's going on in his life?" Fiona asked.

"Always." Realising her mistake, Angie said, "He always has up until now, which is why I think you've got it all wrong. My Will is a good lad, but that Shelby is rotten to the core. It wouldn't surprise me if she hasn't made the whole thing up for attention."

"Why would she do that?"

"I don't know. You'll have to ask her that," Angie said. "All I'm saying is she's not the sweet, innocent girl she wants everyone to think she is. Maybe she shot her current squeeze, or maybe it was her local drug dealer. Who knows with that one?"

"Do you have evidence that Shelby is a regular drug user?" Fiona asked.

"Well, no, but she could be."

"Have you ever worried about Noah being her care?"

"I felt a lot happier knowing my Will was there to keep an eye on things."

"Oh, what sort of things?" Fiona asked.

"You know. Treating him bad and stuff. Neglecting him. You see it on the news all the time. These women with a parade of different boyfriends. Sometimes, it's their blokes preying on the children. Shelby spends all her time worrying about herself and how she looks instead of watching over Noah. You don't think that's what happened, do you?" Angie asked. "She discovered her new bloke was abusing Noah, and she lost it. Then she made up this cock and bull story to drag my Will into it. She was worried that Noah might say what really happened, so she shipped him off to one of her dodgy friends."

"That doesn't seem likely, but we'll be looking into all possibilities," Fiona said. "Let's focus on Will for now. When did you last see Will?"

"It's hard to remember."

"Could you try?"

Properly to speak to? That would have been last Friday afternoon after work. Then, with it being the weekend, we were both in and out. You know how it is."

"When did you first report him missing?"

"That will all be in your files. I can't remember off the top of my head."

"It was Wednesday morning," Fiona said. "But then you rang later that day to say you received a message from him."

"Yes, that sounds about right."

"On your phone? Did you receive the message on your phone?"

"No, no. It came through the post."

"Can you show it to me?"

Angie made a show of making a dramatic effort to pull herself up from the chair before walking over to a side cabinet. "You're lucky I've still got it. It's only a fluke that I didn't throw it out." She returned with a page ripped out of a notebook. "Here you are."

Fiona read the simple message that ended with, 'Love you, Mum. Will.' "Do you have the envelope it came in?"

"Sorry, that did go in the bin on the day it arrived."

"When are your bins collected?"

"They went yesterday morning." Angie stopped to hold back the curtain to look outside before returning to the chair.

Fiona folded the sheet of paper. "Can I hang on to this?"

"Be my guest."

"And the last time you spoke to Will was Friday afternoon?"

"Oh, hang on, no. I think it was a couple of mornings before the day I reported him missing," Angie said vaguely. "It might have been Monday. I made him breakfast, as I do every morning, and he went off to work as usual. That's the thing with routines. It's hard to tell one day from another. When he didn't come home that night, I thought maybe Shelby had gotten her hooks back into him, and I thought I would leave them to it. He would come to his senses soon enough. When I relented, I didn't get any reply from his mobile, so I rang his boss. He said Will hadn't turned up for work, and that's when I rang Shelby. When she said she hadn't seen him, I went around the station to report him missing."

"And this was all on Wednesday?"

"Or it could have been Tuesday," Angie said.

"But it was after the weekend?"

"I think so. Yes."

"Was it usual for you to speak to Will daily?"

"We chatted most days, even when he was shacked up with Shelby. That in itself suggests she didn't give him the support he deserved."

"Shelby said he would always turn to you when he was

troubled."

"That's what mothers are for, don't you think?" Angie asked. "You would know that if you had children. I don't suppose it's possible in your line of work. Well, I can tell you that nothing can replace a mother's love. It doesn't change just because they've grown up and moved away."

Ignoring Angie's barbed assumption about her being childless, Fiona asked, "Are you upset that he hasn't contacted you in the last couple of days?"

"That note you have there explains it. He needs some time alone to sort his head out. That's what he's off doing if you ask me. Not running around shooting people," Angie said. "There were no sightings of him in the area when I reported him missing. Have you anything to prove he's even in the area?"

"Apart from yourself, who else would he turn to if he was troubled?"

"Not Shelby, that's for sure," Angie said. "I can't think of anyone, but I don't think he's done the terrible things you think he has. He's away somewhere trying to work things out. You'll see. He'll turn up in a couple of days and be able to prove none of it has anything to do with him."

"You don't think he has Noah?"

"I don't think he's been anywhere near the house."

"Where do you think Noah is then?" Fiona asked. "Because we don't think he's with one of Shelby's friends."

"I don't rightly know," Angie said, starting to look confused.

"Are you worried about an armed stranger having your grandson?"

"Of course I am. What sort of question is that?"

"Where do you think Will has gone?"

"I don't know. Away someplace by himself. The coast, maybe."

"The coast? Any coast in particular?" Fiona asked. "Is that somewhere you might have taken him when he was little?"

"We always used to go to Burry Port in Wales on the train when he was little. That's a place that would hold special memories for him. You should contact someone there to look out for him,"

Angie said. "We used to stay above a pub just along from the train station. Sorry, I can't remember the name, but it was a big old building near the sea."

"Okay, we'll check that out and leave our conversation here for now. I'm sure we'll be speaking again soon."

Outside the front door, Humphries said, "It's a three-mile walk to the nearest supermarket."

Fiona walked over and photographed the Corsa's cab and registration plate. "I'll circulate this. I want to know where this car has been recently. Also, let's see if we can trace Will's father. But first, I want to organise surveillance of this house. Her confusion about dates and lack of concern about Noah's whereabouts is telling. I'm convinced she knows where Will is and is possibly helping him." Nodding towards the reporters back in their van, she added, "We can't guarantee they won't get bored and drive off."

Closing the garden gate, Humphries looked back towards the house. "You don't think it's worth bringing her in for questioning?"

"I don't think we'll get anything out of her without some evidence, so no. Not yet, anyway," Fiona said. "We'll get someone watching her, and if we're lucky, she'll lead us straight to them."

CHAPTER FORTY-FIVE

Fiona received the overnight surveillance report on Angie's house halfway through the morning briefing and immediately asked Humphries to check it.

After skim-reading it, Humphries said, "Nobody came in or out of the house overnight. Do you want surveillance continued?"

Temporarily thrown as she had been pinning her hopes on it revealing something, Fiona said, "Yes. Arrange another twenty-four hours," before noticing Eddie was reading his screen. "Anything new?"

Eddie put his phone away. "We've just located Will's father. He's in Newcastle, living with his third family. He's been settled there for nearly twenty years. He has a record for minor offences but no custodial sentences. I'll try to contact him later, but we may need to request the local force pay him a visit."

Fiona nodded and looked around the room of tired eyes. "I know it's a Saturday and how hard you've all worked this week, but there's a frightened little boy out there. We've loads of information to sift through, and the sooner we get started on it, the sooner we'll find and return him safely to his mother." She turned to face the board, and said, "The lack of sightings of his car concerns me."

Kerry half-stood. "I've passed on the new car registration number."

"Do we know anything about more about this car?" Fiona turned around to face Kerry. "How did he come by it? Did a friend lend it to him?"

"None of his work colleagues knew anything about the car, but I haven't checked where it did come from yet," Kerry admitted, blushing. "Do you want me to do that now?"

"If you could, yes," Fiona said, concerned about Kerry's lack of progress. She had asked her yesterday to enquire about the car. "We urgently need to know where it came from."

"I'll do that straight away."

"He can't have just disappeared," Fiona said to the room. "Not without someone helping him, and the only person I can think of is his mother, but as you've just heard, she didn't leave her house yesterday."

"Does she realise she's being watched?" Rachael asked.

"I asked them to be discreet, but two reporters were outside her house yesterday. Can someone check whether they're still out there?"

"Will do," Rachael said.

"Maybe someone else is helping him," Abbie said.

"Who? We've established he has no close friends. We've spoken to his work colleagues and the few other people he's known to socialise with. They all refer to him as an acquaintance rather than a friend," Fiona said. "Now the public is aware we consider him armed and dangerous, if they have any intelligence, they will have connected him to the murders. Who is close enough to him to protect him in those circumstances? I can't think of anyone apart from his mother unless we're missing something."

"How about his therapists?" Andrew asked.

"I didn't know he had any," Humphries said.

"It's in one of the reports," Fiona said crossly. "Good thinking, Andrew. He had problems with anxiety a couple of years ago and was sent to see someone. Follow up on it. He has regular checkups at Birstall because of his leg. Follow up on that as well."

"I'll get on to it now," Andrew said.

"Do you think he's gone to ground somewhere nearby rather than left the area?" Eddie asked.

"We widened the search for his registration plate, so unless he's travelling at the speed of light, he's here somewhere."

"He could have changed cars again," Abbie suggested.

"There are no major withdrawals from his bank account, so it's unlikely he bought another one," Eddie said.

"Maybe he's switching plates or decided to steal one," Humphries said.

"Is it worth checking recently stolen cars?" Abbie asked.

"If we could pin down the area he's in, it might be worth checking, but at the moment, we would be looking at too wide an area," Fiona said. "And don't forget he now has a small child with him, so he won't be able to move about as freely as before."

"Do you think he plans to start a new life with his son?" Rachael asked with forced hopefulness.

"No," Fiona said before pausing to look slowly across the room. She guessed most of them already believed what she was about to say, including Rachael. "Everything he's done so far reinforces that he thinks the people who are left behind are the ones who suffer, the same as he has since his car accident. So, no. I'm not a psychiatrist, but my best guess is he will be killing his son and then himself," Fiona said, starting to pace in frustration. "We have to find them as quickly as possible."

"He may have already done so, which is why there have been no sightings," Abbie said.

"It's too soon to be thinking that way," Fiona said sharply. Softening her tone, she added, "One thing we haven't considered yet, is what sparked his rampage. Was it the breakdown of his marriage, or did something else happen? Was it his plan to kill Shelby's new partner and snatch Noah from the start, or is he making it up as he goes along?"

"Fiona," Kerry said, jumping up from her chair. "A confirmed sighting of the car he's driving has come in."

"Where?" Fiona walked over to the map on the whiteboard. "Show me." Seeing Kerry frowning at her screen, she said, "Take a look, Rachael. Kerry doesn't know the area."

Rachael looked from the enlarged map on Kerry's screen to the board before walking over and pointing out a point on a busy B road. "Here, travelling east."

"There's nothing out there except small villages and farmland." Fiona stopped and looked again. "And the aqueduct."

Eddie said. "We can't be sure that's where he's heading," as the team grouped around the map.

"Has he any connection to the area?" Fiona asked.

Rachael said, "It's not been mentioned by anyone," and the team nodded their agreement.

Andrew looked up from his phone. "It has had several suicides recently. It has become more popular, as it's out of the way and not monitored like the major bridges in and around Birstall. The area is isolated, and no cameras are installed at either end. There is a steady traffic flow during the day, but passing cars are few and far between at night. Oh, hang on. A little further along, two vehicles were driven from the clifftop last year. There have been calls for concrete bollards to be put in, but it's currently protected only by barriers that can be driven through at speed. It's a popular picnic area in the daytime, but again, once night falls, the area is empty."

"We've several hours to find them before it gets dark," Fiona said. "Let's hope he plans to wait rather than seek a daytime audience."

"Umm," Rachael said, looking up from Kerry's screen. "The sighting was shortly after Noah was taken."

"How shortly?" Fiona asked.

"Less than fifteen minutes later, and there have been no sightings since."

"So, he hasn't left the area, and we will assume they're both still alive and well," Fiona said with a determined look.

CHAPTER FORTY-SIX

Tired and losing hope, Fiona quietly trudged through the thick woodland behind the picnic area alongside Humphries. The temperature had dropped beneath the trees, but the bulletproof jacket remained hot and uncomfortable. The mood had been positive at the start when officers had ushered surprised families and couples away from the area. Now, shoulders were slumped with disappointment as the light started to fade, and movements were weary rather than buoyant.

She stopped to check for messages from the officers hidden on either side of the bridge. There had been nothing since their messages confirming they were in place, and the bridge and picnic park were eerily empty.

The woodland that ran along the clifftop stretched for miles, and searching it was a painstakingly slow process. They were in the second wave, prodding and poking the undergrowth behind the line of armed officers moving slowly ahead.

Fiona was concerned that Will would have been scared away if he had been nearby, watching the area when they arrived. Confirmation that his vehicle had not been spotted leaving the area, or anywhere else for that matter, gave her little reassurance. In the pit of her stomach, she dreaded them finding two corpses. Or worse, finding nothing and never knowing what happened to Noah while fearing the worst. She doubted Humphries felt much more optimistic but decided to keep her concerns to herself.

Up ahead, an armed officer walked back towards them, and

Fiona prepared herself for bad news. He explained he lived locally and pointed out the wood covered a vast area, with plenty of places where a car could be parked, hidden from sight. More worryingly, he said that a determined driver could follow the off-road tracks to the cliff edge in numerous additional places in the dry conditions.

"So, what are you suggesting?" Fiona asked.

"Nothing really, other than we could search the area all night and not find anything. I've just been told to update you and ask if you were considering halting the search at some point and resuming tomorrow morning."

Not wanting to shoot the messenger, Fiona replied, "Dog handlers have recently arrived, and until we have confirmation that they have left the area, the search should continue."

Shifting his weight from foot to foot, the officer asked, "What evidence is there that they are here?"

"The search continues," Fiona repeated.

The officer shrugged and walked away, leaving Fiona to question her stubbornness. She acknowledged it was a large area that was difficult to search, but it was the most logical place for Will to have taken refuge. Nothing had been heard from the dog handlers so far, but they only needed one of the dogs to pick up the scent for the search to be successful.

"Do you think he might have a point?" Humphries asked. "Would it be better to start afresh tomorrow?"

"No." Fiona set her jaw and continued forwards, poking at the undergrowth. After a short pause, she heard Humphries following suit. As they made progress in an awkward silence, her mind wandered.

Eddie and Andrew were behind the armed team, watching the aqueduct, while Rachael, Abbie and Kerry monitored the situation from the station. Fiona had complete confidence in her experienced team but had concerns about Kerry. She had been thrown in at the deep end in a new area, but her delays in following orders were worrying. It would take a lot of work to turn her into a useful addition to the team, and she wasn't sure Kerry was keen to learn and improve or even how long she would be with them.

Humphries hadn't softened his attitude and had pointed out Kerry's assertiveness and sense of self-entitlement sprung from her private education. Fiona hadn't noticed those traits, and Kerry hadn't made any reference to who her father was as far as she was aware. If anything, she sensed Kerry was trying to distance herself from her father and his influence, contrary to whatever Humphries might think. But she was starting to question whether that was because she wanted to be judged on her own merits, or because she had been pressured into joining the police by her father and had no genuine interest in the career. That was more worrying than the silly class issues that Humphries kept bringing up. Her lack of interest meant she would continue making mistakes and not following orders even after she had time to fully explain what was expected of her.

"Hey, Fiona! Come over here and have a look at this."

Fiona hurried over to where Humphries was examining the ground. "What have you found?"

"Looks like recent car tracks to me," Humphries said. "Unlike others that we've seen, these haven't been made by a heavy off-road vehicle or a motorcycle."

"Where do they lead?" Fiona asked, trying not to hope for too much.

"The ground is so dry they peter out, but here they are going in a straight line to over there," Humphries said, pointing to what looked like an impenetrable overgrown bush.

Branches and brambles scratched at Fiona as she forced her way through the overhanging branches. "More car tracks! And broken branches!" She forced herself through the tangle of overgrown weeds, which reached to the overhanging branches with renewed vigour. "I've got something. It's a car!"

Pushing his way in behind her, Humphries asked, "The right registration?"

"The number plate has been removed, but it looks like the right make and model. It's not an old wreck that's been here a while."

Humphries pushed his way past Fiona to the front of the car, holding his phone. "Can you get in to release the bonnet, and I'll check the chassis number?" Breaking a branch off the tree, he looked back at Fiona. "Other side."

Fiona squeezed her way around to the other side of the car and tried the handle. "All the doors are locked. We'll need to break a window to get in. Have you got anything to use?"

"I'll try with one of the branches, but I doubt they'll do the job."

"While you're doing that, I'll call it in," Fiona said. "I'll return to the track so they know where to find us."

Humphries joined Fiona on the track. "I couldn't find anything strong enough to break the windows. Are they on their way?"

"They should be here any minute," Fiona replied. "You've cut your face."

"Have I?" Humphries said, rubbing his face. He pulled a handful of leaves from Fiona's hair. "But I haven't been crowned princess of the trees."

Pulling the last of the leaves and small twigs entangled in her hair, Fiona heard more officers approaching. After pointing to where the car was hidden, she stepped away, leaving them to break into the car and release the bonnet while she made a call. Five minutes later, it was confirmed that it was the car Will had been driving when he had driven away from Shelby's with Noah.

"Where are we going?" Humphries asked, following Fiona out of the wooded area. "Aren't we going to carry on searching for them?" Not receiving a reply, he tried again, "They've abandoned the car, but they could still be here on foot. Are we abandoning the search?"

"No, the search continues," Fiona said. "Nobody has spoken to the garage that sold him the car. Kerry traced it to a used car place about five miles from here but didn't follow it up with a call. That's where we're heading."

"At this time?" Humphries asked, checking his watch. "Are you sure it'll be open?"

Away from the trees, Fiona had a clear enough signal to contact Simon Prior, the owner of the used car sales company, but received no reply. They drove past the garage on the off chance, but it was locked up and in darkness. After getting out of the car and giving the locked gates a good shake, Fiona accepted it would have to wait until the morning.

Slumped in the car seat, she scrolled the missed calls from Stefan. She sent him a brief note saying she was up to her ears in work but would call him as soon as she had the chance and started the car engine. Driving away, she regretted her message. She missed hearing his voice, and it wasn't him she was avoiding - it was thinking about the prospect of changing stations.

CHAPTER FORTY-SEVEN

Fiona woke up early and checked for overnight developments. Finding none, she tried the number for the garage owner. Simon Prior was disgruntled by being woken by the call but agreed to meet Fiona at his home. Humphries was equally unimpressed by being dragged from his bed so early on a Sunday morning. He only stopped moaning when Fiona offered to drop him in the woods to rejoin the search party instead.

Simon Prior's home was a ramshackle bungalow crouching in a large, poorly maintained yard littered with vehicles and vehicle parts. One thing that was well-maintained was the metal security gates with security cameras and lights. Within moments of them pulling up to the gates, a stocky man in his late fifties limped across the yard to check their ID and let them in.

He led them into a dimly lit kitchen area, where he sat at a table to continue eating his full English breakfast. With a mouthful of bacon, he said, "Sit. What do you want?"

Fiona and Humphries lifted piles of trade magazines and logbooks from the chairs to comply with the request. Unable to spot a clear space on the counter, they put them on the floor under their chairs.

"We're here about a car you sold towards the end of last week," Fiona said.

"Jesus! I sell loads of cars," Simon said through another

mouthful of food. "Which car was it?"

Once Humphries had given details of the vehicle, Simon said, "Yeah. I think I remember." After forking a couple of mouthfuls of food into his mouth and giving them a thoughtful chew, he added, "It was a good little runabout and was all above board. If it's been involved in an accident, that's nothing to do with me. It was in perfect working order when it left here. I check all the cars over myself, and it had a valid MOT certificate."

"It hasn't been involved in an accident," Humphries said. "We're trying to trace the owner."

"Has it been involved in a crime? That also is nothing to do with me. I can't be responsible for what people use their cars for."

"We're not saying you are. We're simply asking for the buyer's details. Do you have them?" Fiona asked.

"Somewhere. I'll find the paperwork once I've finished my breakfast."

"A child's life is at stake here," Fiona said. "You'll find it now."

"Keep your hair on." Simon mopped the last of the grease mixed with brown sauce from his plate with a slice of buttered bread and walked to a pile of paperwork on the kitchen counter next to a sink full of dirty plates. After sifting through it, he pulled out an oil-stained invoice. "Here it is. An anxious little woman. Her old car had been written off, and she desperately needed a replacement."

"A woman?" Fiona said, reaching for the invoice. "Can I see?"

After reading an unknown name and address she passed the invoice to Humphries. "Other than anxious, how would you describe her?"

The clogs in Fiona's mind slowly turned as Simon gave a description that fitted Angie. "Did she have anyone with her?"

"Not that I could see. I think she said she had caught a bus and walked, but she could have been dropped off around the corner, for all I know. All I remember is that she was in a real hurry to have something she could drive away in there and then," Simon said, walking to the fridge and pulling out a beer. "Anything else?"

"No, thank you. You've been very helpful. Can we hold onto the invoice?"

"I need it for my records. My accountant gets very twitchy about missing invoices."

Looking around the cluttered room and wondering what sort of paperwork he provided his accountant with, Fiona said, "Of course. We might need to come back for it later, but for now, is it okay with you if I take a photograph of it?"

"Be my guest."

Once they had driven out of the gates, Fiona said, "Angie's been playing us from the start. If she bought that car for Will, she probably also bought whatever he is driving around now. He could be anywhere if they swopped vehicles after he snatched Noah."

"Is that what you think happened?"

"It makes sense. Angie drove the car to the aqueduct as a decoy, knowing the registration number would be tracked. We need to check how long it would have taken her to return home. Rachael said she was walking along the pavement towards her home when the first response team turned up."

"With two shopping bags," Humphries reminded Fiona.

"Which automatically led us to assume she was returning from a shopping trip."

"Could she afford to buy two cars just like that?"

Fiona shrugged. "We're only talking about cheap runabouts, and we know Will's good at fixing things. Contact the station and ask them to pass her description and the fake name she gave to all the small car dealers."

"Okay, but they're not going to get too many responses this early on a Sunday morning," Humphries said. "I still don't understand why she reported him missing. We wouldn't have been on to him so quickly if she hadn't."

"I agree that doesn't make sense. I think he initially went on the run after the first shooting. That's probably when he holed up in the old hut above the pond. At some point, he did what he always does. He ran back to his mother for help," Fiona said.

"We haven't any clear motive for the first shootings, but from everything Kerry said, I bet Angie was behind Noah's abduction. I think she has some crazy idea that they can play happy families somewhere when this all dies down. She's not worried because she knows exactly where they are."

"Do you think he could be with Angie now?" Humphries asked. "In her house?"

Fiona stopped and banged her palm against her forehead. "Contact the surveillance team and ask if they've seen anyone leave. Forget what I said about him using another car. The front seat of Angie's car was pulled back because Will had driven it there with Noah inside, straight after swapping cars with his mother. While Angie was a decoy, Will smuggled Noah into the house using her car."

"I'll check the timings and the bus timetable, but I'm not convinced she had time to hide the car and catch a bus home," Humphries said. "And how could Will have been in the house? A team descended on the house shortly after Noah was taken."

"There was a delay between the shooting and us connecting it to Will. They had plenty of time if they had prearranged everything," Fiona said. "It's less than a ten-minute drive between Shelby's and Angie's."

"But the team checked the house when they arrived, and a liaison officer has been in and out since then. As have we. And Rachael and Abbie," Humphries said. "Are you saying Will has been hiding in the house with Noah all that time?"

"Does Angie have a garden shed, and was it checked along with the house?"

Humphries pulled up the report on his phone. "She does, but it was locked. It looks like she unlocked it for the first officers on the scene, and they quickly glanced around."

"He was there. I'm sure of it," Fiona said. "I was right earlier. Who else would protect him other than his mother?"

"What about the note he sent her?"

"You mean her excuse for un-reporting him as missing? She made up the story about receiving a note from him when he turned up on her doorstep and told her what he'd done. It was just a scribbled handwritten note without an envelope," Fiona said. "And Abbie said she didn't think she was that bright. When Will confessed to the killings, she was determined to protect him. And then she saw a way to get her grandson all to herself as well."

"What do we do now?"

"Get an armed response team to Angie's house and tell the others what's happening. We'll drive out there but stay well back until the team has been in. Oh, and see if you can get plans for the house. It's an old-style council house, so there may be a coal cellar or something similar."

After completing his calls, Humphries said, "You're not going to like this."

"Don't tell me he was in disguise, and they've let him leave the house with a small child."

"No, nobody has left the house," Humphries said. "But Kerry was worried about Angie. She's gone around there to sit with her while they wait for news."

Fiona stepped hard on the accelerator. "Update the armed response team that there's an officer inside. We might get there before them."

CHAPTER FORTY-EIGHT

Kerry desperately wanted to make a good first impression, but she slipped up somewhere no matter how hard she tried to get everything right. If only she had made the connection with Will going missing earlier or watched the garage forecourt footage when she was first asked to. Shelby's boyfriend would be alive, and Noah wouldn't be missing. If she thought it, what must the others think of her? She had been so determined to make a good start and stand on her own two feet, but everything had gone wrong. She was useless and couldn't survive in the force without her father's help. There was no one else to blame. Everything she touched blew up in her face because she failed to recognise crucial evidence.

Abbie and Rachael worked well together, and while they had been polite, she kept finding herself in their way. They seemed as relieved as she was when she suggested she visit Angie to see how she was coping. She genuinely liked Angie and wanted to support her through this difficult time, but she also hoped that she might uncover a vital piece of evidence that led them to where Will was hiding before it was too late. She couldn't possibly make things any worse than she already had.

Nobody was openly saying it, but everyone thought Will would harm Noah. And probably himself, although nobody cared too much about that. Her gut feeling from the first time she met Angie was that her son was in a bad place mentally. If only she had doubled down on her concerns and looked deeper into his past. If she had followed up with Will's employers, she might have realised the connection to the first shooting. Instead of being the station failure, she could have been the star who prevented the killing of Shelby's new partner and Noah being taken. As it was, she was the idiot who delayed identifying him and the cause of additional death and misery.

She should accept she wasn't cut out for a career in the police even though it was all she had ever wanted to do. As a child, she had felt so proud of her father in his smart uniform and looked forward to him coming home every evening. As she grew older, she was enthralled by his acts of bravery and how he had progressed through the ranks to his senior position. She had wanted him to be proud of her achievements, not embarrassed by her failings.

She had failed spectacularly as an officer, but at least she could show Angie some empathy as a human being. However bad she felt, Angie would feel a hundred times worse, and she doubted she had a wide circle of friends. Even if she did, they would stay away in the circumstances. People were always quick to judge when there was a child involved, and poor Angie would become known as the mother of a serial killer. She hadn't seen anything yet but was in no doubt that the media would already be picking through Will's childhood and blaming Angie for how he had turned out. It was always the parents' fault, or to be more exact, the mothers'.

As the daughter of a senior police officer, she knew how painful the media's misinformation could be. All they wanted was an eye-catching headline. The facts were irrelevant when it came to increasing readership.

It bothered her that the family liaison officer had only popped in for a quick visit before leaving Angie alone to wait for news. She had read her reports twice, and it was clear from her tone that she hadn't built any rapport with Angie. She shouldn't be alone at a time like this, and Kerry felt she had made a connection with Angie when she first came in to report Will missing. With her first-hand knowledge of press intrusion, she could support her through the next few hours and days until they found Will and Noah. Afterwards, she would decide what to do with the rest of her life.

Kerry had to fight off reporters bombarding her with questions outside Angie's house. She would let the station know how intimidating they had been when she had a moment. Before pushing past the reporters and walking up the garden path, she looked back at the two constables chatting in their car and taking no notice. They probably thought there was little point in staying alert while there were so many reporters camped on the doorstep. Will was hardly likely to turn up now, but she thought one of them should be watching the rear of the house. When she left, she would check to see if reporters were also skulking around there.

Kerry wasn't surprised to see all the house curtains drawn. Poor Angie would feel like a prisoner, and the reporters' presence would dissuade any friends who did decide to visit from venturing any closer. She kept her lips firmly sealed and her back to the reporters, who continued to shout questions as she waited for Angie to open her front door.

Angie's worried face peered through the gap in the partially open door. Her eyes were watery, and the lines on her face had deepened since they last met. But the hounded look on her face shocked Kerry the most. "Hi, Angie. Can I come in?"

"Oh, it's you. Sorry I didn't come to the door straight away. I thought it might be one of those reporters chancing their luck."

"Are you going to let me in?" Kerry asked. "I thought you could do with some company while we wait for news."

Angie pulled the door closed to release the chain. "Come into the hall away from the reporters, but there's no need for you to trouble yourself."

"You shouldn't be alone while all this is going on," Kerry said. "I was worried about you."

"No need to worry about me," Angie said. "I should be used to handling things alone by now. That's the way it's always been."

"Just because you can doesn't mean you should," Kerry said, stepping into the narrow hallway. "I can stay for as long as you need me."

"That's very kind of you, but I'm doing fine by myself. Sometimes it's easier that way," Angie said, blocking any further progress into the house.

"Well, okay," Kerry said, feeling less sure of herself. She was expecting Angie to be more pleased to see a familiar face. "I thought you would appreciate some company at a time like this. You must be worried sick about Noah."

"Poor Noah. He's all I can think about," Angie said, although she looked more nervous and distracted than upset. "The house is a mess, but as you're here, do you want to come through to the kitchen for a cup of tea before you leave?"

"That would be lovely. I'm here to see you and won't be looking at anything else. Housework should be the last thing on anyone's mind," Kerry said as she was led through to a spotless kitchen at the rear of the house. She suspected it looked out over the rear garden, but as the blind was pulled down, she couldn't be sure. "While I'm here, would you like an update on our progress? We've found the car Will was driving."

"Oh? That's brilliant news." Angie bustled around the kitchen, making the tea. With her back to Kerry, she asked, "Where was it?"

"Parked up in the woods near the aqueduct. Do you know where I mean?"

"Yes. Funnily enough, I've been to the picnic area many a time with Will's father. I take it as you've only mentioned finding the car they weren't with it," Angie said. "I suppose they could be camping out in those woods. My Will was always a fan of nature. He was always a quiet, gentle boy and never into loud music and drugs."

"We have sniffer dogs up there," Kerry said. "If they're there, we'll find them."

"Those woods go on for miles, so that might take a while. You can't stop with me all that time. I expect a pretty girl like you to have a young man waiting for you at home."

"I can stay for as long as you like."

"Take a pew. The tea will be ready shortly."

Kerry picked up a child's baseball cap from the chair before sitting. Assuming it was Noah's, her first thought was to hide it in case it stirred painful memories for Angie. She looked up when she sensed Angie hovering over her.

"Oh, that's Noah's. He left it here the last time he visited. Let me take it from you."

Watching Angie put the hat in a drawer without any show of emotion, Kerry thought back to the first time she met Angie. Didn't she say the weekend was going to be the first time Shelby allowed Noah to stay over? She told herself to stop being so silly. Noah must have been over plenty of times for a visit before Shelby and Will split up. "When was the last time you saw Noah?"

Angie brought over two mugs of tea and sat opposite Kerry. "It was a while back. Will stopped by after picking Noah up from a friend's birthday party in the next street. That's when he left the cap behind. How long will those reporters be hanging around outside?"

"I'm afraid they are a law unto themselves, and it's not an offence to stand out on the pavement. If it were, I would ask them to move on. As it is, they'll probably be there for a while."

"Is there nothing you can do to make them leave?" Angie asked.

"Not much, I'm afraid, unless they're causing a nuisance. If you feel intimidated, I could ask them to move back away from your front gate."

"But they would still be there, watching my every move. It gives me the creeps, them being out there. Can't you persuade them to go away?"

"I could try, but I can't guarantee they'll take any notice," Kerry said. "But I do understand what an invasion of privacy it is. The thought of being watched all the time can be very unsettling. I do understand how it feels."

"Is there somewhere I can make a complaint about how much

they are upsetting my state of mind?" When Kerry nodded, Angie looked down at her empty hands. "It's because of them that I brought the hat down. I had forgotten about it until this morning. Cooped up in here with those reporters outside, I don't feel like I can breathe. I started to wander about the rooms like a caged tiger. Opening cupboards and prodding about for no good reason. That's when I found the cap. I brought it down here because I thought it might comfort me."

Kerry sipped her tea. There was logic to Angie's tale, but somehow, it didn't ring true. Angie appeared fidgety and nervous but not emotional - not like she had been in the police station when she thought Will was missing. Something was wrong, and the family liaison's comments started to make sense. "Hopefully, it won't be for much longer. We're close to finding Will and Noah, and once we do, the reporters will soon lose interest and move on to the next story."

"Close, you say? Where do you think they are?"

"Probably not too far from the aqueduct," Kerry said. "As they're on foot, they can't have gone far. Did you take Will there for picnics when he was younger?"

"Now you mention it, I did take Will and Jason over there a few times when they were little boys. They loved it by the water. We would have a picnic at the top and then follow the path down to the river. There used to be an hourly bus service." Angie stopped as though she had just remembered something important. "Have you checked with the buses whether a man and a child caught the bus from the picnic area? Assuming it still runs. So many services have been cut in recent years."

"I'm not sure. I'll check as soon as we finish our tea," Kerry said. Feeling increasingly uncomfortable and keen to check whether the local bus company had been contacted, she wanted to finish her tea and leave. Unfortunately, the tea was still piping hot, forcing her to take small sips.

"I heard an appeal for sightings of them on the radio this morning," Angie said. "Shall I put it on to see if we can hear another one?" She pushed back from the table to cross over the room to the radio when suddenly there was a loud crash from upstairs, closely followed by a high-pitched scream.

CHAPTER FORTY-NINE

Angie quickly said, "These walls are paper-thin. I hear everything that's going on next door."

Kerry shot up from her chair, nearly knocking her mug from the table. Her heart was pumping so hard she thought it must be audible. No way did that noise come from next door. She knew a child's shriek when she heard one. There was a child in the house and, in all probability, his father, armed with a gun.

She forced herself to take a deep breath and think. If she hadn't leapt to her feet, she could play it cool, but it was too late for that. She could add her extreme reaction to the noise to the long list of failures she'd made since arriving in Birkbury. She started to edge towards the door. "Well, I had better get back to the station before they send a search party out for me. Thanks for the tea."

"Not so fast," Angie said, quickly crossing the kitchen to block Kerry's exit. "You're not going anywhere."

"Sorry? I don't understand," Kerry said. "You said you wanted to be alone, and I need to follow up things with the bus company. I don't expect anyone thought to check the bus timetables." She swallowed a scream, which escaped as more of a whimper when she realised Angie had swiped a large chef's knife from the counter before dashing across the room. "Angie? Don't be silly. Everyone back at the station knows I'm here."

"I like you. Really, I do. But I can't let you leave." Holding the knife out before her, Angie reached behind to open the kitchen door. Keeping her eyes on Kerry, she shouted, "Will! I need you down here. Now!"

Kerry backed away from the table towards the kitchen window above the sink. She could open the blind and call for help. Her heart sank when she remembered the two constables chatting in the car out the front. There was still the possibility there were reporters out there. She wouldn't give up hope of calling for help just yet. The longer she kept Angie chatting, the more chance she had of attracting attention. "Angie, this is crazy. Put down the knife, and we'll talk."

"No, you're the crazy one if you think I'm going to give up now. Not when we're so close."

"Close to what?"

"Like you said, that lot out there will soon lose interest. Then, the three of us will leave together to start a new life. I'll have my two boys again."

"That's not going to happen if you harm me," Kerry said. "People know I'm here. This is the first place they'll look for me."

"She's right, Mum," Will said, squeezing himself through the half-open kitchen door behind his mother. His hair was dishevelled, and he had dark rings under his eyes. The boyish round cheeks in the recent photograph had deflated, and he looked gaunt and strained.

"Good boy," Angie said as though she hadn't heard Will's comment. "You've brought your gun with you."

Will looked down at the gun hanging loosely from his hand as if surprised to see it there. His eyes widened in horror. "I can't just shoot her."

"Of course you can. Just like the others," Angie said. "Do I have to remind you how all this started?"

Will shoved the gun into his back pocket and placed his hands on either side of his head. "It was that awful girl's fault. She looked so much like Jen. I wanted her to see what it was like to be surrounded by dead people."

"And the man in the garage?"

"He was the school bully. He was so arrogant and rude to that poor woman. Like his time was more important than anyone else's," Billy said. "I just saw red."

"Well, you can just see red again and shoot this one," Angie said.

"But she hasn't done anything to make me mad. And I'm so tired," Will whined like a child. "So very tired. I've had enough of all this. I want it to stop."

"Listen to Will, Angie," Kerry said. "It's time to put an end to this and do the right thing."

Angie lunged forward, pointing the knife at Kerry. "Don't ever tell me what I can and can't do. It's surprising what someone can do when they put their mind to it. I thought I would never survive the loss of Jason. But I did. I somehow dragged myself through each pitiful, empty day. And now I have Noah to think about."

"What are you going to do, Mum?"

Will looked as defeated and scared as Kerry imagined Noah was. She wondered where he was. Was he bound and gagged upstairs to keep him quiet? How had the other officers not realised he was in the house?

"If you're not man enough to shoot her, this is what we're going to do," Angie said. "She's right that people will come here looking for her. I'll have to arrange an accident while you take Noah and start walking across to the allotments over the back. Walk, don't run. The last time I checked, there was no one around the back watching the house, but you don't want to draw attention to yourself. Act casual and try to make it look like you've come from a different direction."

"I don't see how I can do that. They'll see us for sure," Will said. "Why don't I take Noah back to the garden bunker to sit things out? Like we planned before. We'll be fine in there for as long as it takes, so long as you keep us fed."

"Don't be stupid, Will. That's not an option anymore. What the hell were you doing up there? I told you to keep quiet until I got rid of her."

"You shouldn't have let her in."

"Don't you dare criticise me! If you hadn't set off on a crazy shooting spree, I wouldn't have to sort your mess out," Angie said. "Get going like I said. Keep walking out across the fields and stay away from roads. Take the phone I gave you, and I'll come to collect you as soon as I can get away. Get Noah and go now."

"What are you going to do, Mum?"

"It doesn't concern you. Get going, and I'll figure it out."

CHAPTER FIFTY

Fiona screeched the car to a halt outside Angie's house. She jumped out of the car and asked Humphries to find out when the armed response team would arrive. A pushy group of reporters instantly surrounded her. She brushed away their questions and asked, "Have you seen anyone entering or leaving the house in the last couple of hours?"

"Yes. One of your people went in and left about ten minutes later. That would have been getting on for a hour or so ago. Shortly after she left, another of your lot went in and is still in there. Have there been any developments?"

"And there's been no other movement from the house? No one else in or out?"

A reporter pushed himself to the front and held his phone up in Fiona's face. "Can you tell our listeners why you are so interested in this house? Do you think he's in there?"

"No comment," Fiona said, knocking the phone away. "Has anyone been in or out of the house recently?"

"Nope. And as you can see, all the curtains are drawn." The cameraman raised his camera to his shoulder and moved into position while another reporter produced a microphone. "Do you have an update for us, DI Williams? Are you close to making an arrest?"

Fiona pushed the microphone away and stepped away from the camera. "Do you have anyone watching the rear of the property?"

"We did to start with, but there is no clear view other than from those allotments up there," the reporter said, pointing to the rising ground behind the row of houses. "We tried to set up there and speak to some of them, but we were shooed off pretty sharpish."

Humphries, who had asked the same questions of the surveillance team parked along the road, joined Fiona at the front garden gate. "Haven't you lot got anything better to do? Can you step back from the gateway?"

The reporters shuffled their feet, moving back a fraction, while Humphries opened the gate. On the other side, he said, "Kerry went in about half an hour ago. They've been wandering around the back to check for movement every fifteen minutes. There's only one access road around the back, leading from some garages, and it joins the road opposite to where they're parked."

"How about access on foot across the allotments and the fields behind to freedom?"

Humphries gave an unconcerned shrug. "To be fair, we only asked for the surveillance team on the odd chance Angie might lead us to where Will was hiding. It wasn't considered a remote possibility that he could already be in the house until recently."

"Didn't you mention it when you called them?" Fiona asked.

"We were already on our way over, and I thought I could explain the situation when we arrived. I just asked them to be extra vigilant until we arrived."

"Do you know what's beyond the trees up there on the ridge?"

"I'm sure that's the quarry and it should be fenced off."

"How sure?"

Humphries shrugged. "I'm guessing for safety."

"I'm pleased you're thinking about safety issues while being so casual about an officer being trapped in a house with someone who has already killed seven people."

"If he kept himself hidden from a whole team of officers, why would he reveal himself to Kerry?"

"Kerry turned up alone and unannounced after the liaison officer left," Fiona said. "What if during that time, Will had thought it safe to come out of hiding?"

"I think you're panicking over nothing," Humphries said. "She's probably in there with her feet up, drinking a cup of tea. Are we going in to collect her or waiting for the cavalry to arrive?"

Fiona was in two minds. She looked up at the silent house. Was it too quiet? Humphries being wounded at the end of their previous case played on her mind. At one point, she thought they were going to lose him. Could she take the risk a second time? "Go back and send one of the officers around to watch the back of the house. Once he's in place, if they still haven't arrived, we'll knock on the door."

While waiting for the officer to say he was in place, they spotted the curtains twitching - first in one of the upstairs rooms and then downstairs. Fiona looked nervously at Humphries: "Well, they know we're here. Where the hell is the armed first response team? Call them again."

"It's no wonder she's on edge with the press outside. I think if I were in there, I would be taking the odd peak out the windows every now and again. We've probably put the fear of God into her by saying her son is armed and dangerous. I wouldn't read too much into it."

Despite working hard to play the situation down, Humphries jumped as much as Fiona when they heard the front door click open. They turned to see Kerry in the open doorway with Angie directly behind her.

"Ma'am, I'm here keeping Angie company," Kerry said. "Has there been a development?"

Fiona instinctively knew something was wrong. She hadn't known Kerry long enough to get a strong sense of her, but she seemed too stiff and formal. And the way she stressed 'Ma'am' when she had told her to call her Fiona several times. "The search is ongoing, but we haven't found anything of note since the car."

"That's what I've told Angie." When Kerry shifted slightly to the side, Angie closely shadowed her movement. "We've been talking, and Angie used to take Will and his brother up there when they were little by bus. Have we checked with the local bus company? It's a good suggestion."

"Yes. Photographs have been given to the drivers on that route," Humphries said. "Can we come in?"

Kerry's smile, posture and position, which partially blocked Angie, were unnatural. The hairs on the back of Fiona's neck told her something was wrong, and she wouldn't relax until she had a full view of both women. "It's a lovely day. We can talk out here in the garden if that would be easier," she suggested.

Kerry glanced around at Angie before saying, "Angie is uncomfortable with the news reporters hanging around. She wants us to be left alone to await news."

"We can get rid of them," Fiona said, looking over her shoulder and glaring at the reporters, who had gathered around the gate taking snaps. "Get out of here, now."

Fiona hoped the glare she gave the reporters was enough to make them realise she needed them to back away. Most didn't get the hint, but one did and started pulling his colleagues back. The cameraman nearly tripped and dropped his camera as he stepped back, drawing everyone's attention.

Fiona turned back just in time to see Kerry launch herself into Humphries, shouting, "Careful, she has a knife."

Time stopped for a split second. Fiona was too far away to react immediately, and she thought for one terrible moment that Humphries was going to freeze, as visions of him bleeding on the floor after their last case flooded her mind. Time sped up without warning. Humphries pushed Kerry behind himself to safety and, with one fluid move, had hold of Angie's wrist. He twisted her arm, and the knife clattered to the doorstep and slid to the garden path. Fiona quickly retrieved it and handed it backwards to the constable, who came pounding along the path.

Seeing Humphries had control of Angie, Fiona helped Kerry up from the ground. "Are Will and Noah inside?"

Kerry scrambled to her feet. "Yes, but they're heading out the back door and over the allotments."

Humphries pushed Angie, already in handcuffs, towards the constable. "Call this in, then read her rights and get her to the station."

Fiona had taken one step into the hallway when they heard a gunshot.

CHAPTER FIFTY-ONE

Fiona dashed through the corridor with Humphries hurrying behind her, through the kitchen and out the back door into a long, narrow garden with an overgrown hedge and a shed at the end. A rusty metal gate led out to the access drive for a row of garages. Beyond the driveway ran a fence to the allotments. The constable Humphries had spoken to moments before was in a foetal position by the fence. Fiona glanced behind to see Kerry halfway across the rear garden. She pointed and shouted back to her, "Organise an ambulance and stay with him until they arrive."

Fiona leapt over the post-and-rail fencing with Humphries alongside her. She hadn't settled into a running rhythm, and her breathing came in ragged, painful puffs as she hit the incline. She could see Will's long legs clearing the ground up ahead, but he was slowed by dragging Noah along behind him. With their head start, they had already almost reached the far end of the allotments. Beyond that, a field sloped steeply upwards to woodland.

Fiona lowered her head and powered on through the carefully maintained allotment gardens, closing the distance between them. Will reached the far fence of the allotments and threw Noah over. He looked behind before leaping over. On the other side, he scooped Noah into his arms and sped up the hill.

Humphries overtook Fiona as they sped towards the allotment fence. They were gaining on Will but not fast enough. Once he was in the woods, it would be harder to track him. Fiona looked behind to see a couple of reporters following them. She looked forward in time to see Will stop and twist towards them. She screamed, "Get down."

Fiona dropped heavily to the ground and crawled towards a row of runner beans as shots fired out towards them. Face down, she turned her head and was relieved to see Humphries had taken shelter behind a potting shed. She couldn't see the two reporters and could only hope they had ducked for cover and would decide the potential scoop wasn't worth risking their lives.

The shooting stopped, and she raised her head. Will was on the move again. She hauled herself to her feet and started running. Reaching the fence, she shouted ahead to Humphries, "Keep a close eye on him. We'll only have the protection of the long grass if he fires again."

She pushed her aching legs up the steep hill as fast as she could, desperately trying to reduce the gap between them. They would be sitting targets if Will turned to fire down on them from inside the woods. Their only hope was that he felt they were too close behind him to risk stopping. The sound of an approaching helicopter came from her left. She hoped it was the police chopper, but she wasn't going to waste time looking up to check.

A short distance from her, Humphries was closing fast, but he wouldn't reach Will before he entered the woods. Fiona pumped her legs as hard as they would go over the last incline before the trees started. Inside the treeline, Fiona folded forward with her hands on her knees, trying to control her ragged breathing. Humphries put his finger to his lips as he listened for sounds of movement. Hearing none, Fiona realised what that meant. "Get down," she shouted, dragging Humphries behind a fallen tree. They ducked behind it just in time as a bullet whistled past them, embedding itself in a tree trunk behind.

Catching their breath, they listened for movement, but all they could hear was the helicopter circling above. Fiona pressed hard on her side to reduce the pain from her stitch. She consoled herself that the helicopter would track Will as soon as he broke cover.

"What do you think?" Humphries asked. "Is he watching and waiting for us to make a move, or is he creeping quietly away?"

There was a sharp crack of a branch being snapped underfoot. "There's your answer," Fiona whispered, lifting her head over the trunk. "I can't see anything. I think we should follow. Carefully."

Humphries slowly raised himself to his feet. "It sounded like it came from that direction."

Fiona agreed. "That's where the shot came from." She moved forward, sprinting between the larger trees and stopping to listen. The deeper they moved into the woods, the more the undergrowth hampered their progress.

"I don't think he came this way," Humphries said. "We're going to have to double back."

"Or sideways," Fiona said, pointing to a small gap to their right.

Humphries was about to disagree when they heard a child's shriek followed by a loud splash. They rushed through the gap, ignoring the brambles scratching their hands and faces. Fiona was close to giving up when, after a last push, she found herself in a small clearing. A clearing that ended abruptly a few short strides in front of them. They stepped forward and peered down the steep quarry sides to a lake beneath them. They could only see one head that quickly disappeared beneath the water below them.

The helicopter was hovering overhead but wouldn't reach them in time. Fiona kicked off her shoes and threw her jacket behind her as she slid down the bank on her bottom. Her speed quickened as the sides grew steeper. Dirt dislodged by Humphries above, scrambling down to join her, rushed past. Then, she was sliding out of control. She could do nothing to stop the momentum, so she concentrated on maintaining her balance, keeping her weight back and her feet in front of her. She bounced and skimmed the sides of the bank as gravity took over. Her descent came to an abrupt halt as she was slammed into a tree growing out of the bank at a precarious angle.

She hung onto the tree trunk and looked down to see Will

resurface and disappear under the water again. Clinging to the branch, she saw a sheer drop into the water beneath her. If she leapt out away from the bank, there was a good chance she would hit the water. And if she didn't, it was going to hurt.

Ignoring Humphries shouting, "No," from his position above her, she launched herself over the edge. She felt stranded in mid-air like a cartoon character for a split second. There was a whoosh, and she felt herself falling. She closed her eyes and awaited the impact.

When it came, it knocked all the air out of her lungs. As she dropped lower into the gloomy water, she fought hard not to panic and gulp in the cold, murky water surrounding her. Her lungs were screaming for air when her descent slowed, and she was able to start kicking for the surface. She popped up, gasping for air, facing Will. He gave her a panicked look before taking a deep breath and diving under again. Fiona reasoned there was no point searching for Noah in the same place. If Will had been holding the boy in front of him, then Noah would have gone under further out. She looked back at where Humphries was standing and swam the short distance to where she thought Noah might have gone in and dived under. Her eyes stung as she forced them open to search the murky water. Her ears popped as she swam deeper. She knew she couldn't stay under for much longer before having to return to the surface. But she also knew Noah had been under for far too long. This might be her one and only chance to bring him up alive. When she reached the point where she felt she couldn't go on, she told herself just a few more kicks, and I'll resurface.

Something red caught her eye. Was he wearing red? She couldn't remember. She forced herself down and, through the murk, saw it was the boy. She grabbed him under the arms and started to power toward the surface. Every second counted as her tired legs kicked with everything she had left.

Bright lights danced across her vision when she reached the surface, gasping for air. Noah was lifeless in her arms, and she looked in despair at the distance to the shore. She squinted her eyes against the distracting lights that blurred her vision. She had to get Noah to the shore. She twisted around to hold Noah above her and started to swim.

She lashed out when she felt arms pulling Noah away, thinking it was Will trying to pull them under to their watery grave. She swallowed a mouthful of water as she flailed her arms and legs. More bright lights shot across her limited vision, and she felt herself sinking.

CHAPTER FIFTY-TWO

Fiona came to coughing and spluttering. Her thoughts were foggy and confused, and she couldn't stop shivering. She felt her wet shirt being peeled from her. Her urge to fight was dulled by a calm, gentle voice assuring her everything was going to be okay. Maybe it was wishful thinking, but she leaned into the voice and relaxed. Surrendering herself to the gentle, melodic voice was like floating on a cloud without a care in the world. After a final tug, she was free of the cold, damp, clinging shirt and was enveloped in a rough blanket. The material scratched her cold skin, but it felt so warm and comforting that she wanted to curl up and sleep.

A tight constriction in her chest grew into a stabbing pain, snatching the possibility of sleep away. She tried to throw the prickly blanket off her shoulders when she felt something block her airways. She folded forward with the searing pain and gagged. Fighting for breath, with her head pushed between her knees, a gush of water spouted from her mouth. She wiped her mouth as the rising panic subsided. She felt the blanket being wrapped tightly around her again. Her thoughts were still vague, but they were becoming clearer.

She raised her head from between her knees and looked around her. Humphries and a grey-haired man in a wetsuit took turns giving CPR to Noah. His tiny body lay between them. She watched, mesmerised. She wanted to ask the grey-haired lady kneeling next to her if she was an angel and whether Noah was going to survive, but her brain couldn't form the words. She wrapped her arms around her legs and waited.

Above her came the sound of an ambulance siren. She turned to look and saw uniformed officers running down the steep steps to the beach. The thought of the cavalry appearing over the horizon too late made her want to laugh hysterically and then cry. She turned at the sound of gurgling. Humphries rolled Noah's body onto his side as foaming water gushed from his mouth. Fiona dug a thumbnail into her palm, praying it meant that Noah would survive. Paramedics appeared from nowhere, pushing Humphries and the other man aside.

So intent on watching Noah's recovery, she didn't feel herself being lifted from the ground and placed on a stretcher. The jolt when it rolled over the rough ground brought her to her senses. Despite her pounding headache and nausea, she sat up, asking them to stop. The stretcher slowed but didn't stop.

"We need to get you into hospital to be fully checked out."

"I haven't got time for that," Fiona said, swinging her legs over the side of the stretcher. That brought the stretcher to an abrupt halt.

"Hey! What do you think you're doing?"

"Getting off. Thanks for the ride."

Humphries appeared at her side. "What's all the commotion going on over here? Are you causing trouble again?"

"I was just explaining to these guys that I'm getting off."

"Whoa. Are you sure that's a good idea? You were out of it for quite a while."

Fiona waved his concerns away. "How's Noah?"

"They'll be taking him to the hospital shortly," Humphries said. "Where you should be going."

Fiona hopped down from the stretcher. Her head spun when she held her full weight, forcing her to grab hold of Humphries to steady herself. "Is he …?"

"He's breathing again and has a pulse. Hopefully, he'll make it."

"And Will?"

Humphries nodded to the blanket-clad man sitting on the sand with his head in his hands. He offered no resistance when he was handcuffed and hauled to his feet. "On his way to the station, by the looks of it."

The world stopped spinning, and Fiona tentatively let go of Humphries, testing her balance. "I think I'm okay now. But it's probably a good idea if you drive back to the station."

Humphries risked an apologetic look at the paramedics before saying, "How about I get you home and into some dry clothes first? You're shivering."

"Okay. But then onto the station."

Humphries caught Fiona around the waist when she swayed and nearly fell. "Come on then. I'll crank the car's heating up."

CHAPTER FIFTY-THREE

Fiona felt nauseous when she stood up from her bed and sat back down again. As her head stopped spinning, snatches from the previous evening started to come back to her. Humphries had tricked her. She suspected he had concocted the agreement with the paramedics when she was struggling to remain upright walking from the beach. Despite his promise to take her to the station, he had driven her straight to the hospital. After poking and prodding her, they had said they wouldn't release her until they were sure there wasn't still water in her lungs. Despite several calls from Tina, which she guessed were complaints, Humphries had stayed with her throughout the tedious process until they finally agreed to let her go. Or had she insisted she was leaving? She couldn't quite remember.

She reached for her phone, which she always left on her bedside cabinet, before remembering it had been destroyed along with her watch when she'd jumped into the water. No way was she going to lie in bed, not knowing how Noah and the wounded officer were. She needed to at least get downstairs to the home phone. If she could make it downstairs, she could probably make it into the office. But first, she had to stop her head from spinning when she tried to stand.

Attempting and failing to stand again, she accepted she would have to wait it out a short time longer while she tried to remember all she could about last night. She recalled, after discovering her water-damaged phone, pestering Humphries to call the station for updates and to find out about Noah and the constable who had been shot. She sighed in relief when she remembered being told that the officer had undergone surgery and was expected to recover fully, but she couldn't see him because he was asleep.

She almost allowed herself to lie back and get some sleep herself when she recalled that Humphries had been far less forthcoming about Noah. Hard as she tried, she couldn't recall hearing anything positive about his recovery. She prepared herself to stand up when remnants of her conversation with Humphries about calling Stefan returned to her. When Humphries had suggested it, she had decided not to call Stefan from the hospital. There was nothing he could do other than to worry. She hadn't had the energy to ring him when she arrived home.

After another attempt to stand, she sat back down on the bed, waiting for the spinning to slow. As the minutes clicked by, she wondered what her reluctance to contact Stefan meant. She hadn't reached any conclusion when she dragged herself from bed and steadied herself by holding onto the wall while she dressed for the station. Her nausea settled, but her body felt battered and bruised as she carefully negotiated the stairs. After eating a dry piece of toast and washing down painkillers with the coffee, she pronounced herself well enough to drive to the station if she took it steady.

After failing to find her car keys, she looked outside. Of course, her car wasn't there. Humphries had it. She called a taxi and made another coffee while she waited. Sitting next to an open window during the short drive cleared away most of her brain fog, and she felt almost human by the time she was dropped off in the station car park a little after midday.

Seeing the reporters, the taxi driver had stopped directly outside the station entrance to let her out. Sykes waved and mock frowned at the clock when she walked through reception. Climbing the worn stairs with layers of paint peeling from the iron railings and the tired cream walls, she felt nostalgic. It was a powerful sensation that caught her by surprise and caused her to wonder if, somewhere deep down, she accepted that, despite her protests, she would shortly be leaving the station to live with Stefan.

As she opened the door to the operations room, the buzz of voices and clicking keyboards assaulted her. Everyone was there except Humphries, who was entitled to a lie-in. Rachael brought over a coffee as she was taking off her coat.

Fiona sat and gratefully took the offered mug. "You're a lifesaver. Do you know how the injured constable is this morning?"

"Recovering well, I understand," Rachael replied. "But what about you? We weren't expecting to see you today."

"Really?"

"Okay, knowing you, I thought you would be in at some stage. But you need to take it steady," Rachael said. "Is Stefan coming up to make sure you take good care of yourself?"

"And Noah? How's he?"

"It's too soon to say whether he'll fully recover, but he's comfortable and with his mother."

"Talking of mothers. Was Angie brought in?" Fiona sensed Kerry reacting to the name and turned slightly away to stop her from overhearing their conversation. She would speak to her later.

"She's been held overnight. We can charge her with harbouring Will if nothing else."

"Oh, she's responsible for a damn sight more than that. She possibly knew nothing of the first killings until after the event, but I suspect she planned the killing of Shelby's new partner and Noah being snatched," Fiona said. "What's the situation with Will?"

"He has confessed to everything but insists his mother knew nothing. He says he snuck into the house, and she first knew he was in the house yesterday afternoon."

"Who interviewed him?"

"Eddie and Andrew."

Fiona glanced across the room. "I'll speak to Kerry later, but her statement, along with that of the guy who sold the car to Angie, should put a stop to any nonsense about her not being involved. I want to see them both charged." Fiona lowered her voice and asked, "How's Kerry been? She trusted Angie and wanted to help her."

"She'll learn." Rachael shrugged. "She's been quiet this morning and very apologetic. She thinks she should have tied the two cases together sooner, and everything is her fault."

"If anyone's at fault for that, it's me. I'll have a word later," Fiona said. "How do you think she's fitting in generally? She's made a few mistakes, but I've been too busy to keep an eye on her or explain what we want from her."

"She's had a rough start, but I think she'll do."

"I need to have a word with her about a few things, but I'm hoping so, too," Fiona said, turning to her desk. She wasn't so sure, but Rachael was rarely completely off with her judgements, and only time would tell. "I had best make a start on the paperwork as I have a feeling that I'll be summoned by Dewhurst soon for my full account of yesterday, which will end up taking the rest of the afternoon. At least we have Will and Angie in custody, so they're not going anywhere, and Noah is with his mother."

Eddie ended his phone call and walked over to join them. "I think he's arranged a press conference for later today, but what are you doing here? Humphries gave us strict instructions not to disturb you today. He said he would pop around to yours after lunch to see how you were."

"He did, did he?" Fiona asked in mock annoyance. "What time's the press conference? I expect Dewhurst will want me to attend while he takes all the credit," Fiona said, dropping her forehead to the desktop. "That's all I need, the way I feel."

"You shouldn't have to," Rachael said. "You shouldn't even be in today. You should be at home in bed with Stefan fussing over you. Eddie can attend the conference."

"But I'm here, and you know Dewhurst. I'll be fine."

Rachael folded her arms. "But you shouldn't be."

Fiona raised her head and said, "Humphries may get some trouble from Tina, but let the team know after the conference drinks are on me in the pub. Say six o'clock?"

"Will Stefan be joining us?"

"I don't know," Fiona said. "Probably not." She looked up when she heard the door opening, expecting to see Dewhurst. Her heart did its usual happy dance. Who was she trying to kid? Nobody had ever made her feel the way Stefan did when he entered a room. She could no more walk away than she could fly. Her earlier nostalgic feelings were a premonition, and she knew it.

Stefan pulled out the chair next to her. "Humphries told me what happened when I couldn't reach you last night, and I drove up. I was going to check your home first, but I thought you would be here. Where else would you be?"

Fiona reached for Stefan's hand. "We can talk about that later."

The door opened again, and Dewhurst walked in. He stood in front of Fiona with his hands on his hips. "A good result, but I wasn't expecting to see you today. As you are here, there's a press conference at five o'clock. Are you up to attending?"

"We were just discussing that," Rachael interrupted. "Eddie conducted the initial interview and is ready to attend."

"Oh, okay, then," Dewhurst said, looking doubtfully at Eddie. "Do you have something smarter to change into?"

"I can pop home for something."

"Be in my office ready to go ten minutes before." Dewhurst turned his attention to Fiona. "Good to see you up and about, but as that's sorted, why don't you go home?"

"Do you want me to write a report before I go?" Fiona asked, unsure how she felt about her instant replacement by Eddie. Maybe it was time to put herself and her future with Stefan first.

"You can do that in a couple of days when you're fully rested," Dewhurst said, turned on his heels and marched away.

"Well? It looks like we both have a free afternoon," Stefan said.

Smiling, Rachael asked, "So what are you both still doing here?"

"Okay," Fiona said. "But drinks are still on for six o'clock. Can you let everyone know?"

Rachael nodded. "We'll see you both later."

"And you will call me if there's any news on Noah? My mobile is out of action, so use my home phone and leave a message if I'm not there."

"Yes! Now go!"

Kerry caught up with them in the corridor, holding an envelope. "Can I give you this?"

Suspecting what it was, Fiona asked Stefan to go ahead and wait in the car. Not taking the offered envelope, she asked, "What is it?"

"My resignation." Kerry looked down. "I'm so sorry I messed up and let you all down."

"You're being too hard on yourself. If anyone's at fault, it's me. I missed the connection as much as you did. How about you put that away, and we have a proper chat somewhere quiet tomorrow?"

"But if I had followed up on things when you asked, it would have made a difference. Aren't you furious?"

"Unfortunately, you joined us at a chaotic time, but that wasn't your fault," Fiona said. "We need to work on your time management, but you have shown me something else. You stuck to your guns and prioritised the missing person case because you cared. Not everyone does. It was more than a tick-box exercise to fill your time for you. That's as good a basis for a start as anything. Will you delay your decision until after we've talked?"

Kerry slipped the envelope into her pocket. "Okay, Ma ... Fiona."

"And I'll see you in the pub this evening at six o'clock. It will give us the chance to get to know one another better," Fiona said. "I'll be looking out for you."

Kerry nodded. "I look forward to it."

Thank you so much for reading my book. I hope you enjoyed reading it as much as I enjoyed writing it.

I love to hear what readers think of my books. If you have time I would love you to write a quick review.

BOOKS IN THIS SERIES

DI Fiona Williams Mystery

A Fiery End

Time to discover a brilliantly twisty mystery series.

A tradesman is set alight in his vehicle on an isolated road. His daughter is missing. And time is running out.

"I was on the edge of my seat and couldn't read fast enough."
"Totally riveting."
"Superb murder mystery and police procedural."

DI Fiona Williams is a driven detective who cares deeply about getting justice for victims and their families.
Driving home late at night, she comes across a vehicle engulfed in flames. The driver is at the wheel, oblivious to the inferno surrounding him. There is no explanation for why the vehicle was on the road or why the quiet tradesman was murdered in such a macabre way. The only witness to the fire, claims she saw nothing. Whatever she did see goes to the grave with her when she is brutally strangled. Frustration grows when the driver's daughter disappears. With time running out to find the daughter alive, Fiona is drawn into a web of powerful men determined to keep their deadly games secret. Juggling a family crisis and a growing suspicion her boss is corrupt, her judgement is hampered by her attraction to the man central to everything.

A Mother's Ruin

A single mother is brutally murdered in her garden.

DI Fiona Williams interprets the crime scene differently from her colleagues but fears her history of failed relationships taints her judgment. The wrong decision will change the lives of three children forever.

In a male-dominated department, with mounting evidence pointing in the other direction, will she find the courage to trust her instincts and narrow the investigation?

An intriguing mystery that blurs the distinction between the villain and the victim.

A Relative Death

An eye for an eye. A death for a death.
Some people will do anything for revenge.
And one detective will do anything to stop them.
DI Fiona Williams returns from a short break to a station stretched by the antics of a gang of youths, staff absences and three murders in quick succession. With unconnected victims and widely different murder methods, the only link is they seem motiveless. Forced to work in small groups rather than as a team, frustrations and jealousies flare-up between the officers creating a minefield of tension and a headache for Fiona.
As the most experienced officer, she is pulled from the initial case of a poisoned pensioner to investigate the shooting of a wealthy landowner's wife. She is annoyed the murder of a defenceless war veteran is given lower priority and thoughts of the pensioner's last moments are never far away.
The two victims have never met, and the only similarity is their murderer was someone who knew them well. The chances of it

being the same person are remote.

When a breakthrough comes in the investigation, it seems Fiona's nagging thought that the cases are connected may be correct. To fit the missing pieces together she will have to risk her life for an enemy she has worked hard to condemn.

An Educated Death

The best-kept secrets are the deadliest.

When a private boarding school pupil drowns in a lake on the grounds, DI Fiona Williams is called in to investigate. Security around the school grounds is tight, making it a closed community.

Fiona thinks the death was due to a secret society initiation rite that went wrong, but the school denies the societies exist, and her investigation hits a wall of silence.

A second pupil dies, but the silence continues.

The school is concerned with its reputation and upholding traditions, the influential parents care only about protecting their children, and the pupils have secrets of their own.

Nobody wants Fiona to expose the whole truth.

A Deadly Drop

New truths to uncover and a killer to catch.

With a family crisis looming, Detective Inspector Fiona Williams is hoping to take a break when she is called to a suspicious death in an isolated barn conversion, home to a quiet middle-aged couple.

Duncan returned home from the pub to discover his wife dead at the foot of their cellar steps. There are no signs of a forced entry or robbery, but the evidence says Pat's death was no accident. His reaction is strange, but he has a solid alibi for the time of death.

Fiona will have to dig deep into the victim's past to uncover the shocking truth. Pat's anti-blood sports stance had split the close-knit local community and created a rift with her sister. Could her sister or another hunt member be responsible?

Things escalate when Fiona discovers Pat had been about to expose a dubious police appointment. There's a second murder, and the police officer implicated disappears.

While Fiona struggles to solve this troubling case, DCI Peter Hatherall is battling demons of his own.

A Sudden Death

Who is willing to fully face up to their past?

A group of teenagers promise to never tell.
Ten years later one of them feels compelled to reveal their closely guarded secret.

DI Fiona Williams is pursuing an unusual house burglar who takes personal trinkets while leaving valuable items behind when she is asked to review a case ruled as suicide. She's reluctant to choose between the cases, but there's a second unexplained suicide and she's forced to make a harder decision between making an arrest and saving a colleague. As she digs deeper into the deaths, seemingly unrelated current events entwine in a way she never thought possible.

Can she defy the odds and kill two birds with one stone?

BOOKS BY THIS AUTHOR

The Skeletons Of Birkbury

Bells On Her Toes

Point Of No Return

Who Killed Vivien Morse

Twisted Truth

The Paperboy

Trouble At Clenchers Mill

Trouble At Fatting House

Trouble At Suncliffe Manor

Trouble At Sharcott

Trouble At Crowcombe

Debts & Druids

Fool Me Once